THE
UNREMEMBERED
GIRL

ALSO BY ELIZA MAXWELL

The Kinfolk
The Grave Tender

UNREMEMBERED
GIRL

ELIZA MAXWELL

LAKE UNION
PUBLISHING

Text copyright © 2017 Eliza Maxwell
All rights reserved.

Published by Lake Union Publishing, Seattle

www.apub.com

Amazon, the Amazon logo, and Lake Union Publishing are trademarks of Amazon.com, Inc., or its affiliates.

ISBN-13: 9781542045858
ISBN-10: 1542045851

Cover design by David Drummond

Printed in the United States of America

For Dad.
Thank you for your unsinkable faith in me.
You see it even when I don't, and you always have.

CHAPTER ONE

Death was heavier than Henry expected. More than the sum of its parts, it would seem.

He shifted the load on his shoulder, wishing he could unknow what was wrapped inside the bundle he was struggling with. He had to find a way to shake free of it—the knowing. If he didn't, it would keep adding weight, pressing his feet farther into the ground, pushing until he sank below the surface of the earth and finally disappeared altogether.

The shack loomed ahead, balanced precariously on aged, water-marked piers, jockeying for a piece of the night sky among the stately cypress that dripped Spanish moss—a struggle it was always going to lose.

Forcing one foot in front of the other, Henry moved toward the rickety steps. He pictured himself sloughing off his doubts, his horror, and his regrets in a trail of moldy bread crumbs behind him.

Henry knew what he had to do. Wishing otherwise served no purpose. That would only fill him up, leaving no room for the strength he needed to dig deep and find somewhere, somehow.

The steps creaked beneath his feet, giving a voice to the night that stood witness to his actions. A reminder, in case he'd forgotten.

As if he could forget.

The door, which hung crookedly on its hinges, swung wide as he pushed it with his foot, revealing a mostly empty space. Moonlight shone through the windows, save for the dark lines of the iron bars installed over the cracked, dirty glass. The place greeted him, and his heavy load, with the resignation of a bookie who knows desperation when he sees it, or a drug dealer who can spot a junkie at a mile. The place knew the score.

Henry could smell it, clogging his nostrils—the thick stench that fear leaves behind. It was rolling off him, mingling with what was already there.

Tonight would be different, but no less the same.

Dropping the bundle on the floor with a thud that echoed through the bare room, Henry took a moment to catch his breath.

A mistake.

Unbidden, thoughts of his mother crowded in. He didn't want her here, but he was powerless to stop her. The smile lines around her eyes crinkled as she sent him that look, the one that said she knew what he was thinking. The wink she'd toss his way when she slid the last pancake onto his plate at breakfast.

Henry squeezed his eyes shut.

"There's no other way, Mama," he whispered to no one, wondering if she'd understand if she were there.

Putting a thing off never made it easier, Henry heard his mother whisper in his mind, something she'd said to him countless times.

Wishful thinking, maybe, but it was the closest thing to absolution he was going to find.

It would have to do.

Grasping the corner of the blanket at his feet, he pulled, rolling out the body cocooned within, flipping it until it broke free and sprawled, lifeless and indignant, in front of him.

Steeling himself, he reached into the bag slung over his shoulder and removed the tools he'd need, setting them neatly in a row.

There was no going back. It was too late for that.

His only hope, the one he clung to during the long nightmare that followed, was that these atrocious acts he was committing had a purpose. That they fanned a distant flame of flickering light at the end of a deep tunnel.

Or so he wanted to believe.

CHAPTER TWO

Six months earlier

The girl watched. All day, she'd silently observed. Mostly the woman who walked like she had a sickness. She saw the way the woman stood straighter and spoke stronger when others were around. When the woman was alone, the girl saw how her shoulders dropped and the truth showed through, though no one saw it. No one but the girl.

As the hours passed, and the woman went about her routine, a longing grew in the girl. Not just hunger, which had begun to rumble in her belly and would grow sharper by the hour. The girl was used to hunger. It was more than that.

The woman and the young man and the old man who strutted and crowed like a banty rooster, they were part of a set that made up a whole.

She'd seen families before, but she'd never known that feeling.

She stayed hidden, not daring to draw too close. Not close enough to be seen anyway.

She'd watched, and she'd wondered. She'd seen them come and go, then come back again. Did it feel different to go from place to place when you knew there was a spot in the world you belonged and had people to return to? Or did they take it for granted, never realizing they'd be noticed—a missing piece—if one of them never returned?

She crept closer, all the way to the edge of the woods, as evening came on.

The mosquitoes buzzed around her, and she heard the bullfrogs singing off-key from the marsh far to her back, but she paid them no mind. She watched the house—no, the *home*—with a single-minded intensity.

Smells from the kitchen reached her, ribbons floating on the breeze. They pulled at her, teasing her hunger for food and a deeper hunger for things she couldn't name.

She followed those ribbons, stepping from the shelter of the woods. It wasn't dark yet, it wasn't wise, but she gave no thought to consequences.

Closer and closer she came. Her steps were light, and she disturbed nothing as she found a window to peer inside. Her stomach grumbled, and her heart ached in new ways, but the family took no notice. They were together, unconcerned about the gathering dark outside and unaware of the girl who was watching.

Lost in a trance, she couldn't look away and didn't want to.

For a time, she closed her eyes and listened to their voices, muffled and sharp and soft, and she forgot everything. She forgot that she was dirty and alone in a place she didn't understand. She forgot the troubled road that had brought her to this place. She forgot the gnawing hunger in her belly.

It was the laughter, such a foreign and joyous sound, that pierced her daydream. It was a careless thing. She'd never laughed like that. And she knew she never would.

With a gasp, the girl ran. She didn't belong in this place any more than she'd ever belonged anywhere.

The shadows of the trees and the night swallowed her again.

CHAPTER THREE

Henry's brow drew together as he watched his mother emerge from the dense span of woods on the east side of the house. He stood in the bed of the pickup he was unloading, shading his eyes from the morning sun opening its arms above the trees, and raised a hand in her direction.

She ambled, and she did it slowly. Not quite a shuffle, not yet, but a far cry from the easy stride she used to have. But Caroline Doucet wasn't quite the woman she used to be.

She waved in return, then made her way slowly toward him.

Henry went back to moving crates, but his mind was elsewhere and the empty bottles rattled carelessly around inside.

The sharp cry of distress brought his head back up with a snap.

He saw her totter, one arm thrown out instinctively, circling the air for balance, the other bracing itself to meet the ground as her legs wobbled beneath her.

Henry leapt over the crates, launching himself from the bed of the truck in his mother's direction. His feet landed and he was already running before she'd made it all the way to the ground.

The dark-garbed figure materialized from nowhere. It swooped toward his mother, and Henry squinted, trying to comprehend the sight, while fighting off the panic that gripped him, the panic that was always waiting just beneath the surface, waiting for this moment.

His feet moved faster, his heart pumping, as he tried in vain to reach his mother before the shadowy apparition beat him to her.

It wasn't a race he could win.

The fleeting sense in those seconds that Death, incarnated before his eyes, was hurtling toward his mother was irrational. Impossible. But he couldn't deny his confusion when, instead of swallowing Mama whole within the folds of its hooded black wings, the figure stooped low, catching his mother just moments before she fell to the ground.

It wasn't Death. Of course it wasn't. That was crazy.

"Mama," Henry gasped, drawing near to the pair and skidding to a halt, adrenaline still coursing through him. "Are you all right?"

"Well, yes," she said, shaking her head and sounding nearly as confused as Henry had been. "Of course. I tripped, that's all. Thank you . . . ," she said, looking over at the stranger who'd come to her aid, seemingly out of thin air.

Henry spared a glance for the person his mother was leaning against, registering the dark and dingy clothing hanging like tattered bat wings, the cloak pulled up that obscured a face in shadow. He could almost excuse himself the fantastical notion that Death had come swooping out of the trees to claim his mother as his own. Considering all things.

Shaking off the morbid thought, he moved to his mother's side, bending to support her and letting her lean on him to make her way back to the house.

"Don't fuss, Henry," she said to him, clucking like a hen. "It's nothing. Just the perils of age and daydreaming. I tripped over my own feet, that's all."

But she leaned on him all the same. He wondered if she'd twisted an ankle.

"Mama, I don't understand why you have to wander around in the marsh every morning, alone," he said.

She glanced up at him, faint irritation mingling with affection.

"Henry," she said, lightly mocking his prissy tone, "I don't understand why you have to be so bossy. Besides, I wasn't alone. My guardian angel was with me today . . ."

She looked over her shoulder, speaking to the stranger, but the hooded figure had slipped from her side and was standing two paces back.

Henry and his mother both turned.

He didn't know the etiquette for greeting a dirty stranger he'd mistaken for Death, but his mother had no such hesitation.

"Please, I'd like to thank you . . . for your help . . ."

Mama's voice trailed off as the stranger took a step backward at her words. A barely perceptible shake of a head came from within the shadows of the cloak.

"I don't even know your name," his mother said, raising a hand, palm up, toward the figure.

But the stranger took a quick step backward again.

"Please," Mama said again, her voice soft and calm, like she was speaking to a wild animal spooked at finding itself trapped in a cage. In a way, perhaps she was. The stranger turned toward the pines that bordered the field where they stood and bounded off, back from where they'd materialized, the dirty folds of clothing flapping in the wind behind them.

Henry had to stop himself from running after, demanding answers to the same questions his mother no doubt had, though in a less compassionate tone. But his mother was his first priority.

"Come on, Mama," he said, nodding toward home.

She didn't answer, just looked toward the woods, where her sudden savior was blending into the shadows of the trees.

"Well, if that doesn't beat all," she said in a low voice, speaking more to herself than to her son.

Henry shook his head, pushing back the surreal oddness of the situation and reaching for the comforting familiarity of reality.

"Let's get you home," he said.

She nodded, turning away from the woods.

"I'm fine, Henry. You worry too much," she said, her tone falling into the familiar pattern of soft chiding he was used to.

"And you don't worry enough. You could have hurt yourself," he said.

He couldn't help one last glance over his shoulder as they made their way toward home.

Just on the edge of the pine woods, he could see the outline of the stranger who'd stopped his mother's fall. Something intangible pulled at him, and his eyes widened ever so slightly as the figure took half a step forward and pulled back the folds of the cloth that had covered their face.

It was a girl. A dirty, unkempt girl. A girl whose face held such profound sadness as she watched the two of them walk away that it felt like a weapon. Something sharp and painful that pierced through the center of him.

And then she was gone.

Shaking his head at his own thoughts, he forced his attention back to his mother.

"Surely you've memorized every twig and leaf there is to see out there by now," he said to the top of her head, trying to reel in his overactive imagination.

"Oh, Henry, where have I gone wrong with you, love?" she said lightly, but she was clearly distracted.

"I'm serious," he said, his voice sharper than he'd intended. The thin layer of irritation that coated his words couldn't disguise the worry at the heart of them.

She glanced up at him in surprise.

"So am I, son," she said, giving him a bemused smile.

"What if something happens? What if you fall again, or . . . I don't know."

"Henry," she said gently. "If I fall, then I'll pick myself up."

"Mama—"

She held up a hand to cut him off. "You're worried. Okay, I know. It does you credit. But try to understand," she said softly. "Mornings out there, with the quiet and the mist hanging low over the water . . ." Mama shook her head. "I know it sounds silly, but out there? That's where God lives."

Henry sighed. "Livingston might have something to say about that."

"Your father has his own kind of relationship with the Lord, a more complicated one than mine."

Henry bit back the retort before it broke free, but he could hear it, plain as day, in his head: *Not my father.*

"About as complicated as a bully has with the rock he's about to hit you with."

"Henry!"

"Sorry, Mama," he said, abashed, at least a little.

"He has his reasons, you know."

Henry did know, and he regretted the words that put those creases in his mother's forehead. Even if they were true.

"Things changed for him, Henry. He's never been the same. Not since . . ."

Since Mari, Henry thought. But they rarely said her name out loud.

"Ms. Watson's roof is leaking again," Henry said, changing the subject as they drew close to the house.

His mother nodded and glanced back toward the trees.

"I've got some mayhaw jelly you can take to her when you go," she said, her voice quiet.

Henry followed her line of sight, but there was no sign of the strange girl. No sign that anything out of the ordinary had just happened.

If he hadn't witnessed it himself, he wouldn't have believed anything had. But there was a nagging ache where the stranger's sadness had touched him that lingered, undeniable.

His mother glanced back at him.

9

"There were people at the shack again last night," she said.

Henry had heard the voices too, traveling over the night air, before the fat drops of rain had started their chorus, blanketing the sounds. The wind that came close on its heels had shaken the trees and pulled the shingles from Ms. Watson's often-mended roof.

Was that where the girl had come from?

"Tell me you're not poking around in those people's business, Mama."

"I beg your pardon. I do not *poke*. I mind my own, thank you very much."

And she normally did, at that, but the world seemed tilted a little left of center that day.

"The place was empty when I passed by this morning. Those folks were there, then gone. As usual."

"Fine by me."

Henry didn't know what those people were up to over there, but he had enough on his own plate to keep him from eyeing what was on his neighbors'. At least, until they began showing up here, flitting about in the woods with shadowy eyes that burned through him.

His mother let go of Henry's arm and moved slowly to head up to the house.

"Come by the kitchen and pick up that jelly for Helen Sue before you go, Henry. And be back by suppertime. Del and Alice are coming, and you know how your father gets."

"He's not my father," Henry called to her retreating back.

"He most certainly is," she called over her shoulder in a familiar refrain. "Lots of different ways to be a father, Henry. Livingston's no worse than most."

Henry had heard it so many times in his twenty-three years that he could—and did—mouth the words along with her. But only while her back was turned.

"And no better than some," he muttered under his breath.

Henry walked back over to his truck, going through the motions of a life he tried to live without resentment.

He put the girl from his mind. Or tried to. He didn't count the times his eyes were drawn involuntarily back to the woods. Instead, he tried to focus on the tasks in front of him.

The bottles he'd wash and sanitize, then make ready to be filled again with the booze that helped other people to celebrate, or grieve, or just get through the day.

He didn't drink himself. Not as a habit anyway, not past testing the batches. Not because he was sitting on any sort of moral high horse—a bootlegger doesn't have the luxury of high horses, moral or otherwise.

No, he didn't drink because he'd seen every kind of reason for diving into a bottle, seen them up close and personal. But he'd never seen a solitary soul come out the back end of a bottle any better off than they had gone in. Mostly they just came out hungover and in need of a shower.

Once the truck was unloaded, he gathered up his toolbox. He raised it over the side of the truck bed, but something caught his eye, and his hand stilled. Squinting, he stared into the darkened canopy of trees.

He lowered the heavy metal box of tools and set it gently in the bed of the truck, keeping his eyes turned toward the place where he'd seen the shadow.

Henry wiped his hands on his jeans, and after a split second of hesitation, he gave in, unable to help himself. He walked toward the break in the pines.

The brushy undergrowth had been pushed back long ago, giving way to a maze of pathways that his mother had wandered along every morning for many years, communing with nature, or God, or whatever. According to her, they were one and the same.

As he stepped into the dim light, the woods enveloped him. Henry's eyes scanned the familiar surroundings. In this place, it was easy to forget that the world had turned the corner into the twenty-first century.

Time was different here, as if a spell had been cast that slowed the revolution of the earth. Those who lived and died nearby were touched by it, carrying the traces on their fingertips, in their lungs, woven through their hair. It was inescapable.

The mystical qualities that so enchanted his mother weren't lost on him. He'd walked these paths by her side as a boy.

Maybe she was right. Maybe God did live here. It was a place as full of divine beauty as any he'd ever seen. But if that were true, there was no denying God had a cruel side.

The tall, stately pines that grew in drier soils soon gave way to the curving, dripping beauty of the cypress that thrived in the swamp. The ground sloped downward, giving a body the subtle sense of being pulled into the bottomlands that waited patiently just around the corners, where the dark heart of the marsh beat with a symphony of life. Stinging, singing, ancient, and deadly life, where the alligators were king, the snakes and snapping turtles were barons, and the woodpeckers were court jesters jangling their bells from the tops of the trees.

For the moment, though, all was quiet.

There was no sign of the girl.

Shaking off his unease, Henry walked back toward the morning sun, leaving the woods and the girl to their business. He had his own to be getting on with.

CHAPTER FOUR

Jonah's day had turned sour. He clutched his yellow Mustang Matchbox car in his left hand and walked back to the boat, his steps slower than before.

He heard the rumble of a truck coming up the gravel road behind him and moved over to the side to let it pass, but he didn't bother raising his head.

The truck slowed, keeping pace with him.

"Hey, Jonah," he heard.

At the sound of Henry's voice, his day brightened some and his head came up with a small smile on his face. Henry was his friend.

"Hop in, buddy, I'm headed your way."

Jonah opened the passenger door with a creak and settled his hefty frame into the seat.

"Why so blue, man?"

Jonah tilted his head, then looked down at his hands, but they were the same tanned brown color they always were.

He didn't understand, but that was okay. There were lots of things he didn't understand, but he didn't worry around Henry. Henry was nice. Not like some of the others. Not like Tinker's daughter.

"Sad," Henry explained. "You look sad today."

"Tinker wasn't where he always is," Jonah said. He showed Henry the yellow car, sweaty now from being clutched in his hand.

"Ah," Henry said, understanding dawning. "Tinker's daughter was minding the store?"

Jonah nodded glumly.

He'd tried to give her the yellow car for the red licorice. Wednesdays were for red licorice. But her face had pinched up when Jonah walked into the store, and it pinched more when Jonah tried to explain. Finally, he'd left, taking his car back with him.

"Tinker's visiting his grandkids up in Oklahoma for a few days, Jonah. He'll be back next week. Why don't you take a look in the glove box there?"

Next week sounded like a long way away.

As the truck bumped and rattled over the road, Jonah reached out and unhooked the latch on Henry's glove compartment. He didn't know why people called it that. He'd never seen anyone keep gloves there, but he thought he might. If he had a glove box, he'd definitely keep gloves in it, just so it wouldn't get confused about what its job was.

Jonah found a bag of peppermints instead of gloves, and his day got a lot better.

He glanced over at Henry, a question on his face.

"Course, man. I brought them for you. They're the soft ones that kind of melt on your tongue."

"Thank you, Henry."

Aunt Helen told him to always say thank you, and he was proud he remembered before tearing open the wrapper.

"These are good," he said around the candy in his mouth.

Henry pulled over at the edge of the marsh, where Jonah's boat was sitting under a willow tree. He threw the truck into park and killed the engine.

"I'll stop by Tinker's and see if I can soften Linda up for you."

Jonah didn't see how that would work. She seemed pretty set in her pinched way, but he didn't question Henry, who had a better way with people than Jonah did.

Henry loaded the pirogue with his toolbox and a crate, and Jonah put the candies and his toy car in his pocket and pushed off from the shore. The flat-bottomed wooden boat wobbled on the water when Jonah stepped in, but it was good at its job. It had been doing it a long time, and it stayed the course, settling down into the murky water.

Jonah took the long pole and pushed them along, levering it against the muddy bottom.

"Ol' Brutal took down a doe right over there yesterday. Saw him do it," Jonah said, motioning to the far-right bank.

"You're not gonna go messing around trying to bring Brutal down yourself, are you?" Henry asked.

Jonah shook his head. "Aunt Helen says we got us a understanding with the big boy. We don't bother him, and he don't bother us."

"Ms. Watson's a smart lady."

"Says he's been here long as she has, which stretches far back as ever, so we gotta have respect. I got a line I throw out chicken for him on now and then, keep him happy."

Henry nodded. He understood how things worked in the swamplands, just like Jonah did. It was folks that gave Jonah trouble. He never could seem to figure out folks. Henry helped him with that, and Jonah helped Henry with the things he knew best.

The rest of the short ride went by in silence, the only sound the easy splash of the pole as the boat cut through the green on the top of the water.

That was one of the things Jonah liked about Henry. He didn't need to fill up the air with a bunch of words. Too many words made Jonah feel like blackbirds were flying at his face, too fast and too many for him to catch. Made him want to duck down and hide.

The two men pulled the pirogue up to the shore when they reached the swamp island. That was where Jonah lived, with his aunt. He liked it there in their big old house up on stilts. He was hardly ever confused on the swamp.

"Henry Martell, I see you there toting your toolbox," Aunt Helen called down from the ladder she'd perched against the side of the house.

"Mr. Flannigan told me you'd come by and picked up shingles this morning. Figured you could use a hand after that storm last night."

"I'll just bet you figured. I may be old, boy, but I can still patch a hole in my roof without the likes of you coming to save me."

"Course you can. I'm just here to give you somebody to boss around, since Jonah's not real fond of climbing on the roof."

Aunt Helen snorted as she clambered down the ladder.

"Well now, since you put it that way, I'll be happy to show you a thing or two, child. Jonah, bring that crate on inside, and we'll visit awhile. The roof will wait till you've had a glass of iced tea."

Jonah led the way while the other two passed words back and forth. He followed the trail of the conversation until it got away from him, then let the birds flutter on past.

"How's your mama doing, Henry?"

"Well as can be expected, I suppose."

"And that horse's ass she's married to?"

"Fit and hearty. Mean as ever."

"The mean ones live the longest, you know. I figure when the end of the world comes, it'll just be me and that old fool Livingston left rattling around the whole empty expanse of the earth."

"And Ol' Brutal," Jonah added.

"I do believe that gator'd be better company," Aunt Helen said.

Jonah went down the hallway to put his toy car away in the box under his bed with the space rocket blanket. It was a grown-up bed. At twenty-six, and big with it, as people said of him, he didn't fit in a small bed no more. But he liked his space rocket blanket, even if the edges didn't make it all the way to hang down the sides. It might not fit just so, but that was okay with him. He didn't fit just so either.

He'd take the yellow car back to Tinker's again next Wednesday.

Jonah couldn't hear the words anymore, just muffled people noises, but he heard his aunt's cackle of laughter. Henry was good at making her laugh.

Jonah thought about having another peppermint but decided against it. He'd save them. Next week still sounded like a long way away for Tinker to be back where he usually was. He wandered down the hallway toward the kitchen, where the voices were.

"She'd understand, Henry. She would. If she knew that's what you wanted."

"Sure she would. And she'd put on a brave face and tell me to go, but what kind of person would that make me? What kind of son?"

"The kind that has to start living his own life one of these days."

"One of these days will be here soon enough, Ms. Watson."

Jonah's aunt put her hand, which always made Jonah think of a wrinkled paper bag, over Henry's and sighed. It was a sad sound. He could understand that.

"I suppose it will, Henry. I suppose it will, at that."

"And besides, if I run off and join the army, you'll just insist on fixing your own roof."

"And perfectly capable of it I am too."

"I have no doubt. But since I'm here anyway . . ."

"Well, hop to it then, boy. Daylight's burning."

"Yes, ma'am."

Jonah held the ladder while Henry patched the leaky roof. That was good. Jonah didn't like it when the storms outside felt like they were getting inside. Made him wonder if the weight of the storm would push the roof all the way in one day, and he and Aunt Helen would just float off in the house like it was the pirogue.

"I'll talk to Tinker's daughter for you, Jonah. I won't forget," Henry told him when Jonah had taken him and his toolbox back across the marsh to his truck.

"Thank you, Henry," Jonah said.

Henry was his friend.

CHAPTER FIVE

"What is it, Mama?" Henry asked later that night.

His mother shook her head, but she looked rattled.

"Nothing. Nothing, I just thought . . ."

"Is there somebody out there?" he asked. *The girl, back again?*

Henry saw his mother staring out the window, before she knelt down to pick up the pieces of the dish she'd dropped.

"No. I'm just clumsy tonight."

"Sit down, Caroline. I'll take care of that," Alice said.

Alice and her husband, Delwyn, Henry's sister-in-law and step-brother, had joined them for dinner, a weekly ritual that almost everyone dreaded. Henry believed they came more for his mother's sake than any familial obligation to Livingston, Del's father.

"I've got it, don't fuss."

"Caroline, sit down and let the girl clean it up," Livingston barked.

Henry saw Alice's face tighten at the unnecessary reprimand in his voice, but only for a moment. Alice was good at masking her disdain for Livingston. Better than Henry was, in any case, although it couldn't be any easier to be Livingston's daughter-in-law than it was to be his stepson. *Or his son,* Henry thought, glancing at Del.

"The cake," Mama said. "I nearly forgot. I'll get the cake."

She made a move to rise again from her chair, but Henry stood first.

"I'll get it, Mama."

Henry almost mentioned their run-in with the stranger that morning, but shut his mouth. Something about his mother's face . . . If she wanted to discuss it, she would.

"If you ask me," Livingston said, continuing his conversation with his son, "you ought to have better things to do with your time than harass Clayton Simmons anyway. He's a good, God-fearing Christian, boy, and you could take a page out of his book, you know."

"Dad, we're not harassing the man. And good Christian or not, Clayton's crazy as a jaybird. You can't go waving a knife around in the middle of the Winn Dixie, even if you think you're fending off Satan's minions."

"It's those doctors pumping him full of chemicals that are throwing him off-balance."

"Those chemicals are the only thing keeping him from being thrown in the loony bin over in Rusk, Dad. If he'd take them like he was supposed to, he wouldn't be seeing demons in the frozen-food section."

"That man is your elder, boy, and one of my flock. You ought to show some respect."

Livingston's voice was rising, along with Del's frustration. From experience, Henry knew this conversation was going nowhere good, but it was like a runaway train, and there was little he could do to stop it from its inevitable destination.

"Respect? Dad, he came at Brady with a knife!"

"Brady's a fool, and so are you! You two strutting around with your badges acting like the whole damn town needs to roll out a carpet at your feet, to do your bidding just because you're sporting a uniform. Neither one of you inclined to actually do anything useful. What about those criminals using the marsh over there to run drugs and Lord knows what else through here? You do anything about that?"

"Dad—"

Henry kept silent, placing plates of cake on the table.

"You and Brady." Livingston snorted. "My hind end's got more smarts than the two of you put together. And neither one of you can be bothered to show up on a Sunday morning to receive the word of God. It's a travesty!"

"Show up where, Dad? In the middle of the damn woods, with you standing on a tree stump, throwing the same tired old sermons at the same half-dozen crazies that come to listen to you yell? That's not a church, Dad, and you're not a preacher anymore! When are you going to get that through your head?"

The whole room stilled. Delwyn had stepped over a line, and they all knew it.

Livingston's fists came down on the table like the double barrels of a shotgun, but his voice was cold and calm, a far cry from his usual angry bellow.

"I will not tolerate that kind of disrespect in my house, at my own table."

"Livingston—" Mama said, trying to soothe him.

He ignored his wife.

"Get out of my house."

"Livingston, you don't want to—"

"Don't tell me what I want, Caroline. I know my own mind. And I want you to leave, boy. You and your wife both."

Alice stood quickly from the table, meeting Henry's eye as she did. He could see she couldn't get out of there fast enough to suit her.

Del, though, Del tried. "Dad, I—"

"I said get out."

"I'm sorry, Dad. I didn't mean that. I was just—"

"I know what you meant, boy. You don't have to sugarcoat it now that it's sitting out in the middle of the room like a rotten egg. You don't have any respect for me, and worse, you don't have any respect for the Lord. Your sister, God rest her soul, she was the better of the two of you."

Del reared back like he'd taken a physical blow, and Alice gasped. "Livingston!" Mama rebuked.

"No, Caroline. There's no need to walk on eggshells around the boy's feelings. He's a man now, or so he thinks. It's time he heard some hard truths. Maribel was the better of the pair, and that's a damn shame."

"What's a shame, Dad?" Del asked quietly. "That Mari's gone, or that Mari's gone and I'm not?"

Livingston sat back in his chair and folded his arms across his chest. He'd drawn his line in the sand, and he wasn't backing down. "You take it however you like, boy."

"Livingston Renard Doucet! That is quite enough of that foolishness," Mama said, shocking them all. She rarely disputed her husband's nonsense in front of others. Henry had heard them hash it out behind closed doors but never in front of the family.

Livingston looked as surprised as the rest of them, before his jaw set with a stubborn intractability that Henry had seen many times before.

"Don't bother, Caroline. It's not like it's ever been a secret," Del said, rising from the table.

"It was a fine dinner, Caroline, thank you," Alice murmured, following her husband toward the door. Henry rose to see them out, feeling like an usher at the picture show. The question he'd yet to figure out was if the show was a comedy or a tragedy.

Alice made it to the doorway of the kitchen, but she turned and spoke once more to Livingston's back.

"You all forget sometimes, I think. I was friends with Mari. Probably knew her better than any of you did."

Her words were soft, but there could be no doubt that Livingston was listening.

"You've painted that picture in your memory, sir, with a rose-colored brush. And that's fine. Just fine. Right up until you use it as a weapon against your son. Mari was no angel."

"I thought I told you to get going," Livingston said without turning around to face her.

Alice ignored his bluster and patted Henry on the shoulder on her way out the door.

"You take care, Henry," she said.

"You too, Alice."

Henry closed the door behind them and walked back to the kitchen in time to see his mother pick up the slice of cake that Livingston's fork was poised over and sweep it away.

Without a word, she dumped it in the trash and left the room.

CHAPTER SIX

It was late. The part of the deep night when it's impractical to do anything useful, but sleep won't come, so the mind swirls around in the dark, skirting past old memories and bumping against unvoiced desires.

With a sigh, Henry threw back the blankets and went in search of a distraction.

Muffled noises from the kitchen told him he wasn't the only one rattling around the quiet house. He found his mother in her nightgown and robe, heaping leftovers onto a tray.

Considering she hadn't had much of an appetite since her diagnosis, and Henry had passed Livingston snoring on the couch in the study, to where he'd been banished, Henry was confused by the sheer volume of food she was piling up.

"Hungry?" he asked.

Mama gasped and swung around, her hand at her throat.

"Oh Lord, Henry! Didn't anybody ever teach you not to sneak up on an old lady like that?"

"What in the world are you doing?"

His mother opened her mouth, then closed it again. No words came out, and Henry was surprised to see a flush creep up her neck. Was she embarrassed? He couldn't think of a single time he'd ever seen his mother embarrassed of anything.

He watched as she squared her shoulders under the dim kitchen light and tightened her robe.

"Since you're here, you can carry this for me," she said.

"Carry it where?"

"Just follow me, and quit with the questions."

Henry turned his head and watched her walk out of the kitchen. Finally, seeing no other way to satisfy his curiosity, he picked up the tray filled with roast beef and vegetables and a large slab of coconut cake and followed his mother.

His step faltered when he saw her open the front door and glance back at him.

"Well, come on, then."

The stray thought occurred to him that if it weren't for women, in all their cloaks of unfathomed mysteries, men would lead very boring lives.

Pulled along like a small boat in a strong current, Henry followed.

In bare feet, with the breeze blowing her faded robe and nightgown around her ankles, Mama walked down the steps of the porch and into the surrounding starlit night.

She walked through the field and toward the edge of the woods, and Henry followed.

When she came to the same break in the trees where he'd been just that morning, she stopped.

"There," she said.

He looked at her. "You want to have a picnic? At the edge of the woods . . . at two o'clock in the morning?"

"Of course not. Don't be ridiculous."

Henry's brows shot up, but luckily for him, it was dark and his mother couldn't see his face clearly.

"Set the tray there," she said, motioning to the ground again and turning back to the house.

Henry watched her retreating back outlined only by the low lights coming from the windows of their home, then, seeing no other choice at this odd juncture, did as she asked.

He trotted to catch up with her but didn't bother with questions.

When they reached the porch, she settled down on the swing that hung from one of the beams and crossed her ankles.

"Don't you have anything to say about that?" Henry settled next to her, listening to the old swing creak as he did.

"Nope." She chuckled and patted him on the leg. "You remind me a great deal of Weston sometimes."

Henry didn't remember his real father, who'd died before he was two, but he'd heard her say that before, and it always left him feeling adrift.

They lived their lives in his father's house. Everything here had belonged to his father's family for a hundred years. Even the moonshine still, which provided a large chunk of the family's income, had belonged to Weston Martell. Many of the tools that Henry toted in his toolbox doing odd jobs around the county were branded with the initials "WM" on their wooden handles.

But with no memory of the man, Henry couldn't help but feel that a line of history had been broken with his father's death, and Henry had never been able to repair it.

So he floated along with his father's features staring back at him in the mirror, using the things the man had left behind, and always, there was the feeling that he was surrounded by ghosts. Ghosts who were disappointed in him and his inability to understand what they wanted him to know.

Or maybe the night was playing games with his mind. He'd always had a tendency to grow contemplative in the night.

"You think the girl is still out there?" he finally asked.

"I do," his mother replied.

He didn't question her conviction. He'd learned long ago that was a waste of time.

"You realize that girl might be dangerous." There'd been an untamed wildness about her, and Henry sensed it went deeper than the dirty skin and clothes. He didn't mention the lingering uneasiness she had left in him. He didn't know how to put it into words, that sense as he'd met her eyes of being untethered from what was real.

Mama nodded. "I've considered it."

"That doesn't concern you?"

"Not particularly, no."

"Can I ask why?"

"Because I've found that most people are generally a danger only to themselves."

Henry thought about that for a moment but found he couldn't agree.

He'd been eleven when Mari had died. The quake of grief and pain had been devastating, leaving behind a changed landscape, full of shaky, uneven ground. The aftershocks were still happening, a dozen years later.

He glanced toward the trees shrouded in inky-black darkness.

After a moment, he did feel compelled to ask, "So you've decided to feed her?"

She nodded. "Yes. Yes, I have."

His mind rifled through the various responses he could give right now but came up short.

"Hmm."

"Aren't you going to tell me not to go looking for trouble?"

That had been one of the responses he'd considered, then skipped right past. "Nope."

"Thank you."

They sat in comfortable silence, staring at nothing and listening to the night sounds. But the comfort only lasted until she broke the silence.

"Henry, I know how badly you want to join the military. And I know that I'm the reason you've stayed here."

"Mama, I don't—"

"Henry. I'm your mother. Give me a little credit. I know my boy."

Henry's face was troubled. "I'm not going anywhere, Mama."

She nodded, looking off into the distance. "A better person would tell you to go. Go start your life."

"It wouldn't matter, even if you said it. I'm not going anywhere."

She patted his leg again. "I know. And I'm not so selfless anyway. I'm glad you're here." She let the subject go. "Del and Alice are trying IVF again. Alice told me before dinner."

"What is this, the third time?" Henry asked.

Alice and Del had been trying, unsuccessfully, to have a baby for nearly as long as they'd been married. In the past year, they'd pinned their hopes on in vitro fertilization.

"I'm praying for them, Henry. A baby would be a fine thing. Not just for them, I think, but for Livingston too. He needs something to keep his feet firmly on the ground. I won't be here to do that forever."

He hated how cavalier she could sound when speaking of her own death.

Mama rose. "It's late. I'm going to turn in. Goodnight, Henry."

"Night, Mama."

In the distance, he couldn't make out any movement, but he had a sense that there was plenty going on that he couldn't see.

It was a familiar feeling.

The next day, the food was gone. In spite of the late night, Henry rose early to check.

He stared down at the dishes as the sun began to light up the day. Raccoons hadn't stacked the plates neatly upon one another.

The stranger was still in their woods. There could be no doubt. The real question was, what kind of person was she, and why was she there?

Whatever the answers, there was no sign of her now.

Henry took the tray and headed inside the house. He needed coffee.

Mama had also risen early, as was her habit, even now. Henry set the tray on the kitchen counter and poured some fresh coffee into his thermos, noting his mother's face as she took in the sight of the stacked dirty dishes.

"You were right," he said. "She's still there."

She peered out the window over the kitchen sink that faced the woods.

"Yep," she said softly. "I usually am."

CHAPTER SEVEN

While Livingston's congregation, such that it was, gathered, Henry fell into the words of the book in front of him, fitted snugly inside the cover of an old Bible.

He'd found the Bible in Mari's room when they were cleaning it out after her death. What she'd done with the original text inside, Henry couldn't guess, but when he'd opened up the worn white leather cover to flip through the pages, he'd found an Anne Rice novel tucked inside, rather than the Scriptures he'd expected.

It was then that he'd understood his stepsister's absorption with the thing, particularly during her father's long-winded diatribes in church. Mari, a far cry from devout, had always been happy enough to attend on Sundays. At that moment, it finally made sense.

Not one to look a gift horse in the mouth, Henry had asked his mother if he could keep Mari's Bible, and the tradition had continued with him, though he'd long since given up Anne Rice's dark tales and moved on to whatever struck his fancy that week.

It was a connection to his dead sister. One that Henry cherished. He'd grown up on the words of Ian Fleming and Jack Kerouac. On S. E. Hinton and Louis L'Amour. All borrowed from the town library. All with Mari's blessing, her ghostly hand on his shoulder while she sent him a sly wink.

It was the only way he managed to get through Sunday mornings, truth be told. And the only way he managed to get out of this town, even if his travels were confined to his imagination.

Livingston no longer had a real church to preach from. After his daughter died, he'd gone off the rails. The powers that be had eventually tired of his drunken rants and ravings, his eyes and his discourse fiery, with a madman's spittle flying from his lips behind the pulpit.

But losing his church didn't stop him. No, sir. Not Livingston Doucet. Hardly one to go gentle into that good night, Livingston had taken a chainsaw from the barn the next day and set to felling the largest tree in the back forest that he could find.

With a tremendous crashing death, the pine had come down. Not done yet, Livingston wiped the sweat from his brow, then set to work again.

The roar of the chainsaw was egregious as he cut the tree into sections. As loud and grating as any father's cry of grief, and no one dared interrupt. Not the wildlife, which had all darted away at the first rumble, nor the family, who could hear the saw whine all the way back at the house, as they waited with tense shoulders and bated breath to see what Livingston had in store.

Glancing around the clearing under hooded eyes, Henry noted that not much had changed since that first Sunday Livingston had called his new congregation to him to hear his version of the Lord's word.

The sections that Livingston had cut from the sacrificial pine sat in two semicircular rows around the three-foot stump that Henry's stepfather, the ousted preacher, hoisted himself onto each week, come rain or shine.

Most of the flock had stayed true to the Second Baptist Church of Blackwater, happy to have the man and his harsh words banished to the backwoods.

But there were a few die-hard fundamentalists who were drawn like moths to Livingston's way of seeing the world. Not many, it was true, which gave Henry a modicum of hope for the future of humanity, but a few all the same.

The sections of bark-covered pine that served as uncomfortably hard seating for the makeshift congregation, perhaps by design, had never been full, but that didn't seem to bother Livingston. In fact, Henry thought the man found a self-righteous sort of satisfaction in the empty seats, which provided him with a visual representation to gesticulate at while he decried how very far society had fallen from grace.

"And the first commandment . . . yes, I did say *commandment*! Not *suggestion*! Not *recommendation*! Not pretty-good-*idea*! Nay, the Lord *commands* us to honor thy father!" Livingston expounded from his self-made pulpit.

Henry tried valiantly not to roll his eyes.

"Amen," Clayton Simmons added vehemently from the front row, nodding in agreement. Apparently he was out on bail after the Winn Dixie incident.

Henry glanced over at his mother, and his mouth twitched as he caught sight of the arch in her brow. Clearly she was aware that Livingston had decided to reorder the commandments to suit his own purposes, not to mention truncating the phrase "Honor thy father . . . *and mother*."

If memory served, Livingston had altogether skipped over the ones about the one true God, not taking the Lord's name in vain, and how idols were a no-no. There was another one in there too, although Henry couldn't bring it to mind.

It had been a long time since he'd picked up a Bible. Just after Mari had died, in fact. Not the faux version he now held in his hands, but his own copy, the leather cover brown instead of Mari's white, with his name and the words **HOLY BIBLE** embossed in gold.

In his youthful search for answers to questions he could barely comprehend, he'd read the thing from cover to cover, a little bit each night before bed. It had taken him nearly a year.

When he was done, he started again, thinking perhaps he'd missed something.

But after coming to the end a second time, Henry had realized that there were no answers to be had in those holy words. Not for him at least. He knew now that unless a person already had the faith to believe in them to begin with, those words were just words. Like the fire under a hot-air balloon, faith was the fuel that gave them shape and meaning, allowing them to soar. It was a catch-22.

At twelve years old, he'd felt profoundly disappointed. And somehow lacking.

His own copy of the Good Book was sitting on the shelf in his room, where it had sat, gathering dust, ever since he'd snapped that leather cover closed after the second read.

"And so the Lord God did *recognize* that the father holds dominion over his household. He did *affirm* that this is as it should be, for so long as the father shall live. For so long as the father shall live, the honor to be bestowed upon him by his earthly children should reflect the honor that the children of the earth bestow upon our father the Lord in heaven. And so *shall* it be!"

"Amen!" came another interjection from Clayton. "Amen, Brother Doucet!"

This time Henry couldn't hold back the eye roll, so he was sure to keep his head tilted downward to the pages of the spy novel, though he couldn't help but send a glance toward Del and Alice before he did.

Henry was sure that Del realized his father's words were aimed at him. Del might not be the sharpest tool in the shed, but sometimes a blunt instrument was all you needed.

From the corner of Henry's eye, he could see Alice shifting on her stump next to Del, probably regretting urging him to come that morning. He'd overheard her speaking to Mama when they'd walked into the service.

"He didn't want to. And frankly, I can't blame him. But it doesn't really matter how much of an ass Livingston can be, he's still his father. God willing, he'll be our children's grandfather one day."

Mama had hugged her. "I'm glad you're here. Both of you."

"I traded a shift at work. I didn't think Del would come on his own."

Alice was a labor and delivery nurse over at the hospital in Cordelia. She normally worked Sundays, giving her a legitimate excuse to miss out on these weekly shenanigans.

Henry felt Alice was probably grateful for that.

He saw Del tug at the collar of his dress shirt. The temperature was creeping up as the sun rose to take its rightful place above the trees, and it was too damn hot out to be wearing a tie. A gathering in the middle of the sweltering humidity of the pine woods didn't exactly call for a dress code, but Del was clearly trying to make amends with his father.

"The son that forsakes his earthly father shall be *cast* away from the heavenly father, not *worthy* of his kingdom."

Del's efforts seem to be working out for him, Henry thought.

But seeing Del brought Henry's thoughts back to the night before.

His mother hadn't mentioned anything about the stranger in the woods to anyone, as far as Henry knew. Livingston, he could understand, perhaps. But she was barely speaking to her husband, who had refused to call Del and Alice and apologize.

Henry wondered if he should say anything to Del. He'd heard all the rumors about what went on at the shack next to their place. Everything from Satan worship, to prostitution, to a traveling band of gypsies. None of the stories could be verified, of course, but that had never stopped a small-town rumor before.

If anyone would know the truth, it was Del. And the more Henry thought about it, the more convinced he became that the girl creeping around the woods must be associated somehow with the people who came and went at the old shack. It was the only thing that made any sense.

And that didn't make him feel any better.

Mama wouldn't like it if he spoke to Del about the matter behind her back. But he couldn't shake the sense of foreboding that had gripped him since he'd spotted those neatly stacked plates.

As if his wandering mind had brought the ghost girl into being, Henry spotted a shadow floating through the trees. He kept his head aimed at the book in front of him, cutting a sideways glance toward the woods that surrounded them.

His heart picked up speed, adrenaline spiking in his veins.

She was here.

Playing it calm and unconcerned, Henry debated his next move. Should he charge after her, demand answers?

As Livingston brought his sermon to a close and people began to rise and gather, full up on their weekly dose of sanctimony and bullshit, Henry made a calculated decision.

CHAPTER EIGHT

She saw them gather within the odd clearing in the woods.

At first, she hung back, worried they were coming together to hunt her down and send her back to the men who'd brought her there.

But it became clear soon enough that their agenda had nothing to do with her and everything to do with the brash little man who made a great deal of noise.

She'd heard his words, clanging about like dented pots and pans banging together, but words alone, even loud ones, had long since lost their ability to frighten her.

Instead, she'd turned her attention to the others, studying them from a distance, as she kept herself back within the pines.

When the little man was done with his stump preaching, and the small pockets of people stood and drew together then apart, heading out of the clearing back to where they'd come from, the girl kept herself still and quiet behind the brush where she was hiding. Still and quiet she could do very well.

The young man left quickly, trotting off to catch up with some of the others.

When the field was clear and the voices had faded to nothing, the girl crept forward slowly, making her way into the quiet den of green and sunlight.

She ran her fingertips over the cut stumps the people had used for chairs, feeling the ring of bark that circled the outside and must cut into the backs of their legs.

On the ground, next to the place the young man had been sitting in the back row, she spotted the cover of the white book he'd held in his hands, forgotten and left behind.

Unremembered.

Kneeling, she dared not pick it up, but she couldn't help but caress it, her dirty fingertips a sharp contrast against the worn, but pristinely clean, white cover.

There were words on the cover, and she wondered what they said.

"That was my sister's," came a quiet voice from much too close.

Her head whipped upward, and she fell back onto her butt in surprise.

The man's hands came up slowly, palms outward, and his voice was gentle, but still she scrambled away from him until her back came up against another piece of tree trunk, stopping short her retreat.

"I'm not going to hurt you," he said slowly.

Although she understood the words, she couldn't stop the slow rumble that came from her throat when he took a small, slow step toward her. Her eyes darted around as she desperately calculated her options for escape.

He was close. Too close, and moving closer.

Her breath quickened in anticipation.

Able to see her fear, he stalled, looking like he was searching for the right words.

His image began to blur in her mind with men who had come toward her at other times, their steps slow, their intentions clear. None of them had ever cared about her thoughts on the matter.

She knew instinctively that this was her best chance. This brief split second when he was second-guessing himself.

Launching herself from the ground, she flew at him, catching him by surprise, turning the tables.

The two of them tumbled backward onto the ground, and her hands found his throat.

She could feel the power of him beneath her, knew that he had the advantage. She was small and weak in comparison. She'd never last against him once the element of shock was gone. She had to run, she had to do it now.

And yet . . .

His hands came up to hers, and she squeezed, almost involuntarily, against his vocal cords. Not to hurt him, but in anticipation of those hands hurting her. It was inevitable.

Her breath was hot and ragged, her eyes wide as she met his gaze. He did nothing. Simply looked into her face.

He laid his hands, palms up, on the ground next to his head.

"I'm *not* going to hurt you," he said again, quiet and intense.

Those eyes. That face. She'd never seen eyes look at her like that. He stared, his eyes begging her to believe him, while his body followed his words, lying still and prone beneath hers.

He had the power. He *could* hurt her if he chose to. All he had to do was reach up and take hold. She wasn't strong enough to defend herself this close for very long, not without a weapon of some kind, and she had nothing. She'd always had nothing.

Yet he was giving that power to her, holding back, waiting to see what she would do. And all the while, he was looking at her. Really looking. She couldn't seem to move away from the raw newness of that. Had anyone in her life ever actually looked at her before? She couldn't remember a single time.

There was something alive in that connection, pulsing and electric. It shocked her, and held her. She felt exposed before him, like he could read her past and present and future right there.

She let go of him and pulled away as if his skin were on fire and to stay too close would mean burning alive.

She turned to run. She didn't want to be near this man, who'd already seen more of her than anyone ever had. She had to get away.

With a start, she realized the woman was standing between her and the route back to the safe anonymity of the forest. The stranger's face was set in a picture of compassion, and the girl's heart seized at the expression she barely recognized. Her legs stalled, and she had trouble staying upright. Her senses were overloaded with the proximity of these two people, both so different than anyone she'd ever known.

She felt as if she'd wandered too close to the surface of the sun.

Losing her will to run, the girl felt her legs fold beneath her, and she dropped to the ground. Her face crumbled and she tried in vain to hide her head, to hide her heart, from whatever pain would inevitably come from getting too close to such searing warmth.

CHAPTER NINE

Mama fed the girl, of course, after they'd led her back to their home. While his mother was occupied with the task, Henry had taken the opportunity to step outside and call Del before his brother had a chance to get too far down the road. He was going to need backup. For what, he wasn't sure yet, but it sounded like a good idea to plan ahead, all the same.

When he entered the house, Mama was stepping out of the kitchen to come find him, a concerned look on her face.

He met her in the living room, but his vantage point from where they stood allowed him to glance through the doorway into the kitchen. Henry was shocked to see the girl hunkered down on the floor in the far corner of the room with a plate of food balanced on her knees. A curtain of greasy dark hair shrouded her face, and she was busy scooping food into her mouth with her hands, looking warily up from time to time.

The kitchen chairs sat empty and ignored.

It made Henry profoundly uneasy.

"Mama, I really think you should reconsider feeding the strays around here," Henry said in a low voice.

A snort broke from his mother, and she raised a hand to her mouth, shocked at her unladylike display.

He took a good look at her face, which was pale save for the two spots of color high on her cheeks, but if he wasn't mistaken, there was a definite spark in her eyes. A spark he hadn't seen there in a long time.

"That was unkind, Henry," she said, gathering herself in a cloak of dignity.

"Unkind or not, that girl needs help we're not qualified to give."

The front door opened, bringing Livingston into the room with them. As usual, he paid little attention to anything other than whatever it was he was planning to say next.

"Caroline, I'd like to speak with you, if you could spare a few minutes," Livingston began when he spotted his wife. "In private," he added to Henry.

His timing was laughable.

Mama turned to him, squared her shoulders, and boldly stated, "Livingston. There is a girl in our kitchen who's been living in the woods, for whatever reason. She is my guest, and I expect you to treat her as such. Anything less, from you or any other member of this family," she said with a hard glance in Henry's direction, "and I assure you, you will answer to me."

And with that declaration, she turned and walked away from the two men, heading back into the kitchen to join the girl.

Livingston blinked at her retreating back. He looked at Henry, but all Henry could do was shrug and tilt his head toward the kitchen, where the girl in question was handing her empty plate back to Mama for a second helping.

Livingston followed his gaze.

"What in the Sam Hill?" he said in a low voice.

Henry was saved the necessity of an answer by the opening of the front door, and just like that, they were three.

"Hey," Del said as he joined them. He clearly had matters on his mind as well, if the determined look on his face was any indicator. "Now, Dad," Del began with a hand raised in Livingston's direction. "I know you said you don't want me here, but Henry called and Alice had some errands to run, so I told her to leave me here and pick me up when she was done, so if you insist on holding a grudge, I suppose

I could sit out on the front porch, but that'd be awful uncharitable for a man who . . ."

Del trailed off when he realized that neither Henry nor Livingston was sparing more than a glance in his direction.

"What's going on?" he asked, craning his neck to see what had them so interested. "What in the Sam Hill?" Del asked.

The two men looked at Henry, expecting an explanation, but he could only shrug and shake his head.

He'd be a fool to even try.

CHAPTER TEN

"So she just showed up in the woods?"

Henry nodded. It was the third time in as many minutes that Livingston had asked the question, each time with a touch more disbelief than before. The answer hadn't changed, in spite of that.

The three men had moved outside after Caroline had glared at them, but they kept their voices low, not interested in incurring her wrath.

"She must have come from the shack," Del said.

"That was my thinking as well," Henry agreed.

Del shook his head. "That's not good, man. Not good at all," he mumbled.

Henry squinted and took in the sight of his brother's growing discomfort with the strange situation.

Del tugged at his tie. Henry got the sense his brother was missing his sheriff's uniform, a thing he usually wore like a mantle of superiority about his shoulders, pulling confidence from it almost unconsciously.

Henry had always had doubts about Del's suitability for his chosen profession. It seemed to him that a man with a gun ought not be the same sort of man who thought dick and fart jokes were the height of entertainment. But he couldn't argue that Del had flourished in the job.

At the moment, though, Del had an uneasy expression on his face that struck a sharp chord, chiming with Henry's own misgivings.

"Isn't there somebody we can call?" Livingston asked.

Henry inclined his head toward Del. "Like the Sheriff's Department?"

Livingston turned on his son. "Well? What are you gonna do about it?"

Del ignored his father. "Has she said anything? Why she's here? How she got here? Who she came with?"

Henry shook his head. "Haven't heard her say a word, actually. She did growl at me."

"She growled at you? You let your mother bring home a woman who looks like she's been dug out of a shallow grave, and you're telling me she *growled* at you?" Livingston asked.

Henry threw a look at his stepfather's scandalized face. "For the record, I didn't *let* my mother do anything. When's the last time you managed to talk her out of something her mind was set on, Livingston?"

The little man drew himself up, words shooting out of his mouth like they were under pressure from his puffed-up chest. "Well, she can't stay. That's all there is to it," he said with a dramatic finality.

"As much as it pains me to say this, I agree with you," Henry said. "The trouble is going to be convincing Mama."

Del shook his head. "It's not just a bad idea, buddy. It's a real bad idea."

Henry waited for him to say more, but Del just stood there shaking his head and looking like he'd swallowed a mouthful of something past its expiration date.

"You know something about this you're not saying?" Henry prompted. "Because if you do . . ."

Del shook his head again, but he wouldn't meet Henry's eye.

"No. No," he said. "Nothing official anyway."

"And unofficially?" Henry asked.

Del ran a hand across his face. "An unsubstantiated report. A rumor really, that's all."

It didn't look like Del had any intention of saying more, but Henry's frustration was starting to grow teeth. "Care to elucidate, brother?"

Del sent him a blank look. "What? Don't hit me with those college words, Henry. What the hell does that even *mean* anyway?"

"Just spit it out, Del!"

"Fine! Fine. Jesus. There may have been a . . . an incident. With that group out at the shack a few nights ago."

"What kind of incident?" Henry asked.

"A man was attacked. Supposedly, he was hurt pretty bad. We got a source, Brady and me."

"A source? You and Brady have a source?" Henry asked, one eyebrow up.

"Yeah, a source. This badge didn't come out of a cereal box, you know."

Henry held up his hands at Del's defensive posturing. "All right, Del, all right. I'm sorry."

Slightly mollified, his brother went on, "Apparently, after this scuffle, they packed up and moved on again."

"And what did you and Brady do about that?" Livingston interjected. "Why weren't you out there arresting somebody? Too busy harassing Clayton and watching reruns of *Miami Vice*?"

"Dad, lay off already. Nobody made a report. We didn't even hear about it until after the fact."

"Hmph. From your *source*?"

"Yes, Dad. Look—"

"They may have packed up and moved on, but it looks like they left some of their baggage behind," Henry said.

He had approximately zero interest in watching these two go at each other again.

Del nodded. "And that's the problem. Because rumor has it, the attacker was a female."

Henry nodded. He'd had an idea where this was headed. Only Livingston was taken by surprise.

"A female? *That* female? The one sitting alone in the kitchen with my wife?"

Del shrugged. "I don't know for sure, but it's a possibility."

"A dangerous possibility," Henry murmured, glancing back at the window to the kitchen.

"She can't stay. Henry, you can't be around every minute of the day, and it'd be irresponsible to leave the woman here. Caroline's sick and Dad can't . . ."

Del trailed off, realizing that he'd stepped in it, yet again.

"Dad can't what, exactly?" Livingston said.

"Look, I didn't mean . . . ," Del began in a placating voice, but at the stubborn set of his father's jaw, he could see that wasn't going to work.

He changed his tactic.

"Fine. You can't protect Caroline. Or yourself, for that matter. You're an old man, whether you like it or not."

But as far as tactics went, that one was the wrong one to take.

"Boy," Livingston said, drawing himself up to his full height, all five foot four inches. "I'll have you know, I may be just an *old man*, but this old man can still whoop your ass."

"Dad, don't be this way," Del said.

"No, sir. That's the second time in a matter of days that you've taken that disrespectful tone with me, and I'm done with you, boy. You get your ass out of here. We don't need help from the likes of you."

"Dad, she could be dangerous. Don't do this."

"Maybe she is, and maybe she ain't, but the day I can't handle a slip of a girl is a day that you're never gonna live to see, son. Now, you take your useless tin badge and get the hell out of here."

Henry and Del watched in shared frustration as Livingston marched himself back to the front door and slammed it behind him.

"Damn that old fool," Del spit out. "Sometimes I think I hate that man."

"Amen to that, brother," Henry said with a sigh.

"Look, stick as close to the house as you can," Del said. "And try to get a name from her, where she's from, anything. If you can do that, I'll have a better chance of tracking down where she belongs, then getting her the hell back there and out of here."

Henry remembered the low rumble that had come out of the girl's throat when she had felt threatened. He thought of the way she scooped the food from the plate to her mouth, like she'd never been around a spoon before. He had his doubts about being able to get anything useful out of a woman who was more wild animal than human.

But he nodded all the same.

All he could do was try.

CHAPTER ELEVEN

With a sensation of warm fullness in her belly that she barely recognized, her hunger was sated. For now.

The room was worn, but clean, and smelled of sweet, delicious things.

She wondered how long it would last.

The woman leaned against the counter, glancing in the girl's direction, but not pressing.

"My name is Caroline," she told her. "The man who helped you, that's my son, Henry. There are more, but . . . well, we'll get to that in time."

Hen. Ree. The girl turned the sounds over in her mind, feeling the shape of them.

"Would you like to tell me your name?" Caroline asked.

The girl was silent. Speaking—pushing words past her mind and out of her mouth in predetermined forms—was placing herself in the path of harm.

It had always been this way. She'd long ago adopted silence. It was easy to do. No one asked her anything anyway. Until now.

Caroline accepted her silence with only a glance over her shoulder. She was busy at the sink, cleaning the dishes. She didn't come too close.

The girl was glad.

"That's okay, if you don't want to tell me," she said, her eyes drawn to the world beyond the window. "Those men outside . . . my husband, my sons . . . they're unsure right now about the best way to move forward. When a man is unsure of what to do, he becomes like a child, sometimes."

The girl listened to the rise and fall of Caroline's voice, though the words spoken didn't matter so much. Only the blanketing calm.

"Don't trouble yourself about them, or what they might say. You're safe here."

Caroline wiped her hands on a towel and turned toward the girl. She didn't move any closer, thankfully, but she did tilt her head, trying to make a connection with her eyes.

The girl folded in upon herself, still hunched in the corner on the floor, looking away from those old brown eyes full of things the girl couldn't understand.

"You have my word," Caroline added.

Savoring the idea, the girl recognized that this woman was the only person ever to give her a gift.

First the kindness, so unknown, and now her word, given so freely.

She watched with her hair lowered in front of her face as Caroline laid the towel to dry along the edge of the sink.

"I'll be right back, okay?" she said.

The girl didn't speak, but forced her head to incline, a small recognition that the words had found a home.

The older woman gave a tiny smile at her nod, accepting it as the gift it was intended to be.

"Okay, then," Caroline said. She moved toward the door.

With effort tinged with fear, the girl opened her mouth and formed the shape of a word in the back of her throat. The sound that came out wasn't what she'd meant it to be, hardly a word at all, but it caught on the other woman's ear.

Caroline stopped and turned back to her.

She tried again.

"Girl," she said, a little stronger this time, clearer, though still quiet as a moth's wings.

Caroline cocked her head to one side and pushed the gray hairs that had fallen onto her cheek behind one ear. Two small, deep lines appeared between her brows.

"Girl?" she repeated back to her.

The girl gave a small nod.

"That's what people call you?"

Another infinitesimal nod.

"Do you have any other name?"

This time she shook her head, short and quick, back and forth.

"Hmm," Caroline said, hiding her thoughts behind a mask. "In that case, would you like another name?"

It was the girl's turn to tilt her head to one side, mulling the question.

Caroline waited.

An unvoiced need was growing inside the girl.

She nodded twice, her eyes wide.

Caroline cleared her throat, looking like she was fighting back her emotions.

"Good," she said. "I'm sure we can do better than that."

CHAPTER TWELVE

"Mama?" Henry called. There was no reply. The house was silent, save for the whisper and clicks of the ceiling fans.

"Mama," he called again, louder this time. It wasn't worry, not yet, but it would be soon, if he didn't hear her voice.

With a bump followed by footsteps from the bedroom in the back of the house, he relaxed somewhat.

"Hush now, son. There's no need to shout. My hearing is just fine, thank you," she said in a low voice as she came down the hallway.

"Where is everybody?" he asked. Henry had stepped into the shed and loaded up his truck for the deliveries he'd have to put off until he was comfortable leaving his mother alone with their guest.

"Alice came by and took Del on home. I think he wanted to change out of that silly tie. I've asked them to join us for dinner tonight, though. A peace offering of sorts. I'm not sure where your father's stormed off to. He was a bit . . . let's say miffed, when I let the girl lie down in Mari's room."

"Mari's room?" Henry said, incredulously. No one used Mari's room. Not ever.

"The child was dead on her feet, Henry. Would you prefer I let her rest in your room?"

He held up his hands, a white flag to his mother's defensiveness.

"No, no. Just surprised, that's all."

He thought of Mari's lace curtains and the pale-blue quilt on the bed, the way it had looked when they'd shut the door after clearing it out following her death. Pristine. Empty. A room without an inhabitant.

"I threw a sheet over the bed," Mama said, with a glance in Henry's direction.

Henry thought of the sour odor of abandonment that surrounded the stranger and couldn't help but feel that was wise.

"Livingston was less than pleased, I take it."

His mother patted him on the shoulder. "You've always had a gift for understatement, my boy."

"Mama, Del said there might have been some sort of incident out at the shack."

His mother's back went up. "Livingston mentioned it."

"Oh, I'm sure he did," Henry said. *Mentioned it loudly, no doubt.*

"Two things, Henry," she said, holding up a finger in his direction. "One, we don't know what's happened to bring this woman to our door, but she very clearly needs our help."

"Mama, if—"

She raised a hand to cut him off. "I'm not done. You hear me out, because this is the last time I plan to say this. I am not, nor have I ever been, the kind of person who is willing to turn a blind eye to someone in need. I would hope that I've raised you well enough that you wouldn't either."

She stopped and looked him square in the eye, plainly judging the effect of her words. After a moment, Henry nodded.

"Good. Now, secondly, even if this unconfirmed report is true, even if a man was, in fact, attacked out there and that girl is the one responsible for that . . ." She glanced over her shoulder in the direction of Mari's bedroom and sighed. "At the risk of sounding like I'm taking potshots at your entire gender, Henry, I feel the need to point out that a woman very rarely attacks a man without a good reason. Now, I might be jumping to conclusions here, but the fact that it wasn't officially reported to the police tells me I'm probably not."

Henry had nothing to say to that. He couldn't fault her logic. He didn't like it, not even a little bit. But she had a point. Somehow, that didn't ease his tension.

"I'll be staying close to the house, until we know the whole story," he said. His mother started to speak, but it was Henry's turn to put his foot down. "And I don't want to argue about it."

She finally nodded, granting him this small measure of reassurance. And small it was, indeed.

Mama suddenly looked very tired. The air of capability that she was normally so careful to keep in place slipped for just a moment, and Henry got a glimpse of the exhaustion and pain she was carrying around. It squeezed the breath from him.

"I believe I'll rest for a little while myself," she said, her words no longer propped up by the strength of her convictions. "It's chicken tonight for dinner." Henry could have howled at the banality of the words. She patted his arm again, and turned to find her own bed. "Don't be late," she called over her shoulder. "You know how your father gets."

Not my father, he heard echoing in the distant caverns of his mind, but the thought lacked its usual vehemence as he watched his mother shuffle down the hallway.

Along the way, she passed the room where the girl rested.

If Henry or his mother had chosen to look into the room, they would have been struck by the contrast of the filthy person curled up on the bed and wearing rags to the clean sunlight streaming through the windows.

Henry's brows would have drawn together in concern for what the future would bring and what part this unnamed girl would play in it. Caroline's thoughts would have been more inclined toward empathy, leaving the practicalities to sort themselves out.

Neither would have noticed the shallow breaths that indicated the girl was still awake, listening intently to their words. Neither would have seen the knife from the kitchen that the girl had slipped between the folds of her clothing, then held tightly to her heart as she lay on the bed.

But neither chose to look, and the girl finally gave in to a sleep that was deep and dreamless, her grip on the handle of the knife never loosening, even then.

CHAPTER THIRTEEN

"What the hell's going on around here, Henry?" Alice asked later that day. "Del said Caroline's taken in a homeless girl?"

They were out at the shed, where Henry was filling jars with the lemon drop vodka that was so popular at the local bar. He'd save a few for Ms. Watson too. He knew she liked it.

"'Homeless' might be too kind. She's more feral than anything else," he said to his sister-in-law over his shoulder.

"You're not kidding, are you?" she asked with a look of disbelief.

"Nope," he said.

Alice chewed on a fingernail, her worried face echoing his own feelings on the matter. "Henry, I realize that nobody likes to talk about it," she said after a moment, "but I know you're aware what the doctor said about the cancer."

He nodded. "That without treatment, it would spread? Yeah, I know."

She watched his face, not unkindly. "Have you considered . . . I mean . . . ," Alice trailed off.

"What? You think the cancer's affecting her judgment?" he asked, genuinely surprised.

"Well, cancer's unpredictable," she said. "There's no way to know where it'll spread. Lungs, lymph nodes . . ."

"Her brain? Is that what you're trying to say without coming out and saying it?"

Alice looked at him apologetically. "Well, it's a possibility."

Henry thought about it for a moment, but only a moment. "No," he said, shaking his head. "Not unless old-fashioned Christian charity can be chalked up to brain cancer. Her mind's as sharp as it always was. It's the rest of her I'm worried about."

Alice sighed. "Have you tried talking her into chemo again?" she asked.

Henry turned back to the sterilized jars on the rack. He didn't want Alice to see the helplessness on his face. "Me, Livingston, the doctors. We've all tried till we were blue in the face. She won't have it. Not again. She says she'd rather have three months of better-than-nothing over a year of living hell."

Alice nodded. "I can't say I agree with her, but I understand, I suppose."

Henry had tried to understand too. He really had.

"Ovarian cancer, at this stage, is nearly impossible to get rid of entirely," the doctor had said after the cancer had come back. "But more chemotherapy can prolong your life, Mrs. Doucet."

Mentally preparing himself for the months of sickness and pain that the second round of treatment would bring about, Henry had done a double take when his mother had smiled gently at the man.

"Thanks, Doc, but I believe I'll pass."

It had been easier to come to terms with her decision four months earlier when she had said the words. And to be fair, Mama had seemed to be doing well. She tired easily but insisted on continuing to do the things she'd always done for as long as she was capable.

Thinking of the exhaustion he'd glimpsed in his mother earlier, he was keenly aware that she was living on borrowed time.

"She was resting, but I'm sure she's up by now. Why don't we go up to the house, and you can judge for yourself her mental state?"

"Henry, you know I didn't mean to imply anything."

He nodded. "No worries, Alice," he said, holding the door of the shed open for her. "I almost wish I *could* blame it on a brain tumor.

But the truth is, she's just a good person. A better person than me, and definitely a better person than Livings—"

Henry stopped in his tracks, and his mouth hung open at the sight that greeted them. There wasn't much that left Henry flabbergasted, but seeing the girl from the woods in the chicken coop, with her dark, ragged clothing flapping about her, clutching a hatchet in one hand and one of Mama's broody hens in the other brought him up short.

"Oh my—" Alice gasped by his side, bringing a hand to her mouth.

The hatchet came down on the neck of the chicken with a gruesome thud.

"God," Alice breathed out.

Oblivious to the dust and blood, the girl dropped to the ground right there in the coop and set to plucking the unfortunate animal, ignoring the squawking and the ruckus the rest of the hens were making at the deadly stranger in their midst.

CHAPTER FOURTEEN

Alice's face was pale when Henry held the front door for her.

They could hear Livingston's perpetual carping from the direction of the kitchen and followed the sound. They arrived just in time to see Henry's mother slam a bowl onto the counter in an uncharacteristic show of temper.

"Enough," Mama said, loudly interrupting her husband, who'd gone somewhat red in the face. His thinning hair was standing on end, as if the frustration of dealing with his wife's pigheadedness had overloaded his circuits, sending a jolt of electric current through him.

"We've been married for seventeen years, Livingston Doucet." Mama gestured with the large knife in her hand. "And I've been a damn good wife. I dare anyone to say any differently."

"Caroline—"

"Shut up and listen to me, Livingston. I don't have a lot of time left on this earth, and I'm getting awfully tired of people interrupting me. And that goes for all of you," she added, waving the pointy end of the knife around the room, first at Del, who was leaning against the counter with his hands in his pockets, then to Henry and Alice in the doorway. When she was sure she had their attention, Mama went on.

"Now, I've put up with your opinions and your loud mouth and all your posturing because I know that, deep down, you are a good man. Are you intending to prove me wrong today?"

"You've got to realize, Caroline, that you can't just drag up with a wild girl in tow and expect to put her in Maribel's room," Livingston said, pleading now. He looked around at the rest of them for support, but Del was suddenly unduly interested in his shoes.

Alice met Henry's eyes uneasily, then glanced back over her shoulder, clearly thinking about the girl in question, who was, as far as they knew, still relieving Mama's prized laying hen, Mathilda, of her feathers. *Mathilda won't need them now anyway,* Henry thought. *Seeing how she no longer has a head.*

Unaware of the carnage in the chicken coop, Mama crossed her arms and faced down her husband.

"Frankly, Livingston, I find it more than a little bit offensive that you've pushed me to this, but might I remind you that this is *my* house? Mine. It was mine before we got married, and it's mine still. And if you don't calm yourself down, then I swear to the good Lord above that I will change my will *today* and leave it to the Second Baptist Church when I go."

"Now see here, Caroline . . . ," Livingston blustered. But the stony look on her face never wavered. "You wouldn't . . . ," he trailed off.

"You think I'm bluffing?" Mama's eyebrows shot up, and her arms crossed in front of her. "Go ahead, call my bluff. See what happens."

The couple's eyes were locked upon one another, and Henry couldn't help thinking of something Mama had told him often: "When you see a fight in front of you, son, there's one thing you need to ask yourself. Is this the hill I want to die on today? Most of the time, the answer to that is no, probably not. But every once in a while, the answer will be yes. Because it matters that much. Learn to tell the difference and you'll be just fine."

His mother had chosen her hill.

"As much as I hate to interrupt, Mama, there's something I think you need to see," Henry said quietly. "Outside," he added with a nod of his head toward the door.

His mother took a good long look at his expression, then nodded. "Okay, then," she said, the fire in her face banking somewhat. "Show me."

Alice moved back a few steps, and Henry gestured for his mother to step through the front door. Out of curiosity, Del and Livingston brought up the rear.

They didn't have to go far. As the five of them stepped onto the porch with Mama in the lead, the strange girl was headed back in their direction, done now with the chicken coop. Mama stopped at the edge of the steps, and the rest of them fanned out behind her.

Henry couldn't see his mother's face when the girl stopped short of walking up the steps, but he could see the darker places on the girl's dirty clothing where blood had soaked in, and he could see the white and brown feathers clinging to her in clumps.

With her eyes lowered, she held out the dead bird with one hand, an offering to Mama.

"Chicken," the girl said in a voice so low that Henry could barely make out the words. "For your dinner," she added.

Unable to contain his curiosity, Henry took a step forward and glanced over to gauge his mother's reaction to that.

Mama's face was decidedly calm, though her eyes had gone wider than normal, and she blinked several times as she took in the scene.

"Well, um," his mother said, then cleared her throat. "Thank you, dear."

She straightened her back and moved down the steps, meeting the girl at the bottom. The stranger held the denuded carcass out for her, which Mama accepted with an impressive amount of grace.

"Thank you," she said to the girl again. "It's a little . . . well, a little *fresher* than what I had in the fridge, but this will do just fine," she added with an encouraging smile, while the girl looked down at the ground.

Henry's mother turned back toward her family, who were gaping at the pair of them.

The girl raised her head for just a moment, her eyes seeking out Henry. When he met her gaze, he felt an uncomfortable pull and the remembered sensation of the girl's hands on his throat.

He broke the unwanted connection and looked back at his mother. The girl's eyes dropped to the ground again, but not before the thought flitted across Henry's mind that the world was spinning beneath them, out of his control, and the best he could hope for was to cling tightly to the surface.

"Well, what are you all gawping at?" Mama asked, pulling Henry back to the practicalities of the present. His mother put a gentle hand on the girl's arm and guided her toward the front door. "Where do you think the other stuff comes from? The chicken fairy?" His mother shook her head at them all, standing speechless as they passed. "Honestly, people."

Henry met Alice's eyes, which were wide and questioning, reflective of the weirdness of the situation. He could only shrug, turning his hands palm up, as if to say, *What do we do now?*

For his part, Del was looking distinctly out of his depth. But Livingston was the one who found his voice first, speechlessness not being a state he was overly familiar with.

"Caroline!" he called to his wife's retreating figure. He followed her with a fresh determination on his face. The rest of them had little choice but to trail along in their wake. "I don't understand what's gotten into you, woman, but if you think for a minute that this is okay, then you have another think coming. I absolutely will *not* allow—"

Henry saw his mother turn to face her husband from the doorway into the kitchen, and the look on her face brought them all up short, including Livingston.

"Test me, Livingston," she said quietly. "I dare you."

He took a step back and peered at his wife like he was looking for some sign of the amiable, gentle woman he'd married. But she wasn't there. Not today.

He sputtered. He hemmed and hawed. He opened his mouth to make sounds into words several times but couldn't manage it. All the while, Mama stared him down, waiting for Livingston to stop flopping like a fish on the deck and accept his fate.

"That . . . that unholy creature will have to accept Jesus as her savior before she can stay in my—"

Livingston broke off when his wife tilted her head and crossed her arms, looking at that very moment as if she were capable of breathing fire into his face.

"In *our* home," he backtracked carefully. "She's got to be baptized, Caroline. Can't you give me that, at least? Please?"

Henry had never heard Livingston plead with anyone before. He thought it might be a brand-new experience for the man, and for a moment, he thought his mother might be inclined to tell him where he could shove his request.

But he saw her soften, then glance over her shoulder into the kitchen at the girl. When she looked back at Livingston, her eyes were kinder.

"All right, then. After dinner," she said with a nod. Livingston gave a sigh of relief that deflated him, though whether it was at the idea of cleansing the girl's soul in the spirit of the Lord, or simply because he felt he'd managed to save some face, Henry couldn't guess.

"A bit of a rinse in the river wouldn't hurt anyway," Mama added. "Now, if you don't mind, I have a chicken to deal with. Go do something useful."

Livingston nodded. It was settled, then.

CHAPTER FIFTEEN

Caroline had tried to explain to the girl about this thing called baptism, but she didn't understand it. Something about giving her soul to the mercy of God.

That sounded fine. God could have it if it meant she could stay here, within this place of warmth she'd stumbled into. Her soul hadn't been much use to her so far, and she didn't think she'd miss it.

The grass rustled under her feet as they walked, Caroline's husband several steps in front of them, striding with a purpose. Where they were headed to, she didn't know and didn't care. Caroline was talking to her, and she was trying to listen, but her thoughts kept darting out of her reach, finding Henry instead. He was a mystery to her, as so much of this place was. When they'd eaten their dinner, she'd moved to sit in the same corner she'd sat in before, but he'd placed a hand on her arm and guided her to a chair at the table.

He hadn't smiled, hadn't spoken, but she felt his eyes on her during the meal and tried to come to terms with the uncomfortable sensation of being seen. The other man, the one they called Del, had leaned forward and fired questions at her that made her shrink back in her chair, until Caroline had insisted that was enough.

But Henry had only watched, his silence somehow louder than the barrage of questions that made her wish he hadn't insisted she sit there, on display.

"What's your name, girl?" Caroline's husband had demanded to know. Caroline had given him a firm shake of the head, but he pressed on. "Have to know for the baptism, don't I?"

The girl's shoulders had slumped lower still as she cast a glance at the only person in the room she believed to be on her side.

Caroline gave a sad sigh, coupled with a small smile of encouragement in her direction. "We're working on that, Livingston," she told him, though her gaze was still on the girl. "A little patience wouldn't go amiss."

He'd blustered on after that, but the girl looked down at the plate of food in front of her and allowed Caroline to field any further questions.

But now, with evening beginning to cascade down around them, Caroline had questions of her own.

"Is there a name you like, dear?" she asked.

The girl bit her lower lip, then said in a low voice, so Caroline had to lean in to hear her, "Don't know any names that don't already belong to someone."

Caroline nodded. "Fair enough," she said, gazing off into the distance. Henry hadn't joined them. Del and his wife either.

"Hmm," she said. "My grandmother's name was Maude." She gave a small chuckle. "Lovely woman, but my goodness, what an awful name. Maude. Sounds like something you'd scrape off the bottom of your shoe.

"No," Caroline continued. "Something pretty, I think. I get the feeling you haven't had much pretty in your life, have you?"

The girl held herself tighter, her throat thick with the truth of just how much ugly she'd known.

Caroline's keen eyes missed very little.

"Her sister's name was Eve. My great-aunt. Evangeline, actually, but everyone called her Eve." Caroline shook her head. "Can't imagine what their mother was thinking, calling one daughter Maude and the other Evangeline. Asking for trouble, in my opinion. And truth be told, they had no use for one another, sisters or not. Maybe that was the root of the problem."

Caroline seemed content to ramble on without expecting the girl to fill in the gaps, and the tension in her shoulders eased a bit with that realization.

They'd come to the edge of a river, north of where the girl had hidden in the woods. The world was different here. Beautiful, yes, but different. Where the marsh was enclosed, a bubble of a world that knew all her secrets and taunted her with them, the river was wide and arrogant. It didn't care about her secrets. It didn't care about anything.

"Eve," Caroline said, tilting her head and trying it out. "I think it suits you."

The girl saw the question in the older woman's face.

"Eve?" she whispered, hardly daring to meet Caroline's eyes. She stiffened when the other woman reached out and took the girl's hand in her own.

"Only if you want, dear."

Breath held close, not daring to let it out, the girl gave a nod. She'd never wanted anything more.

Caroline's smile was gentle as she patted the girl's hand, so grimy and stained between her own, which were cool as old coins worn smooth with age.

"Eve it is, then."

There was a splash from the direction of the river. The two women turned to see Livingston wading into the water, forcing it to part and flow around him. Up to his waist, he turned and gave an impatient wave of his arm.

"Come on, then, girl. Ain't got all day," he called.

With a shake of her head, the girl resisted. "Not girl. Not anymore," she said shakily.

Caroline gave her a wide smile.

"Her name is Evangeline, Livingston. You can call her Eve," she told him over the sounds of the river and the cicadas.

"Eve, is it?" he called back. "Well, isn't that just fine and dandy. Pardon me, then, and thank you very much, *Eve*, but we've got the

Lord's work to be getting on with. Come on, now." He placed his hands on his hips and scowled up at her.

She glanced at Caroline, who gave her a quick hug and a small nod. "Go on, love. You'll be fine."

She hesitated. But in the end, it seemed a small token to give in return for the look on Caroline's face. She stood a little straighter and walked toward Livingston.

Gingerly, Eve made her way down the path to the river. She looked back over her shoulder at Caroline, who smiled and nodded encouragingly, but she couldn't help but wish that Henry had chosen to join them. She couldn't shake him from her mind.

"Come on, girl," Livingston barked.

She whipped around and looked him in the eye.

"Eve," she said, with her head and shoulders held high.

"Ah, got a bit of spirit in there, after all, do you?" He gave her a smirk that had no kindness in it.

The dark water pulled at her, lapping her body, as she stood face-to-face with the loud man who thought of her as no one. But she wasn't no one anymore. She was Evangeline.

"Are you willing to trust your everlasting soul into the keeping of Jesus Christ, in atonement for your sins, and beg his forgiveness in exchange for the promise of eternal life?"

The words were loud, spit into her face with a fervor that made her pull back.

A gleam came into Livingston's eyes, seeing her reluctance, and it spurred him to throw more words at her like a hunter with a spear, searching for weak spots.

"Well?" he demanded. "Are you willing to forsake Satan and his evil works and ways, girl? Are you?"

She inhaled deeply, and with a sense of purpose that had little to do with God and everything to do with proving this little man wrong, she spoke in a clear, concise voice, "Yes. I am."

He raised his eyebrows at her prideful stance, but she wasn't done. "And my name is not *girl*. It's Evangeline."

A flush crept up Livingston's neck, and his hands curled at his sides, but she wouldn't back down.

"Well, then, *Evangeline*," he said softly, stressing each of the syllables of the name with mocking precision, "I now baptize you—"

His hands came at her like whips as he reached out and grabbed her by the arms, pushing her down into the dark, rolling waters.

The world around her was gone, and she was surrounded by nothing but the sound of water rushing into her nose and mouth, the bubbles rising up. The face of Livingston wavered above her through the water. She heard nothing, knew nothing, except for those hands holding her beneath the surface of the water.

With a cry that was borne away by the river, she fought against him, struggling to break his hold and free herself. The river had made its way into her lungs, sucked in by her panic. Livingston's grip grew tighter, digging into her arms, and his voice grew louder, but it was muffled and distorted. She couldn't hear his fevered words, nor the cries from Caroline to let her up.

She could hear nothing but her own death, creeping toward her, cutting her off from a life she'd barely begun to glimpse. A life she realized that she wanted desperately to live.

With all the strength she had in her to give, Eve broke away from the hands holding her. She was free.

But in her struggle and confusion, she lost her way. Death was coming closer now. There had been times in her life she'd begged for him, pleaded for him to take her, but she found she'd changed her mind. She was no longer a girl with no name and no will to live.

But Death didn't care. He was coming, and the river was carrying her to meet him.

The world grew dim.

CHAPTER SIXTEEN

With a grimace, Henry placed the garbage bag containing Mathilda's remains into the trash bin next to the house, turning over the conversation he'd had with his brother while they'd cleaned up the chicken coop.

"The problem isn't just whether Caroline wants to play Mother Teresa with this girl. It's bigger than that," Del had said.

"How so?" Henry asked.

"Well, for one thing, Dad's not far off when it comes to those people at the shack. We *do* have suspicions of criminal activity over there."

Henry shook his head and dumped the mess at the business end of the shovel he was holding into the garbage bag that Del held open for him.

"Then, for God's sake, why don't you do something about it?"

Del shifted his weight from one foot to the other. "It's not that easy. We don't have anything concrete, and you can't just go arresting people based off of rumors and suspicions, no matter what Dad might think."

"So what are you saying?" Henry asked, jabbing the end of the shovel into the ground and leaning against the handle.

"I'm saying, if Caroline's going to keep this girl around, you need to watch your back. Because whatever those people are doing, they'll be back."

"Do you really think she hurt somebody?" Henry asked. He knew what he thought, but he wanted to hear Del's opinion.

Del looked over toward the house. Alice was walking down the steps, heading in their direction.

"I think it's never a good idea to underestimate a woman, Henry. Even under the best of circumstances." He twisted a knot into the top of the trash bag and handed it to Henry. "Just keep your eyes open, okay? Until we know what we're dealing with."

Del and Alice had gone home, but his brother's warnings stayed behind, and Henry couldn't keep his thoughts from circling around the girl. She pulled at him.

Giving in, he slammed the lid on the garbage can and headed toward the river.

When he came to the line of trees that bordered the water, standing tall and proud, he hesitated. Rubbing a hand over his face, he was on the verge of turning back when his mother's shouts broke through his indecision.

Running down the path to the river, he had only a split second to take in the scene in front of him. Livingston was standing midstream, and Mama was starting to wade in, yelling at her husband, "Let her up, Livingston!"

But Livingston was standing, his hands empty. Henry's eyes followed the path of the river, searching, looking for the dark place that would indicate where the girl must be.

At first he couldn't see her. His eyes scanned back and forth, and then, there she was, rushing downriver, caught in the flow of the water.

"No, Mama!" Henry shouted as he ran toward the girl. "Stay back!" The undertow could be vicious.

"Henry, go!" his mother shouted, but it was unnecessary. He was already making his way south to the side of the river, running through the brush and brambles, over downed logs, to try and get in front of the girl, hoping like hell he could get there in time.

There was no easy path to the water here—the banks rose sharply on either side of where Livingston and the girl had been—and Henry had no choice but to take a running leap from the drop-off at the edge. His legs and arms whirled as he flew through the air.

The river came up to meet him, and the sounds of water rushing around him filled his ears as he was swallowed whole. With no time to waste, he fought his way to the surface, knowing all the while that seconds counted. Seconds could be the difference between life and death.

As he broke through the water to the darkening day around him, he was oriented north. He could see Livingston, still standing upriver on the shallow plateau. He could see Mama, her hand over her mouth as she stood at the edge of the water. But as his eyes scanned the river surrounding him, he had a moment of anguish when he couldn't find the girl. Gone, just like she'd never been.

He was too late.

"There! Henry, there!" his mother cried, pointing.

He turned his head, just in time to see a dark form break the surface of the water to his right. He reached out a hand, lunging toward her, but she was too far away. He came back with nothing.

But he'd be damned if he let her go now.

With a burst of determination, Henry sliced through the water, pushing himself to reach her. He had to reach her this time. He'd only get one more chance.

Praying he was close enough, and with a growing sense of dread that he'd come up empty-handed again, he made a grab for the dark fabric being carried away from him.

And missed.

His hand passed just millimeters from the girl's ratty clothing. It may as well have been miles.

Failure exploded upon him in a mushroom cloud as his hand passed through empty water.

Images of another body in the water flashed through his mind. Another girl he'd been too late to save. Those images were so powerful, so debilitating, that when his hand, still open and clutching, came into contact with a limb below the surface of the water, he very nearly fumbled his final chance.

But his hand, reacting before his brain had a chance to battle its way out of the thorny maze of painful memories, had a mind of its own. With a grip that wouldn't allow another one to be taken by the river—not today—it tightened upon the arm of the girl from the woods, holding fast.

The river still carried them, pushing and pulling farther and farther downstream, but now they were two.

Henry yanked the girl toward him, and her head broke the surface, wet hair hanging across her face, but they weren't in the clear yet. She wasn't moving.

He turned her on her back, gripping her beneath the arms with one hand while he fought his way to the edge of the river. His legs and one free arm pulled them closer and closer, until finally, he was able to come near enough that the undertow let them loose.

Henry pulled the girl up onto the bank. She wasn't breathing, nothing but pale skin and dead weight. Adrenaline was pumping through him as he pushed the wet hair away from her face.

With desperation and prayers, Henry brought his mouth to hers, pushing air into her lungs, willing her to live. This girl he didn't know, didn't even want to know, couldn't die on him here. Not like this.

He pushed air in again, then moved to press the heels of his hands upon her chest—one, two, ten, twenty, thirty times.

"Breathe, damn you, breathe," he whispered, over and over, river water dripping from him onto her unmoving body.

But she didn't.

Leaning in, he forced air into her lungs again, with all the crushing weight of loss that was beginning to descend on him.

"Live, damn it. Live," he demanded as he pushed on her chest again. "I don't have room on my back to carry your death too."

Henry didn't know if there was a God listening or not, but if there was, it was his mother's God. The one who lived in the beauty of the woods, the one who had a cruel side, and a merciful side as well.

The girl coughed. River water spewed from her mouth as her body jerked and gagged, expelling the liquid from her lungs and throat.

Turning her on her side, Henry laid his head on the girl's shoulder and closed his eyes while she coughed up death. He sucked in long, deep breaths, trying to quiet the shaking that was taking over his body.

He sent up a prayer of thanks, just in case anyone was listening.

CHAPTER SEVENTEEN

They stood apart, beneath the shared blanket of the night. Eve had been quiet since their return from the river. Henry had no way of knowing the thoughts that must have been churning behind her enigmatic eyes. But he'd given up trying to fight his compulsion to find out.

As she stood with the moon behind her, he watched her with a focus he didn't care to examine. Eve held her arms tightly around herself, and he was struck by how the changes in her managed to highlight the things that remained the same. Her hair hung down her back, revealing a face that might have been washed clean of dirt and grime, yet still gave nothing away. Her posture was tall, claiming more space in the world, but her shoulders still turned inward upon herself. Her clothes were clean, an old sundress of Mari's and an oversized cardigan, but they hung from her frame in a loose way that proclaimed them not her own. She didn't seem to notice, or care.

He'd never seen anyone who looked so apart from the rest of the human race.

Taking the steps down the porch, he approached her, drawn in by her isolation. Once at her side, he searched for words that might let her know that she wasn't alone. If she didn't want to be, that was.

He failed, and settled instead on putting his hands in his pockets and hoping his presence alone could convey that.

After a while, she turned her head to meet his eyes. She didn't smile, and neither did he.

"You saved me," she said, studying him.

It wasn't a question, and he needn't reply, so he remained silent and waited to see if she'd say more.

"Why?" she asked finally.

He drew back. *What kind of question was that?* He opened his mouth to say the obvious things. *Because you needed help. Because it's what anyone would have done. Because I couldn't let you drown.*

But those weren't the words that came out.

"A long time ago, my sister died. In the river. Alone. Her skin was cold and pale when I found her. I still dream about it sometimes."

Eve tilted her head to the side, peering at him. She offered no condolences or sympathy, and he was glad of it. He imagined her as a person who'd been whittled down to the core, with nothing left over for social niceties or expectations. Nothing left but sinew and bone. He shook his head at himself. How would he know?

"You cared for her?" Eve asked.

"Yes," he said simply.

She nodded, then turned her face back to the dark outline of the forest that surrounded them.

"Do you have family? That you miss? Someone that's missing you?" He didn't want to pry, but he couldn't stop himself.

She looked back toward him, but her eyes grew unfocused, and he had the feeling that she was gazing at something else entirely.

"No," she said shortly, turning away.

"Who are you?" he couldn't stop himself from asking. "Where do you come from?"

He saw a shiver run through her, and she held her arms more tightly around her body.

"No one," she whispered, while Henry strained to hear her. "I'm no one. From nowhere."

The words rang with a hollow, haunting note of desolation, pulling at Henry in a deep, dark place that he hardly knew existed. Those words wrapped around his soul, and he yearned to give her better, determined that this was one thing he could do. He could fix it. For this one woman, this one broken soul, he could make things right.

He'd failed before, failed with Mari, and now she was gone forever, nothing left of her save the memories that haunted those who'd loved her but never understood her.

He wouldn't fail again.

"Not anymore," he said. "Not anymore."

The first time Henry had met Eve's eyes, he'd felt pierced through. With these words, he formed the first unbreakable thread that would bind them together. He did it without conscious thought, with no regard to the consequences.

In the weeks that followed, a thousand more tiny stitches were woven through their hearts. When Eve plucked a wildflower to give to Mama—a child's gesture of admiration that lit his mother's face— another stitch. When she turned her silent face to the morning sun, soaking it in like she'd never bathed in its light before, another.

When Mama taught her to weave on her old loom, a pursuit his mother had shown little interest in since the cancer, and they both laughed like girls at Eve's first awkward scraps of cloth, yet another stitch was pulled taut.

When Eve began to make a deep guttural sound in her throat at Livingston's sharp words toward Mama over dinner, a sound that brought to mind a wolf warning of imminent danger, his mother patted her hand and reassured Eve that all was well.

And another stitch tightened.

In quiet ways, a strange love grew. Not with a bang, not with hugs and kisses, but silently, insidiously. Neither Henry nor Eve knew they were resting in the eye of a storm, a storm of their own making.

When the winds of that storm inevitably began to blow, they'd have nothing to cling to but one another. Nothing to shield them from the fallout, when life and death came crashing together with a thunderous roar and a strange, inevitable love became stained with obsession.

CHAPTER EIGHTEEN

One month later

"Henry, my boy, come on back to my office after you unload that whiskey and we'll get your money sorted out."

King Barrett, proprietor of the local beer joint, was in a good mood that day. Henry normally had to hunt him down to get paid. Worse, if it was "his time of the month," as his wife, Raylene, referred to those dark days when taxes came due, Henry would have to sit through an endless rant about the "evil, thieving hand of the guv'ment" before King handed over payment. He'd heard it so many times, he knew just where to throw in the occasional "Obviously," or "Criminal, ought to be locked up, the lot of them," until King ran out of steam.

Henry glanced over toward the bar, where Raylene had given Eve a bottle of orange soda. He could hear the two women chatting. Well, Raylene did the talking, but Eve gave the occasional shy smile as she sipped the sugary drink and listened to the older woman flutter on. It was early, and the place was nearly empty.

"It's all there," King said, handing over an envelope of cash when Henry joined him in his cramped back office.

"Sure it is, you sneaky old SOB," Henry said, opening the envelope to count the money. "And I had to duck to miss the pigs flying past when I came through the back door."

Far from apologetic, King just shrugged. "Can't blame a man for trying."

Opening a drawer in his desk, he pulled out an additional bill and handed it over.

Henry counted it anyway, then raised an eyebrow at the bar owner.

With a sigh, King reached in the drawer again and added another bill to the stack.

"You're heartless, son. Just like your daddy before you."

Folding up the envelope and sliding it into his back pocket, Henry gave King a nod.

"I'll take that as a compliment."

"Intended as one," King said, patting Henry on the shoulder as they walked out of the office. "You know, Henry, there's been lots of talk going around."

"Talk tends to do that."

"Don't give me any guff, boy. I'm concerned."

Henry's brows shot up. "You're concerned? About what?"

"This mystery girl you got hanging around," King said in a low voice, nodding toward the bar. "People are saying a lot of crazy things."

King stood there looking at Henry like a tabloid reporter waiting on the inside scoop.

"And?"

"What do you mean 'And'? Don't you want to set them straight?"

"You'd do that for me, King? Set them straight?"

King leaned in conspiratorially. "Course I would, Henry. You know you can count on old King."

Henry thought about it for a moment, then nodded solemnly.

"All right, then. You tell them . . . You tell them that that girl . . ." Henry leaned in closer to King. "That girl out there is none of their damn business."

King stood straighter and shook his head at Henry. "Go on with you, then. You Martells. A more tight-fisted, closed-lipped bunch of—"

The sounds of shouting and glass shattering interrupted them. Henry turned away from King and ran toward the bar, where the voices were coming from, becoming louder by the moment.

As he skidded around the corner, Henry took in the sight of Eve backing away from a man on the same side of the bar. Her eyes were bright and wide, her breathing shallow. She was holding the broken orange soda bottle by the neck, like a knife, in a tight, unflinching grip.

Raylene was frozen with a bar towel in her hand, shocked into stillness by the sudden and violent shift of what had been a fine morning. But it was the old drunk bleeding onto the front of his shirt from a cut on his cheek who was making all the noise.

"Ah, Lordy, I'm bleeding! I didn't mean you no harm, girl," Dwight Pennick was saying, as he took his hand from his cheek to look at the blood on his palm.

Behind Dwight's words, Henry could hear King speaking on the phone. "Send one of the deputies down to my place, Gladys," he was saying to the dispatcher for the Sheriff's Department. "We got ourselves a problem, and it ain't even lunchtime yet."

Henry came around the corner of the bar and stood in front of Eve. He had to stoop to put his face in her line of sight, and he watched her eyes come back to focus on him.

"Eve, give me the bottle," he said in a voice that was calm but brooked no argument.

She looked down at her hand, as if noticing the broken glass for the first time. It had spots of blood clinging to the sharp parts, bright and red.

He placed his hands slowly around hers, and peeled her fingers from the makeshift weapon.

"Henry, I swear, I didn't mean her no harm. I just walked up to say hey there and introduce myself to a pretty girl. I didn't mean to scare her none."

Henry set the broken bottle on the bar but kept his eyes on Eve as he spoke to the man he'd known his entire life. Dwight was seventy, if he was a day, and he'd spent most of those days avoiding work and searching for his next beer. The only things he'd ever been dangerous to were the fish in the river.

"I know, Dwight, I know. No worries, man. How bad is it, Raylene?" he asked.

The bar owner's wife had come around and was taking a look at Dwight's face.

"Oh, I think he's gonna live," she said. "I got a first-aid kit behind the bar, Dwight. A little disinfectant and a butterfly bandage or two, and you'll be right as rain."

Dwight, God love him, was still trying to apologize as he let Raylene lead him, casting a wide berth around Henry and Eve, to the back of the bar so she could doctor his cheek.

"I'm sorry, Henry. Ma'am, I didn't mean no disrespect, I promise you."

Eve hardly looked at him as he passed by. Her eyes were locked on Henry's.

"Come on, Eve," he said, leading her to a table away from the bar. "Everything's okay. You just sit down in this chair right here. Can you do that for me?"

She nodded and dropped into a chair. Henry knelt in front of her.

"You're okay. You're safe. Nobody's gonna hurt you. Do you understand what I'm telling you? You're safe."

She nodded again.

"Now, I need to go and check on Dwight. You just sit tight, okay?"

Looking down at her hands, twisting one upon the other in her lap, she nodded again.

With one last glance at her, Henry turned back to the three people gathered at the bar. Raylene was dabbing at Dwight's face with a cotton swab, and King was standing by with his hands on his hips.

"Damn, Henry, I feel real bad about scaring the girl."

"He really didn't do anything, Henry. Just sat down next to her," Raylene said, meeting his eyes with a worried look of her own, then looking back at her patient. "Guess you'll think twice before you stick that ugly mug of yours in a woman's face again, won't you?"

Dwight chuckled, then winced as Raylene dabbed some more alcohol on his cheek. "If that ain't the truth."

They all turned as the front door swung open, letting the morning sun come in along with Brady Watson in his brown deputy's uniform.

"Took you long enough," King said.

"It's been all of a minute and a half since Gladys got me on the radio," Brady said, rolling his eyes at King. "You're lucky, I was headed this way anyway."

"Ah, man," Dwight said, shifting in his seat to look at King. "You didn't have to go and call the cops. It's just a scratch. I had worse from trying to shave after a few beers."

"Be still, will you, Dwight, or this is gonna open up again before I can get the bandages on, and I don't want blood on my new blouse," Raylene said, taking Dwight by the chin and turning his head back.

"What happened to your face, Dwight?" Brady asked, leaning in low to peer at the old man's cheek.

"I'll tell you what happened," King said, pointing at the chair where Eve was sitting, staring at her hands. "That girl over there happened."

Everyone's heads turned toward Eve.

Brady whistled low and rocked back on his heels.

"That little old thing did this to you?"

"It's nothing, Brady. I'm telling you. Just a misunderstanding. My fault for coming up on her sudden-like. I ain't gonna press no charges. Nothing to see here, so you may as well go on about your business."

"All right, all right," Brady said, holding his palms out toward Dwight. "Cool your jets, old man. I'm not the gestapo."

"Thank you. Really," Henry said to Dwight, who nodded.

"Even if he doesn't press charges, I don't want to see her back in here again, Henry. You hear me?" King added.

Henry looked toward Raylene, who didn't meet his eyes.

"Sure, King. I understand."

"Okay, then. Long as we're loud and clear," King said.

"Henry, tell her I'm sorry, will you? I truly didn't mean her no harm."

"I will, Dwight. And I'm sorry about your face. I got a few extra jars of moonshine in the truck, if that'd go any distance to making up for it."

Dwight broke into a smile wide enough to make Raylene sigh as she was trying to close up the wound.

"Aw, now Henry, it really is water under the bridge, but since you're offering, I wouldn't say no to any of that Martell 'shine."

"Okay, then. Let me get Eve settled in the truck and I'll bring them in for you. If you're sure you don't want to press charges, that is. I'll understand if you do. Even let you have the whiskey anyway, just to show there's no hard feelings."

"You're a good man, Henry. A good man. Your daddy'd be proud of you. But no, I ain't pressing charges, so you can take Deputy Watson here with you when you go, if you don't mind. Drinking with the coppers hanging 'round always gives me indigestion."

"That's not indigestion, that's your guilty conscience acting up," Raylene said.

Henry held out his hand. Dwight shook it with a grip that belied his age.

"I'll walk you out," Brady said. "Since I can see I'm not needed here. You take care of this old cuss, Raylene. King." Brady inclined his head to him.

Henry walked back over to where Eve was waiting for him, looking frail and confused.

"Come on," he said gently. "You want to get out of here?"

She looked up into his face and nodded silently. He placed his hand lightly on her back and led her out into the shiny heat of the day.

Once she was settled safely into the passenger seat of his old truck, he shut the door and turned toward Brady, who'd walked out behind them.

"Henry, I've been hoping to run into you. That's why I was headed over here when I got the call from Gladys. Thinking I'd catch you on your deliveries."

"Everything all right, Brady?" Henry asked as he moved to the bed of the truck to grab the whiskey for Dwight.

Brady hitched up the pants of his deputy uniform and shifted his not inconsiderable weight from one leg to the other.

"Oh, can't complain, Henry, can't complain."

Brady had played football in his younger days. Blackwater's star quarterback, if you wanted to be kind. Truth be told, the Cougars had never had a season better than four and six during the years that Brady and Del had played, but that was a fact that got glossed over in the retelling.

But the partnership that Del and Brady had started under the small-town stadium lights had endured into adulthood, when little else had, save a few tall tales of glory too often told. The two of them made up the entirety of the Knightsbridge County Sheriff's Department, unless you counted Sheriff McKinney, and hardly anyone did.

"Is it Jonah? Ms. Watson? I was heading over there later to drop some supplies by."

"No, no. Far as I know, Jonah and Aunt Helen are doing fine. I went by to see them myself just a few days ago," Brady said. A cloud passed over his face as Brady spoke his younger brother's name, but it was gone as quickly as it'd come.

Brady and Jonah had been raised by their aunt Helen after a car accident had killed their parents when the boys were young. Brady had grown up and moved away from the house out on the marsh, but Jonah had remained. He was comfortable where he was, with his aunt Helen, and since the other accident, the one that had left him the way he was, no one had expected any different.

"No, actually, I wanted to talk to you about your girl there."

"Eve," Henry said automatically. She didn't like to be called *girl*.

"Eve, yeah. Those folks down at the shack, they came through town again last night."

Henry had heard them. He'd gone looking for Eve—she often got restless at night—and found her up on the roof. As he took the steps up the ladder, he'd made just enough noise so she'd know he was coming, then sat beside her and leaned back to watch the stars with her in shared silence.

He didn't know what troubles she was trying to let loose out in the night air, but it always seemed to do her good, left her calmer, more settled, after she'd come back from her wanderings.

But last night, she'd been agitated. When he'd heard the voices carrying over the wind from the direction of the old shack, he'd asked her if she wanted to talk about it, but Eve just shook her head and hugged her knees tighter to her body.

"I heard them" was all Henry said.

Brady rubbed his hand against his cheek.

"They mostly steer clear of the locals, you know, but there's a few around that we think might have dealings with them. But that class of people, well, they don't trust the cops, and we're having a real hard time getting anybody to talk about what's going on down there."

Henry knew all this. He and Del had talked it over plenty in the last few weeks.

"The thing is, word's bound to get back to them, Henry. Now that you're bringing the girl around town with you. Eventually, they're gonna hear about it, and they just might come looking for her. Maybe not this time, but soon enough, if they have a bone to pick."

"Then we'll deal with that when it happens, Brady," Henry said. The idea of anyone coming after Eve made his skin grow cold. He'd been keeping her close to him. But he didn't know what else he could do. "I got other stuff to worry about just now."

Brady gave him an understanding nod. "I know you do, Henry. Del told me about your mama. I'm really sorry to hear how poorly she's been."

Henry felt his throat go tight at the thought of his mother. She hadn't gotten out of bed again that morning.

"And you know I don't want to add to your burdens, man, but I gotta tell you, you might want to keep an eye on the old man."

"Livingston?" Henry asked in surprise.

Brady nodded. "People are starting to complain, Henry. It's all fine and good when he can keep his preaching in the woods, but when he starts shouting at people from the top of an upturned trash can on Main Street, folks don't much like that."

Henry sighed. "Brady, I appreciate that, but I don't know what you think I can do about it. He's never listened to me anyway, and now that Mama's going downhill, he's been—"

"He yelled at Babs Holstrom that she was Jezebel returned, yesterday. Scared the shit out of her and her kids. And Ronnie wasn't too pleased about it when it got back to him either. And sending Del out to deal with it doesn't do any damn good at all. Just fires Livingston up more."

Henry gave a deep sigh and passed a hand across his eyes. "Jesus, man. Okay, I'll try to talk to him. But to be honest, I don't see it doing much good."

"I understand. Just give it a shot, will you? And hey? I'm sorry about your mom. Give her my best, all right."

Henry nodded, his jaw tight. It didn't matter how many people chipped in to send Mama their best, unless their best happened to be a last-minute miracle cure for the cancer that was eating away at her final days, but he supposed the sentiment was well meant.

"You take care, Henry," Brady added, before heading back to his cruiser.

"Yeah," Henry whispered to his retreating back. "You too."

But Brady was already starting his car, and Henry was left standing in the parking lot with two bottles of bootleg liquor in his hands, a broken girl in his truck, and far too many worries on his mind.

CHAPTER NINETEEN

"Are you mad at me?" Eve asked.

Henry glanced over at her, but she wouldn't look him in the eye. He pulled the truck to a stop and threw the gearshift into park.

He'd gotten used to having her there, a quiet shadow by his side. More than that, he *counted* on having her there, hardly able to imagine a world without her presence. Yet, in many ways, she was as much a mystery to him as she'd always been.

"No," he said.

She looked up into his eyes. "Will you send me away now?"

"Eve," he said, drawing out the word on a sad sigh. "No. No one's sending you anywhere."

She didn't look convinced. Henry took her hand in his own.

"I know things have been . . . confusing. But it'll get better. Easier. I promise you."

She looked away from him. "There are so many things I don't understand. The talking, and the smiling, and the things people mean behind the words they say. I don't know how to *be*, Henry."

"I know, Eve. It'll get better."

"Will it? What if you're wrong?"

He didn't have the words to set her mind at ease. He could only hope that time would do that. He gave her a small, sad smile.

"Come on," he said, trying to lighten the mood. "Let's get this stuff over to the island. Ms. Watson's waiting on it."

She nodded, but the sadness was still there, floating around her like a fog.

After they got out of the truck, Henry pulled a rope that hung from an old cypress. The bell attached high in the tree clanged with an echo through the marsh. He pulled the rope three times in all, the signal to Jonah that visitors had arrived.

Minutes later, the sound of a boat slipping through the water met their ears.

"Hello, Jonah," Henry said, helping the man pull the pirogue up to the shore. "How are you today, my friend?"

Jonah gave a good think to the question before nodding and answering, "Good. I'm good today. Aunt Helen's in a state, but 'twasn't me that caused it this time, so I'm good."

"Her electric's down again, huh?"

Jonah nodded. "She's in a state. But 'twasn't me."

"Course not, Jonah."

The big man gave Henry a wide, toothy smile. "She'll be better at seeing you, though, Henry. You always make her laugh."

Jonah caught sight of Eve, who was watching him solemnly.

"Ma'am," he said, nodding in Eve's direction. She tilted her head, studying him in return. Jonah didn't seem bothered by her odd response. He stepped out of the pirogue and helped Henry load the crates of supplies onto the boat.

Henry watched Eve during the short ride to the marsh house. She seemed calm here, dipping a finger into the water and watching the wake it made. Her face came up and brightened as a frog croaked and hopped into the green water to their left. She didn't smile, not quite, but some of her tightness had come loose.

"Henry," called Helen Sue Watson from the shore when they grew closer. "Am I glad to see you, my boy."

With the boat on solid ground again, Henry reached a hand to help Eve step out. She'd visited the marsh house with him before, though she'd been reserved and mute around the older woman. He couldn't help but hope she'd feel more comfortable this time.

"And you brought me salt, I see. You're a godsend, Henry. That you are."

"I don't know about that, but salt's easy enough to manage."

"My damn electric's out again. Got a pole dropped down in the marsh, and the electric company's in no hurry to get it up and running, since I'm the only one it serves out here in the boonies. I tell ya, Henry, that damn electric's more trouble than it's worth some days. Just like a husband, it is. Sticks around just long enough you start to think you can depend on it, then it goes and lets you down."

Henry laughed. "I can't imagine a man brave enough to let you down, Ms. Watson."

She snorted. "Oh, I've known a few. Brave or stupid. Sometimes it's hard to tell the difference."

"You remember Eve," Henry said.

"Of course I remember Eve, boy. I'm old, but my mind still works just fine. Come on in, then. It's hot, and it stinks of venison and gator meat, but I got a freezer full that I gotta make into jerky before it starts to go bad. Damn electric company. Don't get me wrong, jerky's fine in small amounts, but I don't fancy a whole load of the mess. But what can you do?"

They carried in the supplies, and sure enough, she had a kitchen full of meat in various stages of defrosting. Some was seasoned and ready to go into the smoker, which Henry could smell was already going in the back. Some was waiting on the salt that Henry had brought in five-pound bags.

It looked like a butcher's shop in there.

"You look pale, girl," Helen Sue barked at Eve. Henry dropped the bag of salt he was carrying and turned to see Eve sway on her feet and put a hand out against the wall to steady herself.

"Eve, are you okay?" he asked, coming to her side.

She didn't answer, just brought her other hand up to cover her mouth.

"Didn't take you for the squeamish type, dear," Ms. Watson said. "Not that there's anything wrong with that. My own mother was one hard woman, but any sight of blood and she'd pass clean out every time. Henry, take her out to the back porch and get her some fresh air, will you? There's a nice breeze out there."

Henry nodded. Once they'd left the kitchen and settled down on the porch, some of Eve's color did seem to come back, leaving high red patches on the apples of her cheeks.

Jonah joined them, carrying a shoebox full of toy cars.

"Would you like to see my cars, Eve? I got some new ones Brady brought for me."

Eve took a deep breath and gave Jonah a nod.

"You sure you're okay?" Henry asked her, and she nodded again, then turned her attention back to the red toy El Camino Jonah was handing her.

"Not one for idle chitchat, your girl," Helen Sue said to Henry. "Come with me, son. You can help me bring out some glasses of tea. It's not cold, but it is sweet."

Henry nodded. Eve seemed fine, but worry still nibbled around the corners of his mind.

"How's she settling in, Henry?" the older woman asked with a piercing directness once they were out of earshot.

Henry shrugged. "I'd have said all right, up until she cut Dwight Pennick's face with a broken bottle this morning."

Ms. Watson turned slowly back from where she'd been pulling glasses from the cabinet.

"You're serious," she said.

"Dwight's gonna be fine, but I just . . . I don't know how she's settling in, to be honest."

Helen Sue nodded, cutting her eyes at Henry while she poured the tea into the glasses.

"You two seem awful close," she said. "I know it's none of my business, but I'm too old to be worrying about manners. And I'm worried for you, Henry. Do you have feelings for this girl? Romantic feelings?"

Henry opened his mouth to answer, then shut it and sat down hard on the bar stool pulled up at the old woman's kitchen island.

"I don't know what to say to that. Feelings, yeah. But romantic? That's such a . . . I don't know. A *thin* word. It's not like that. It's less, and it's more. A whole lot more."

Helen Sue just looked at him, waiting for him to go on.

Henry shook his head. "This is gonna sound crazy," he said quietly. "But it's like, when I pulled Eve out of that river, and I breathed air back into her, I gave her too much. Too much of myself, and now she's walking around with part of me inside her and I can't get it back. And I don't even know if I want it back."

"Lord have mercy, boy," she said.

"Have you ever felt like you've met somebody who was the only person in the world who fit into your edges, and you theirs? Somebody who was the other half that made you whole?"

She peered at him, a magnifying glass concentrating sunlight to bore into his soul.

"No, Henry, I haven't. And thank God for that."

He deflated, his shoulders slumping. "I don't know how it happened. God knows I didn't ask for it. But there it is."

"Well, I was hoping you'd tell me something that'd set my mind at ease. Not sure how old I'll be before I learn not to ask questions I don't want to hear the answers to."

Henry shrugged. He didn't like it much more than she did.

"That girl's broken, Henry. She's broken and she's dangerous."

He nodded. She didn't need to tell him that. He'd known it from the beginning.

"And if you think you can fix her, I'm afraid you're destined for heartache, my dear. Some folks are slated for more than their fair share of heartache, and I do believe you're one of them, Henry Martell."

One corner of Henry's mouth came up. "That's why I like talking to you, Ms. Watson. You always make me feel so much better."

Helen Sue shook her head and handed Henry the tray of tea glasses. "You're right. I'm sorry. But since we're already talking of low-down things, tell me how your mama's doing."

"Not good," Henry said, following her back out to the porch. "She's gone downhill faster than anyone expected."

Mama had been in the shed, working on her old loom and teaching Eve the ins and outs of how to weave fabric, the first time she'd collapsed. Henry would never forget Eve's face when she'd run to fetch him.

"What's the doctor say?"

He shook his head. It was a sore point, and one Mama refused to budge on.

"She won't see one. Says when it's her time, it's her time. God's will, and all that."

Helen Sue took a seat and stared off into the trees in the distance. Henry couldn't help but wonder if she was thinking of her own mortality. She and Mama were of a similar age.

"She didn't get to choose how she's destined to leave the world, but she's chosen how much dignity she's taking with her to the end. Your mama's a fine, brave woman, Henry."

He didn't mention that he'd spoken to Alice, and together they'd made arrangements for a doctor Alice knew from the hospital to make a home visit to see Mama that evening. Henry could almost understand his mother's insistence not to undergo radiation and chemotherapy again, but he couldn't sit by and watch her die and not lift a finger. He wouldn't.

"Ran into Brady in town," Henry said, for no other reason than to change the subject. "Said he'd been out to visit recently."

Ms. Watson pursed her lips before answering. "He does that from time to time. Not as often as he should. Jonah loves his big brother."

Henry glanced over to where Jonah was still showing Eve his cars. She looked uncomfortable in her own skin, sitting stiffly, nodding when Jonah asked her a question. But then, she looked like that a lot. Jonah didn't seem bothered by it.

"It's guilt that pulls him out here," Ms. Watson said with a shake of her head. "And guilt that keeps him away so long in between. But that's a crock of shit, you ask me. Brady and Mari were just kids when the accident happened. Kids. And what's done is done. Acting like a fool about it doesn't change things."

Henry was caught off guard. She didn't usually mention the accident that had caused Jonah's disabilities. No one did. The effects had been too far reaching. Jonah, deprived of oxygen for far too long, had been left with the mind of a child, trapped in a body that had continued to manhood.

As for guilt, while Brady might be plagued by it for the rest of his life, he'd still handled it better than Mari had. There was a headstone and a world of unvoiced grief that could attest to that.

"I won't keep you two any longer, Henry. I know you've got other things to see to. But send your mother my love, dear. I'll drop by and visit her soon, if you think that'd be all right."

Ms. Watson's words were kind, but her usual energetic disposition was subdued.

"I'm sure she'd appreciate that."

He and Eve took their leave.

Henry felt bad that he'd let Jonah down. He hadn't been able to make his aunt laugh after all. Not this time.

CHAPTER TWENTY

"I told you, Henry, I've got no interest in wasting what time I have left with doctors."

Mama's words were weak, but she leaned around the doctor in question to deliver a glare at Henry that was anything but.

He stood his ground.

"Just let the man have a look at you, Mama. He's come all the way out here as a favor to Alice. The least you can do is be civil."

"Civil? Henry, are you lecturing me on manners? I've got news for you, son—" But whatever she had to say next was cut short by a bout of coughing that shook her whole body to the bones.

"I understand we're a tiresome breed, Mrs. Doucet, but I promise you, I'm only here to help."

"Hmph," she snorted, once the coughing had come under control. "I've heard that before. But I'll save you a lot of time, Doctor, and tell you now: I've got cancer. It's incurable, and it's catching up with me." Her voice was growing strained and weak as she visibly tried to fight off another coughing attack. "Nothing you can do about that."

"True enough, Mrs. Doucet. There isn't a thing I can do about that. But if you're right, and this is your time, there *are* things we can do to make it easier."

Mama looked up at the man standing by her bedside and gave him half a smile. "There's not much else in life that's easier than dying, Doc. Seems to me, you just go along for the ride till it stops."

Dr. Atkinson chuckled, and Henry wondered if things might have been different if his mother had met a doctor earlier who was willing to listen this closely to her.

Probably not.

"You're right about that. But I wasn't talking about you, Mrs. Doucet. I was talking about them," he said, looking back over his shoulder at Henry and Alice. "I can help make things easier on them. If you'll let me."

He's good, Henry thought. *Damn good.*

He watched his mother lose her smile, and her feverish eyes bored into the doctor, but he'd given it to her straight, and he wasn't backing down either.

"You fight dirty, Doctor," she said.

Dr. Atkinson nodded. "Yes, ma'am, I do. When I feel it's necessary."

"All right, then. But this is the last time I intend to be poked and prodded. And you two," she said to Henry and Alice, "you get out of here and give me some privacy already."

Alice nodded through relieved tears, and Henry leaned over to squeeze his mother's hand before doing as she asked.

"Go easy on him, Mama," he said.

She squeezed back. "I think this one can hold his own just fine."

Henry followed Alice out the door. She had her hands stuffed in her pockets, and her shoulders were hunched against a chill, in spite of the warmth of the house.

"Frank's a good man, Henry. He'll do what he can for her."

Henry could tell that was true, and his focus shifted to his sister-in-law. "Let me make you a cup of coffee, or some hot tea, Alice. You look like you could use it."

"Okay. But I'll make it. I need something to do with my hands."

Alice scrubbed at her face as they walked to the kitchen. Eve was outside, feeding the chickens. Henry glanced toward the window but resisted the urge to check on her. Even so, he was always aware of her.

"I thought while Dr. Atkinson was here, he could take a look at Eve too," Alice said, her thoughts apparently moving in the same direction as Henry's.

"Maybe," Henry said. He had no idea how Eve might react to the suggestion, but it wasn't a bad one.

"Eve seems to be good for Caroline," Alice said. "And for you."

"I don't know, Alice. She's doing okay here, I guess. She spends a lot of time with Mama, but when we're out in town and around other people, it's hard for her."

"And how is Livingston?"

"Honestly?" Henry asked. "He's coming off the rails."

"He's losing his wife, Henry," Alice said.

"Yeah. And somehow he's managing to make that all about him."

"That's a little harsh, don't you think?"

"No, Alice, I don't. Where is he? Why isn't he here?"

"I heard he's been spending a lot of time in town, spreading the word."

Henry snorted. "Is that what he's doing? Sounds a lot like yelling at people to me."

"Just try to be patient with him, Henry. Caroline would want that."

There were only so many words that they could use to fill up the space, and they'd run out of them. Settling on silence, the two of them marked the minutes, lost inside their own heads.

Eventually, they heard a door opening and footsteps in the hallway.

"Well, Doctor?" Henry asked, rising to his feet when the other man joined them in the kitchen.

Dr. Atkinson sighed. "There's no easy way to say this, but it looks like Mrs. Doucet has all the signs of pneumonia."

Alice raised a hand to her mouth, leaning her weight on the counter at her back. Henry sat down hard on the chair behind him.

"If I had to guess, I'd say in all likelihood, the cancer has spread, and she's more susceptible to infection because of it."

"Pneumonia can be treated, though," Alice said. But Henry had an idea what the doctor would say about that.

"It could, if Mrs. Doucet would allow it. But the chances of success are slim at this stage, and she's refusing treatment anyway."

"But . . . but we can't just let her . . . ," Alice trailed off.

"I'm afraid she's adamant, Alice."

"How long, Doctor?" Henry asked.

"Well, at this point, it's hard to tell. She's still lucid, which is a good sign, but I take it she's not eating much."

"No," Henry said. "A few spoonfuls of soup today, but I think mostly just to make me feel better."

Henry looked down at his hands. They were calloused and capable. But they were useless to him right now.

"I think you all need to prepare yourselves for the worst. There's no easy way forward now. She's refusing to go to the hospital, but I did manage to extract a grudging agreement from her to allow someone to come into the home."

There was a pause while his words sank in.

"Are you saying . . . hospice care?" Alice said. "But is it really time for that?" The pitch of her voice was rising. She'd picked up a towel from the counter and was wringing it between her hands. Henry rose and went to her. He pulled her into a hug. She was shaking as she buried her face against Henry's chest.

"I'm afraid it's just around the corner. The spreading cancer coupled with the pneumonia will no doubt be too much for her to fight off for very long. And she knows that. None of this was a surprise to her."

"Will she be in pain?" Henry asked over the top of Alice's head.

"I'm afraid she's been in pain for quite some time," the man said gently. "Hospice can help, although it is, of course, a significant financial decision."

Henry waved away the question in the doctor's eyes. He wasn't concerned about the money. If need be, there was always the money his father had left him. It was hardly a king's ransom, but it was there. Mama had never let him touch it. For his future, she'd said. A future, he now realized, he'd have to face without her.

"I'll prescribe a morphine drip that can be administered through an IV," Dr. Atkinson continued.

"And she agreed?" Henry asked.

"She did." The doctor nodded.

Henry didn't know what words Dr. Atkinson had used to elicit Mama's agreement, but he had a feeling it had to do with how it would affect her family more than her.

"I'll set up the hospice care, and they should arrive tomorrow."

"Tomorrow?" Alice sounded near panic now, glancing up at the doctor, then quickly back at Henry's face. "That soon?"

Dr. Atkinson gave her a sympathetic nod. "Spend as much time as you can with her now, while she's still with you. She's weak, and with the fever, that's going to get worse very quickly, but for the moment, she's still Caroline, and she needs her family around her now. And you need this time as well."

Henry let Alice go, and she buried her face in her hands.

"Thank you, Doctor," he said quietly, moving to shake the man's hand.

"Of course," he said. "I wish there was more I could do."

"You've done plenty, and we're grateful," Henry said.

"Doctor, before you go, would you mind doing one more thing? You remember the girl I told you about?" Alice said, wiping her face and straightening her shoulders with an effort. Her voice was dazed, but she was trying to pull herself together. Or distract herself, Henry wasn't sure which.

"Ah, yes. The girl from the woods."

"Henry, if you could bring Eve inside, maybe we should let the doctor give her a check-up while he's here."

"I have to confess, I'm curious," Dr. Atkinson said. "I was involved with a case early in my career. A young boy found running feral in the wilderness. I'd be happy to give her the once-over. Only if she's willing, of course."

Henry nodded. "I'll go talk to her," he said.

"We don't actually know anything about the way Eve was raised or what kind of conditions she was living in prior to her being left here, Doctor," Henry heard Alice telling Dr. Atkinson, sniffling around the words. Even after a month, there was little they could add to that. Eve had remained mute about her past.

Henry made his way to the chicken coop, trying not to think too deeply about what the doctor had said. There would be time for that when he was alone. Instead of Eve, he found only the hens scratching at the grain on the ground. The bucket used to feed them was hanging from a hook along the wall of the coop, but Eve was nowhere in sight.

Involuntarily, his eyes sought out the place where the hatchet hung in the toolshed that backed up against the coop. It was undisturbed, with no signs of fresh blood. He felt instantly guilty for checking.

"Eve," he called, stepping away from the coop and glancing around the yard. He hadn't heard her go back inside. She had to be out there somewhere.

"Henry," Eve replied, startling him. She was standing directly behind him.

"Oh God, Eve," Henry said, shaking off the scare.

Eve's eyes pierced the veil of calm he was hiding behind.

"Something's wrong," she said. "Is it Caroline?"

His chest grew tight, and he swallowed hard to hold back the emotions that the doctor's words had stirred—emotions that he didn't want to share, even with someone it seemed he couldn't hide them from.

With a phenomenal force of will, he held his voice steady.

"Alice is inside. She's got a friend here with her. Someone she'd like you to talk to."

Eve bit her lip, glancing toward the house, then back at him, but Henry couldn't tell if she was worried about speaking with someone new or about his state of mind. And he didn't know how much longer he could hold it in.

He needed her to go.

"Will you talk to him?" Henry asked.

"Without you?"

He nodded once. "I'll be there in a bit. I just need a minute to clear my head." The tightness in his chest was starting to creep up into his throat, and the words were getting harder to push through.

She stared into him with an intensity that made him look away.

"Okay," she said, finally. "If that's what you want."

The moment she turned away from him, Henry's shoulders sagged. The hated tears he'd been fighting against were there, just under the surface, but even alone, he didn't want to give in to them. Not because of some misplaced belief that men weren't supposed to cry, but because he knew they'd do no one any good.

What good were tears to the woman lying in there, days from death? Or to Eve or Alice, or any of them? He needed to be strong right now, strong enough for others to lean on. What pulled at him, bringing him low, was the realization that he was losing his touchstone. His mother had always been there, the one constant he could rely on. Always. How was he supposed to find strength, or compassion, or faith, if she wasn't there to lead the way?

Torn between the need to hit something and the overwhelming urge to run as far and fast as he could from the grief waiting to devour him, he stalled in place, frozen in a suspended state of denial.

Henry didn't know how long he stood there, immune to the passage of time.

It was the shouting that brought him back to the here and now.

As he ran for the house, the horrible possibilities of what he might find when he got there flashed through his head. Mama was dying. Eve was unstable. Livingston was missing in action. And Henry had been outside giving in to self-pity, leaving Alice to deal with it on her own. It was his responsibility to be there when things went wrong. Only his.

"No! No!" Eve was screaming when Henry threw open the front door.

Alice was standing, wide-eyed with shock, across the living room from where Eve had backed herself into a corner. Dr. Atkinson was a few steps in front of Alice, with his hands raised, palms up.

"I'm not going to hurt you, Eve," he was saying in a calming voice.

"No! No doctors!" Eve was still screaming.

Henry ran toward her to try and calm her down, but she jerked away from him, knocking a lamp over with a crash in the process. The sound of glass breaking made her cringe and set off a bout of hysterical sobbing as Eve curled in on herself and slid down the wall in a heap.

"No doctors, no doctors. Henry, please!"

He sank down beside her, broken glass biting into his knees, and put his arms around her balled-up form.

"Shh," he said. "It's okay."

"It's not! It's not okay!" she sobbed.

Henry looked over Eve's head and met Alice's stunned gaze.

"I should go," Dr. Atkinson was saying to Alice in a low voice. "Eve, I'm going now," he said, louder now, hoping to be heard over her sobs. "I'm not going to hurt you, you won't be forced to do anything you don't want to do, and I'm sorry I've upset you."

Alice quickly walked the man outside. Henry could see her shaking her head in confusion as she apologized to Dr. Atkinson and shut the door behind them.

"Eve, shh. Shh. The doctor's gone now. Everything's going to be all right," Henry crooned, rocking her gently in his arms while her hysterics ran their course.

"I can't, I can't. No doctors, Henry, please," she cried, sounding like something had broken inside of her. "No doctors. Please don't make me."

"No one's going to make you, Eve. No one wants to harm you. Shh. It's okay."

Once she'd calmed enough, Henry walked her to Mari's room— Eve's room now. He opened the door and was momentarily surprised that nothing had changed in the month that Eve had been with them. The room looked the same as it had the first day she'd come there.

"Why don't you lie down, rest for a while. If you need me, I'll be right outside."

Eve nodded, swallowing against the hitch in her throat, and climbed into the bed. She pulled a pillow to her middle and wound her arms tightly around it, squeezing her eyes shut. Henry wondered at the demons she was shutting them against, the ones that haunted her past and had come out to grab hold of her present.

On quiet feet, he left her and joined Alice and Dr. Atkinson on the porch.

"Henry, I don't know what happened," Alice said. "One minute she was fine. Well, fine for Eve. But as soon as she realized that Frank was a doctor, she just lost it. He never came near her, I swear."

The echoes of the earlier conversation with Raylene didn't escape Henry.

Dr. Atkinson had one hand in his pocket while the other fidgeted, rotating his wedding band around his ring finger with his thumb.

"I'm sorry, Doctor," Henry said. "Eve's . . . she's having a hard time." The words felt as lame as a limping thoroughbred.

"So I saw," Dr. Atkinson said. "I'm no psychoanalyst, but between you, me, and the fence post, I'd hazard a guess that that girl has suffered some trauma in her past."

"Do you have any suggestions, Doctor? To help make things easier?" Alice asked.

Dr. Atkinson sighed. "Like I said, this isn't my area, but I would counsel patience. A lot depends on what kind of trauma we're talking about."

"What do you mean?" Henry asked.

"Well, for example, there's a big difference in recovering from an isolated incident versus a lifetime of abuse or neglect. Alice said you don't know much about Eve's situation prior to coming here, am I right?"

Henry nodded.

"Rebuilding trust—trust in ourselves, trust in humanity in general—after a life-altering event can be difficult, even for those of us lucky enough to live healthy, stable lives."

"And for the unlucky ones?" Henry couldn't stop himself from asking.

The doctor raised his brows and puffed air out between his cheeks. "For the unlucky, learning how to trust can be a completely foreign concept. Like trying to teach a concerto to someone who's never heard music before. It could be done, I suppose, with enough time and patience, but it would be a long, hard road."

Alice's mouth twisted in tight, worried lines. "But what if you get to the end of that road and realize your student is tone deaf?" she asked quietly.

Dr. Atkinson gave a serious look to both Alice and Henry in turn, mirroring their somber moods.

"As a doctor, my job is to help when and where I can. But one of the hardest things I've had to learn to accept is that some things can't be fixed."

Henry pulled back at the bald statement.

"Of course, that may not be the case here at all," Dr. Atkinson went on, as if sensing how deeply those words had shaken Henry. "Like I said, it's not my area of expertise."

On that note, the doctor moved to take his leave. Henry and Alice watched him walk to his car, but Henry had one last question.

"Hey, Doc," Henry called. "What happened to the boy? The one they found living in the woods?"

"Institutionalized," Dr. Atkinson said. "He never learned to talk. Had trouble walking upright. There was speculation that the boy had been abandoned by his family because of disabilities, but we never knew for sure. No one ever came forward to claim him. There's no way to know how long he was out there, on his own."

"And did he ever learn? To hear the music?" Henry asked.

Dr. Atkinson winced. "No. I'm afraid he didn't. He died a few years later."

CHAPTER TWENTY-ONE

The ticking of the old grandfather clock had never seemed so loud, nor so insistent, as it did during those next few days. It rang like a gong in Henry's head, marking off with hateful clarity the moments that his mother would never have again. The moments that he would never have with her again.

It was late. Del was sleeping on the couch in the living room. He and Alice had come to lend whatever support they could. Henry appreciated him being here, even if he did spend the evening wandering from room to room with his hands awkwardly stuffed into his pockets.

Eve had sat at Mama's bedside for hours until she'd nodded off. Henry knelt next to Eve and tucked a stray lock of hair behind her ear.

"Why don't you go get some sleep?" he asked. "If you can."

"She's kind. I never knew a woman to be so kind," Eve said.

The hospice nurse on duty was quiet and competent, but her presence irritated his mother all the same, and she'd resisted the morphine drip Dr. Atkinson had recommended. The nurse had acquiesced, but the sterile medical equipment remained at the ready, if and when Mama changed her mind.

Mama's fever worsened in the hours that passed, and with it, her control. They caught a glimpse of how much pain she was in.

"Should we call the doctor?" Alice whispered. She was using a damp washcloth to try and cool her mother-in-law's forehead.

Before Henry could answer, his mother spoke up, though they'd both believed her to be sleeping after the last round of coughing.

"No more doctors," she said in a low, raspy voice.

"Mama, it doesn't have to be this way," Henry said, glancing at the nurse, who was checking his mother's vital signs.

One of his mother's hands fluttered in the air, waving off his words, though she didn't open her eyes. "Alice, lovely girl, I'm so thirsty," she said. Alice leaned over to the bedside to bring a glass of water to her lips, but Mama opened her eyes for a moment and shook her head. "I'm sorry to ask it, but can you fetch me a glass of iced tea? With a little lemon, please?"

"Of course," Alice said, replacing the water and leaping at the chance to fill any request so easily managed. If Mama wanted tea, then Alice would make sure it was tea she would have.

"Could I manage to get a little privacy with my son?" Mama asked the nurse, her tone not nearly as sweet. The woman's face was impassive as she left them alone.

"Henry," Mama beckoned him to her. He sat in the chair that was still warm with Alice's body heat and took his mother's frail hand in his own.

"You'd think when a person's as close to knocking at the pearly gates as I am, they'd be blessed with some sort of wisdom to leave with their loved ones, wouldn't you?" She gave him a small smile that quickly turned into a grimace of pain.

"Shh, Mama," Henry said. "You don't need to—"

"Don't shush me, Henry, I'll speak if I like."

Even in her state, Henry could hear the steel behind her words. Just as there always had been, in spite of her mostly gracious ways. If you were listening closely enough.

"Livingston's not going to take this well," Mama said.

Henry's face hardened. Livingston was a subject he didn't want to discuss. The man had been and gone twice now since the doctor's visit. He'd managed to enter the room where his wife lay dying on the second of those occasions, but Henry didn't know what had been said. What he did know was that Livingston had practically run from the house after that, mumbling incoherently about the Lord's work.

"He's scared, Henry. And fear makes him weak, but don't hold that against him," his mother said, seeing the stony look on her son's face.

Henry started to speak, but seeing the plea in his mother's eyes, he closed his mouth and took a deep breath. "I'll try," he said.

She nodded. "That's all I ask." She shifted on the bed, looking for a position that would make her more comfortable, but comfort was impossible to find at this point. "Losing Maribel like we did . . . It nearly broke him."

Henry didn't need the reminder. He remembered all too well how Livingston had dealt with the aftermath of his daughter having taken her own life.

"It took all the strength he could muster to come back from that, and I worry . . . I worry that he won't have any left to draw on this time."

Henry believed she was right to worry. Because, he realized, Livingston hadn't drawn on his own strength to recover from his daughter's death; he'd drawn on the strength of his wife, so freely given.

Where would Livingston find that wellspring of courage once Mama was gone?

Where would Henry?

"I worry for you too, son," she went on.

Henry shook his head, fighting against the constriction in his throat. "You don't need to do that," he said.

"I do, and you need to hear it. Bringing Eve here . . ." Mama shook her head and looked away. He could see the exhaustion in every line and crease of her face.

"Mama, you should rest," he said.

"To hell with that!"

Henry pulled back in surprise, then leaned in again as her outburst brought on a coughing fit. While she recovered, Henry held her hand, shaken at the sound of the loose rattle in her chest.

"I don't have any time left, Henry," she said. Her voice was weaker, but her eyes were on fire. "These damn tumors won't let me rest anyway. I've made my peace with that."

"Mama—"

"No. Just listen. Bringing Eve here, it was my way of paying penance for Mari. I let that girl down. We all did. Her father, her brother, Brady, Alice, all of us. She needed help, she needed help so badly, and we didn't see it. We weren't there for her. When I saw Eve, I saw another girl in need. I couldn't, I wouldn't, turn a blind eye again. But that's on me, Henry. Not you. You were just a child."

Mama grimaced, closing her eyes, whether against the pain of the past or the pain of the present, Henry couldn't know.

"I don't understand what you're trying to say, Mama," Henry said.

At the sound of footsteps in the hallway, Henry looked up to see Alice coming into the room with a tray. It was the same one his mother had filled to leave for Eve in the woods. Now it carried iced tea and a small bowl of broth.

Alice took one look at the two of them, and moved to set the tray down.

"I'll just leave this and let you two be alone," she said.

"No, Alice. Stay. Please," Mama said.

Alice glanced at Henry, unsure, but he nodded. She pulled up another chair on the opposite side of the bed. His mother accepted when Alice offered her the tea. The ice cubes clinked in the glass as Alice brought the drink to the older woman's parched lips, and she drank deeply.

"I worry I've brought a world of trouble down on you, bringing Eve here," Mama continued when her thirst was sated. "I was selfish, looking to Eve to help me make up for my mistakes with Mari."

Alice raised her eyebrows in Henry's direction, but he could only shake his head in confusion.

"But you're never too old for more mistakes, it seems," Mama said.

"Are you saying you don't want Eve here?" Henry asked, incredulous.

She shook her head. "No, of course not. But even a blind man can see what's happening between the two of you."

Henry sighed. "Then you should explain it to me, because I don't understand it myself."

"I know you don't, son. I can see that too. And I'm afraid for you."

"Eve's not going to hurt me, Mama," he said, trying to reassure her.

His mother gave a short, bitter laugh. "If you believe that, you're a fool."

Henry frowned. His skin was prickling where the hair on his arms and the back of his neck was standing on end.

"A love like that, Henry, where you're so close that one breathes out and the other breathes in the same breath . . . It's a powerful thing. Maybe the most powerful thing."

Henry shook his head, ready to deny her words, even, or especially, to himself.

"Don't shake your head at me. I know what I see. I've felt it myself. With your father."

Henry knew his mother wasn't referring to Livingston this time.

"It's not the same," Henry said.

"Oh, isn't it? You don't feel more *alive* when you're with her, like the sun only rises once she walks in the room? The thought of walking away from her doesn't feel like it will open a wound that your life's blood will pour out of? In that case, I must be wrong."

"I . . . It's not . . . ," Henry stammered, then stopped.

"That's what I thought," his mother said.

Alice sent him a look of pure sympathy that left him more conflicted than ever.

Feeling like a guillotine was hanging over his head, Henry stood, pushing the chair back behind him.

"What are you trying to say, Mama?" he asked, pacing the room. "Even if that's true, do you really think there's anything I can do about it now?"

She didn't answer, and her silence brought his eyes back to her.

An aura of sadness surrounded his mother, pulling at her features and her limbs, and he watched her struggle to hold it back.

"I wish I had the answer to that. It seems like, this close to the end, I've earned the right to have some answers to share, but it doesn't look like that's going to happen."

Henry took his seat again and hung his head. He didn't want her to be consumed by this. Not now.

"It'll work out, Mama," he said, trying to reassure her.

"I wish I could believe that. And I hope it does. But, Henry, son, sometimes a love like that . . . It can be a terrible thing. It's easy—too easy—to get lost in it. It can bury you alive, if you're not careful."

Henry didn't know what to say.

"Love her, if you must. But try not to lose your way, Henry. Hold on to what makes you *you*, if you can. I'm proud of you, son. So damn proud of the man you've become. That man's not a quitter. But sometimes, Henry . . . you need to understand that sometimes love's not enough."

Henry sat helpless as another round of coughing took his mother's words away from her. Once the coughing finally subsided, her eyes remained closed this time, and he watched her give in to whatever sleep she could manage to wrest away from the cancer eating at her from the inside.

There were tears in his eyes as he met Alice's gaze over his mother's deathbed.

And he saw there were tears in hers as well. Henry could only be grateful that he wasn't alone.

CHAPTER TWENTY-TWO

"Repent, ye sinners who walk among men!" Livingston was shouting. "Repent, and earn God's forgiveness. Repent your wicked ways, before it's too late!"

Henry swerved and pulled the truck over. His front tire jumped the curb and he came to a stop on the sidewalk. There was no danger of hitting any passersby, as they'd all crossed to the other side of the street to avoid Livingston's bruising rhetoric.

Henry slammed the gearshift into park and threw open the door of his truck. He marched over to where his stepfather stood perched on an old and battered metal trash can.

"Get in the truck, Livingston," he said, with a calmness that valiantly tried to cover the anger simmering just below the surface.

Livingston ignored him.

"The sins of the flesh and the sins of the mind must be purged in the blood of the lamb, my disciples," he continued to shout. "Follow me, I'll show you the one true path to righteousness!"

"Livingston," Henry said, his voice going up a notch. "Get your ass off that trash can and get in the damn truck."

They were drawing a crowd. The same townspeople who'd turned their eyes away in awkward embarrassment while Livingston made a fool of himself alone stopped to stare openly at Henry's struggle to rein his stepfather in. Henry must have been a sight, dressed in his black suit jacket, his face alternately calm, angry, and disgusted as he tried to get Livingston's attention. Tried, and failed.

"The Lord Jesus did say, 'I am the resurrection and the life. He that believeth in me, though he were dead, yet shall he live. And whosoever liveth and believeth in me shall never die'!" Livingston's words grew louder and more quarrelsome with each passing phrase, and still he ignored Henry standing at the foot of his makeshift pedestal.

"Jesus wept," Henry muttered under his breath. "I'm telling you now, old man. Get down from there and get in the truck, or I swear to you, in the name of all that's holy in your world, I will drag you down."

"And the people *believed!* They *believed,* and now is your time to believe, my children, in the light and the—"

With a great and mighty shove, Henry placed his foot on the silver can and pushed, sending Livingston toppling down. The older man scrambled to his feet and came up swinging.

"How dare you?! How dare you—"

Henry grabbed him by the collar of his shirt and pulled his face inches from his own.

"My mother is getting buried in the ground today, you son of a bitch. And you are going to be sitting in a pew, silent and contrite, or I promise you right here and now, I will put you in the grave next to her myself."

Livingston's face went white with grief, then splotches of color bloomed on his cheeks and Henry could see the pious anger begin to boil up in him.

"Go ahead. Swing at me. I'd love to knock you on your ass one more time," Henry said quietly.

Livingston sputtered, unintelligible sounds that gave away the wreck of a human being he'd become since the death of Caroline.

Henry hadn't known Livingston's first wife, Del and Mari's mother, who'd died giving birth to the twins. But chances were, she'd been too good for him. Mama certainly was. Always had been. Suddenly, Henry realized that Livingston must have known that.

Unbidden, a seed of pity cracked open inside him.

"Just get in the truck, Livingston." He sighed, letting go of his stepfather's collar, his anger draining away.

For one moment, Henry thought Livingston might argue, and he simply didn't have the fight left in him to force the matter any further. But then Livingston lowered his eyes, so full of desperate loss. Slowly he walked toward Henry's waiting truck.

Livingston didn't meet his stepson's gaze when Henry shut the passenger-side door, and he didn't speak at all on the way to the church. And that was fine by Henry.

CHAPTER
TWENTY-THREE

"And where do you expect me to find the money to pay for that, Alice? My God, how many times are we going to do this?"

Henry's steps faltered as he walked into the Knightsbridge County Sheriff's Department.

The place wasn't fancy. In fact, Henry found it downright depressing with its faux wood paneling and glaring fluorescent lights. But he supposed it served its purpose.

Gladys, the dispatcher, had a desk immediately inside of the front door. She was currently trying her best to look occupied with anything other than the marital issues unfolding behind her.

"Good morning, Henry," she said in a loud, cheery voice intended no doubt to let Del and Alice know they had company and to tuck their dirty laundry away.

"Morning, Gladys," Henry said, his eyes on Alice, standing halfway across the room with her back turned to her husband. She was swiping tears away from her eyes. Del looked like he was tamping down his temper, though it was clearly taking effort to do so.

"What's going on?" he asked Gladys in a whisper.

"The IVF didn't take, poor girl," Gladys whispered back.

Henry glanced at Alice again, who was busy straightening her shoulders and putting a brave face on top of her distress. Henry had an overwhelming urge to go to her, pull her into a hug, but he knew there weren't enough hugs in the world to make the pain subside for her.

"Henry," Del called to him gruffly. "What's up, brother?"

"Ah, it can wait, Del. I'll just come back later," he said, glancing at Alice.

"Why don't you come have a seat," Del said, ignoring his wife. "Alice was just leaving."

Alice shot her husband a look designed to melt steel, but Del didn't meet her eyes.

Henry took a hesitant step forward, and Alice gave him a sad smile as she walked away from Del.

Grabbing her hand as she passed, Henry said, "Come by the house later, if you want. Eve'd love to see you. We'll talk. If you're up for it."

She gave him the same distracted half smile, and swallowed back tears. "Sure. That'd be nice." She squeezed his hand, then Henry and Del watched her as she walked away.

"What brings you in?" Del said, clearing his throat and making it clear he had no wish to discuss Alice or whatever they'd been arguing about. Del motioned Henry to the chair across from his battered desk.

"A couple of things, actually," Henry said. "In fact, I can count them on two fingers."

Not his own fingers, but they'd get to that soon enough.

"If this is about Dad, Henry, I gotta tell you, I've washed my hands of him," Del said.

"What's that supposed to mean?" Henry asked.

"I keep getting calls about him bothering folks in town with all his holy roller talk, and every time I go out there, he lights into me about Mari. I can't keep doing it. I won't." Del's face was set in harsh lines that reminded Henry of Livingston.

"I imagine that's hard to stomach," Henry said.

"Hard to stomach?" Del gave a short laugh. "Yeah, you could say that. He loved her more when she was alive, and now that she's dead . . . well, I can't compete with that, can I?"

Henry was thrown by the scowl that had darkened his brother's features. Del had always been a simple man, and while that had its drawbacks, it had its advantages too. One being that Del had always seemed to be able to shrug off his father's hatefulness. It seemed that ability was slipping.

"I tried to talk to him about it, Del, but you know he's never listened to me. It's been months since Mama died, and he slides farther away from reality every day. I don't know where it's gonna end."

"I'm fairly certain I hate him, Henry," Del said, staring at a spot above Henry's head. His eyes were bloodshot, and Henry wondered how much sleep he was getting.

"I think maybe I always have," Del went on. "You know, Mari went to him. Before she did it. Did you know that?"

Henry's brows came together. He didn't know that, but what concerned him the most had nothing at all to do with Mari. He was more worried about his brother's state of mind. It didn't seem to be any more stable than Livingston's at the moment.

"Oh yeah. She went to him, tried to talk to him about how she was feeling. That business with Jonah, she couldn't handle it. Felt like it was her fault. Truth be told, it was," Del said, lost now in the shifting shadows of the past. "She had a vicious sense of humor, Mari did. Always took things a step too far. Like she couldn't help herself."

"Del," Henry said. "I don't know what to say."

"That's funny, Henry. Because I don't either, man. Everybody thinks, since I was her twin, formed in the same womb and all that, that I'm supposed to have some great insight into why Mari did what she did. But the truth is, I don't have a clue. Not one damn clue. Her mind was as much a mystery to me as a stranger off the street. How's that for irony, huh?"

Del leaned back in his chair and ran his hand through his hair.

"But you didn't come here to talk about my sister or my crazy old man, did you?" Del said, his eyes focusing in on Henry for the first time since he'd walked into the building.

"No, I can't say that I did. But I don't know if this is going to make your day any better."

"I don't know if it can get much worse."

"Oh, I think it might," Henry said. He fingered the small bag he'd carried into the station with him. It looked like the kind you'd get from a jewelry store. Black velvet, with a drawstring on the top.

He leaned over and placed it in the center of Del's desk, then rested his elbows on his knees and stared at a spot in the linoleum where the corner had chipped away, waiting for Del to open it. He didn't look up, didn't see the look of curiosity Del sent his way as he loosened the smooth black rope at the top of the bag.

But when Del turned the bag upside down and dumped the contents onto his desk, Henry heard the small, heavy sounds as the two disembodied fingers bounced off the metal desk.

The scrape of Del's chair as he pulled away from the macabre offerings Henry had brought him was loud in the sterile room, but not loud enough to mask the gasp that Del gave when he realized what he was looking at.

"What the shit is this, Henry?" he practically shouted.

"What does it look like, Del? It's fingers." Henry studied his own hands as he said it, studying the place where his own fingers attached to his hands. He didn't care to look at the unattached appendages lying between the two of them, couldn't manage it.

"No shit it's fingers! I can see that! Why the hell are you bringing me fingers in a fucking bag, Henry?"

Henry looked up into the shocked face of his brother. If it weren't for the pale, gruesome digits lying lifeless between them, Henry might have laughed.

"That's an excellent question, Del," he said, shaking his head. "Short and to the point. But I'm afraid I don't have an answer for that."

CHAPTER

TWENTY-FOUR

Eve plucked nervously at the unraveling sleeve of the oversized cardigan she'd pulled around herself like a blanket. She was huddled in the corner of the sofa, with her knees pulled to her chest, trying to make herself small against the onslaught of Del's questions.

"Did you see anyone when you went to the door? Anything that looked out of place or drew your attention?" Del was demanding.

She glanced toward Henry, wishing Del would just go away. She'd tried to tell Henry not to go to his brother, not to go to the police at all. She didn't need them asking questions that she already knew the answers to.

Mute, she shook her head.

"Nothing? I find that hard to believe, Eve. The front yard is a big open space. Henry already said he was with you when somebody knocked on the door, and you went straight to answer it. So I'm having a hard time figuring out where this person must have gone so quickly. They didn't vanish into the air, sweetheart."

"Take it easy, Del," Henry said. "If she says she didn't see anything, she didn't."

But that wasn't exactly true. She had seen something. A man. He'd been standing at the edge of the woods, and he'd wanted to be seen. He'd raised a hand in her direction, making sure that she'd gotten the message, which she had. Loud and clear.

And that was before she'd opened the bag.

Stepping quickly back into the house, she'd closed the big front door behind her, her breath coming short and shallow. She'd known they were there, at least sometimes. And she'd known they wouldn't forget about her, not so easily, yet still she'd hoped.

It was a foolish, childish hope.

"Henry, you didn't see anything either, I suppose?" Del asked, turning to his brother.

"No," Henry said. "I remember I called out to Eve. Asked who it was, but when she didn't answer I got worried and came into the living room. She was standing there, looking like she'd seen a ghost. Or a monster. I saw something in her hands, but I couldn't tell what it was. Not until I got closer."

Henry's face was troubled. Eve couldn't stop her mind from racing ahead, considering what would finally be the last straw for him. Was this it? Would he send her away now? Or would it be weeks, months from now? Not so long ago, she thought she might have been able to come to terms with that inevitable day, but now? Can a blind person who's finally seen a bright and shining light go willingly back into the dark?

When he'd realized what she was holding in her palm, Henry's face had gone stark. She'd seen clearly the disgust, the horror. How long would it be before he looked at her that way?

"It was a message," she said to the two men. They turned to stare at her, and she grew uncomfortable under their combined scrutiny. She rose from the sofa and moved to the window to stare out into the day, so bright and full of promise just a few hours before.

But that had been a dream. A stupid dream.

"A message from who, Eve?" Del demanded.

She turned her head and gave him a withering glance. If he didn't know the answer to that, he was dumber than she'd thought.

"The men from the shack?" Henry asked.

"Yes, the men from the shack," she said with a sigh. "Who else?"

"But why? What do they want?" Henry's voice was rising, and Eve pulled away, cringing from his anger.

"They want me to know they haven't forgotten. That they'll never forget."

"Forget what, Eve? What the hell happened out there?"

She shook her head and turned her face back to the window. She leaned her forehead against the cool pane of glass. She was so tired.

"Eve, you have to talk to us," Henry said, moving toward her and taking her by the arms. He was gentle, as he always was, but when he turned her to face him, she could see the hardened determination in his face. "You have to talk to me," he said. "I can't help you unless I know what the hell I'm dealing with here."

"You can't help," she said, breaking free of his hold. "Just leave it alone, Henry. Please."

Her voice broke, and she ran from the room.

Those fingers had been meant for her, not Henry, and certainly not Del. They were a warning.

If they'd wanted her dead, she wouldn't still be here. It was a warning to keep her mouth shut.

And that was exactly what she intended to do. Nothing was going to take Henry away from her. Not now that she'd warmed herself by his light. Nothing. Not now. Not ever.

Eve knew she was living in a house built of straw. One hard puff, and it would all come tumbling down.

And she was afraid. More afraid than she'd ever been in her life. She'd never had anything to lose before.

Eve would pay any price at all to keep Henry next to her. If that price was her silence, then silent was what she would be. She'd keep their secrets, if that's what they wanted. And she'd keep her own, for as long as she could manage.

Because the alternative was unimaginable.

CHAPTER
TWENTY-FIVE

Henry started when there was a knock on the door for the second time that day. He thought immediately of Eve. She was in the shed with the old loom. He'd known she wanted to be alone, to work through her thoughts in whatever way she managed to do that, but he regretted leaving her on her own. If the people who'd left the fingers came back, if they saw her by herself, without protection . . .

Alice jumped back in surprise when Henry flung open the front door, ready for a confrontation.

"Henry?" she asked. "What's wrong?"

He started to tell her. He wanted to tell her. Alice was a beacon of calm in a storm. She always had been. But one look at her red-rimmed eyes and her pale, puffy face, and Henry put it aside.

"Alice," he said, pulling her into a hug. He could ask if she was okay, but that was a pointless question. Anyone could see she wasn't. When he felt her against his chest, choking on her own tears as she tried to hold them back, his heart hurt for her.

"I'm so sorry," she said, her voice full of grief-laced emotions that Henry couldn't begin to imagine. "I probably shouldn't have come here. I just—" She broke off on a sob, and Henry held her while she tried to find her way out of the other side of it.

"It's okay, Alice. It's okay," he said, rubbing his hand in circles on her back, giving her what little comfort he could.

"It's just that Caroline is who I'd come to. Normally. She'd hold my hand and make tea, and I'd cry and cry—" She broke down again.

"Come on in," Henry said.

"I miss her, Henry," Alice said quietly. "I miss her so much."

He glanced over to the shed, where another woman, one who owned him in a completely different way, was weaving a piece of cloth that had begun with his mother's hands.

"God, so do I," he said. "Come on in, Alice. I'm not Mama, but I can make one helluva cup of tea. I had a good teacher."

Alice tried to smile. She almost managed it, even in the midst of the tears welling up in her eyes again.

They moved into the house. Alice cried and Henry let her. Between the tears, she railed against the unfairness of it all. Lacking options to make it better, Henry listened to her. It was the least he could do.

Curled up in the same corner of the sofa that Eve had tried to disappear into earlier that morning, Alice gripped her tea and tried to make sense of it all. Why? Was God punishing her? Was it just the irony of the universe, that she was destined to help other women bring babies into the world but never to have one of her own to hold?

Henry had no answers for her.

"And Del!" she said. "I swear to God, I don't understand your brother at all. He blows hot one minute, freezing cold the next," she said, shaking her head. "And now, every time we do this, every time we get our hopes up, just to have them crushed underneath the failure, he pulls further and further away. Away from me, and away from the idea of having a baby at all."

Alice was moving from grief to anger, and Henry couldn't help her. She set her teacup on the side table and rose to pace the room.

"And me, I go in the other direction. Once I realized we might not be able to have a baby, there wasn't anything in the world I wanted more. But we're so far apart now, I don't know if there's any coming back together."

"Maybe he's just dealing with it in his own way?" Henry asked.

"Ha!" she burst out. "He's not dealing with it *at all*. One sign of trouble, and Del checks out. I knew that about him. I did. I just never expected him to check out on *me*. Guess that's what I get." She sighed, some of the fight draining out of her. "Don't ever fall in love with someone, then expect them to change, Henry. It's the surest way to find heartbreak I can think of."

She sank back into the sofa in defeat. "And now I have to figure out what to do. And I'm so—so *mad* that I have to do it on my own. Do I let it go, leave it up to fate? I think of doing that, Henry, and it makes me want to crawl into a hole."

She shook her head and stared down at the ring on her finger. "Del says we can't afford to go through any more IVF treatments. And I know he's right. Hell, I don't know where he came up with the money for the first three rounds. I wanted this too badly to ask. But I can't help but wonder if it's just his way of giving up. Giving up on a baby. Of giving up on me."

Her words trailed off, and Henry sat with her and watched them go.

"I should go," she said suddenly. "Henry, I'm sorry I dumped this on you."

"Don't worry about that, Alice. I just wish I could help."

She gave him a small smile. "Me too. But you know what my dad used to say? Wish in one hand, Alice, honey, and shit in the other. See which one fills up first." She sent Henry a sardonic look. "Classy guy, my dad. But now that I've got two hands full of shit, I'm starting to get his drift."

Henry couldn't stop the laughter from bubbling up. Alice looked at him in surprise when the first chuckle broke away from him, and a slow smile started to creep across her face. When she started to laugh as well, just a giggle at first, it was contagious.

"It's not even that funny," Alice said, but that only made them laugh harder and, before long, the two of them were wiping away tears while they howled with amusement.

It was irrational. It was uncontrollable. And it was so very necessary.

Henry didn't know how long they might have gone on if the sound of a vehicle coming up the drive hadn't pulled their attention away.

Oh God, Henry thought. *What now?*

CHAPTER TWENTY-SIX

"Jonah, you see that man there?" Aunt Helen asked.

He looked toward where her hand was pointing and followed it across until he caught sight of the man she must be speaking of.

"The loud one?" he asked, just to be sure. "That's Mr. Doucet, isn't it?"

"That's the one." She nodded.

"Yes, ma'am, I see him, Aunt Helen."

He could hear him too. Jonah figured everybody in town could probably hear him. He looked right upset about something.

"What's he so mad about?" Jonah asked.

His aunt shook her head. "That'd take more time to explain than I got days left on the earth, my boy. Now, you listen up. I want you to go over there, pick that man up, and put him in the bed of my truck."

"All right, then," Jonah said. Without hesitation, he turned to do as Aunt Helen asked.

Jonah paid no mind to the shouting of the man as he walked up behind him and hefted him over his shoulder, nor did he question whether this was something that was okay for him to do. When Aunt Helen wanted something, it was usually best just to get on with it.

After placing his wiggling catch in the back of the truck, it didn't look like he intended to stay put, so Jonah placed a hand on Mr. Doucet's shoulder and held him there.

"Why don't you climb in the back, buddy. You can ride with him and make sure he doesn't jump out," said Helen Sue, nodding and ignoring the racket the man was putting up.

Mr. Doucet had some not-so-nice things to say about Aunt Helen. But she'd always told Jonah to turn the other cheek when people were ugly, so he looked off to the left.

"Okay."

Jonah hopped in and they lumbered down the road. People on the street were watching them go by like they were in a parade. A couple of folks started to whoop and holler, and there was a bunch of clapping and whistling going on, so Jonah raised his right hand and waved. He had to use his left to push the mad little man back down into the truck when he tried to climb out again, and that just set off another round of laughs and a few calls of "Go, Jonah!"

Jonah just sent them a big gap-toothed smile. He'd never been in no parade before.

Aunt Helen pulled the truck out of town, and Jonah settled in to ignore the ugly the man was spouting while he enjoyed the ride.

When the truck turned the corner to go down the lane to Henry's house, Jonah got real glad. He was always happy to see his friend.

When Aunt Helen stopped the truck up near the house, she climbed out and nodded to Jonah.

"You can toss him out of there now, Jonah. But set him down easy."

So he did, placing Mr. Doucet on his feet like a toy doll. The man pulled away from him as soon as Jonah let loose and turned all that ugly onto Aunt Helen.

"You done yet?" she asked, once the man looked like he'd come to the bottom of his big ol' bucket of nastiness.

He gave her a look that said he was just waiting till that bucket refilled off the tap, then he was gonna light into her again, but she didn't give him the chance.

"I ain't never had no use for you, Livingston Doucet. Never made a secret of it neither. But this is just plumb crazy. You get on in that house and you take a shower. Damn, man, but you stink."

"Don't you lecture me, Helen Sue Watson. God created man to—"

"Oh, just shut the hell up. God didn't create man to go stinking up town and scaring little children. I'll tell you what God created. He created soap, you old jackass."

Jonah waved to Henry as he stepped out onto the porch. Looked like Alice was there with him. Jonah liked Alice.

"Hey there, Henry," Jonah called. Henry waved back, but he didn't step down from the porch.

"I tell you, Livingston. I'd hate to have to ask my boy here to pick you up and haul you into the house and throw your skinny behind into the shower. But by God, that's just what I'll do if you don't pull yourself together."

"That boy lays one more finger on me, Helen Sue, and by God, I'll—"

"You'll what?" she asked in a low, slithery voice that sounded like a snake creeping out from under a log.

Mr. Doucet took a good long look at her face, then over at Jonah, who broke into a smile. Jonah thought maybe the man needed a little nice in his life, so he gave him some for free.

"You got no right, Helen Sue. No right, and you know it," he said.

"Right or not, I see you in town again scaring people like that, I'll do the same. Your kind of preaching doesn't sit well, Livingston. People got enough worries without you throwing that mess in their faces."

She got back in the truck. "Come on, Jonah," she said.

He climbed up into the passenger side of the truck while his aunt leaned one arm out the window.

"I realize the likelihood of you taking any kind of advice from me is slim to fat chance, but I gotta tell you, Livingston. You might want to talk to somebody. Losing a person . . . particularly a person as fine as

Caroline . . . that's hard. It'd be hard for even the most sure-footed of men. And you certainly haven't ever been that."

Jonah watched Mr. Doucet go red in the face as his aunt backed the truck out of the driveway. He didn't appear to care much for what she'd said, as he started in on shouting and waving his arms again. He even leaned down and picked up some rocks from the gravel drive to throw in their direction, but they were too far away by that time for the rocks to reach them, so Jonah just watched as the angry man grew smaller in the distance.

CHAPTER
TWENTY-SEVEN

Henry sighed a deep, long-suffering sigh of resignation as he watched his stepfather throw rocks at Ms. Watson's retreating truck.

The commotion had brought Eve out to the doorway of the shed. Henry heard Alice gasp behind him when Livingston turned his ire on the girl.

"What do you think you're looking at, huh?" he demanded as he stomped back to the house. "Nothing but a freeloading gypsy, you are, girl. You just mind your business and be glad I don't toss you out on your ear."

Henry was tempted to remind Livingston that he couldn't do that even if he wanted to, since Mama had seen fit to will the house to her son rather than her ill-tempered second husband. He had no doubt about his mother's reasoning. She'd known that Henry would never kick Livingston out, because that hadn't been her wish. The same couldn't necessarily be said if the situation were reversed.

But Eve didn't seem bothered by Livingston's outburst in the least. She stood there looking at him like a bug under a glass, so Henry didn't bother to correct him.

"You quit that right now, Livingston Doucet. You can't treat her like that," Alice said. Apparently, she didn't have the same sort of restraint.

All she earned for her trouble was her father-in-law turning his blistering tongue on her.

"And what's it to you, Miss High and Mighty?" he sneered, coming up on the porch to join them. "Don't you have better things to do than hang around here where you're not wanted? You have a husband you ought to be seeing to, don't you?"

Alice drew herself up at his insults.

"Del's perfectly capable of seeing to himself, Livingston. Unlike you, I see."

"Now you listen here, missy," Livingston said quietly, wagging a finger in Alice's face. "I've had about enough of the disrespect and the downright disregard for my status as the head of this household. It's one thing when that old bat can't control that big, dumb ox of a boy that she's raising like a heathen over in the swamp, but I will not listen to that kind of sacrilege in my own home."

Again, Henry was tempted to remind him that it was not, in fact, his home, but he knew it would get him nowhere.

"Why don't you settle down—"

"Don't you tell me to settle down, boy," Livingston bellowed in Henry's face. "I'm not some hysterical schoolgirl who just saw what a man looks like down under for the first time. You'll treat me with respect, by God!"

"All right, then. Fine," Henry said, holding his palms up and backing away a step. The man was obviously in no mood to listen to reason.

"Look," Alice said in a soothing tone. "Why don't I go in the kitchen and fix you something to eat. You look like you haven't had a good meal in days. Am I wrong?"

Henry raised his eyebrows at her over Livingston's head. The offer was nice and all but sounded a lot more like something Mama would have said rather than Alice.

Livingston looked a little suspicious himself, but his hunger must have won out. Henry knew for a fact he hadn't been home in several days, and a man can only live on hate and religious mania for so long.

"Well, that's more like it," Livingston said gruffly.

"All right, then. You go take a shower, and by the time you're done, I'll have you a meal fit for a king."

Livingston scratched at the mangy beard he'd grown in.

"That's more like it, indeed," he said, nodding. "I do need to fuel up. I've got preaching to do. The Lord's work doesn't get done on its own, you know. No, sir, it does not."

Livingston wandered into the house, presumably in the direction of the bathroom and a much-needed shower.

Henry met Alice's eyes. "You know you don't have to do that, right?"

But Alice had a determined tilt to her chin. "Oh, I know. But I want to. It's the least I can do," she said, brushing past him and heading for the kitchen.

Henry's brows shot up, and he stuffed his hands in his pockets as he watched her back. For the life of him, he'd never understand women.

CHAPTER

TWENTY-EIGHT

Henry knelt, hands on his knees, and studied the top of Livingston's head. It was lying on his arm, which was outstretched across the dinner table, a fork still clutched in his hand.

Livingston's face was sitting partially upon the edge of the plate that Alice had made for him, tilting it so that brown gravy and bits of mashed potatoes were clinging in a sticky mess to his recently cleaned and trimmed beard.

"He's not dead, is he?" Henry asked, casting a glance at his sister-in-law.

"Of course he's not dead," Alice said as she lifted the unconscious man's head and slid the plate from beneath him. "Don't be silly."

She used a washcloth to wipe the food from the dark-ginger and gray hair on Livingston's cheek, then let his head drop back onto the table with a not-so-gentle thud.

Seeing the look of confusion on Henry's face, Alice put her hand in her pocket and dug out a bottle of prescription pills. They rattled around when she placed them on the table next to Livingston's head.

"Sleeping pills," she said. But Henry had figured that out. "The doctor said I needed to get some rest. I don't care for them much; they make me feel foggy. But they came in handy, don't you think?"

Henry leaned over and lifted one of Livingston's eyelids, but despite giving a rumbling snort, the man seemed totally unaware.

"Jesus, how many did you give him?" Henry asked.

"Just two," Alice said, sounding defensive. "I mixed it in with the food. But he probably hasn't slept in days, and he looks like he hasn't eaten much either. Two was all it took."

Henry's concern must have shown on his face.

"They're completely safe," Alice assured him.

"Okay," Henry said, running a hand through his hair. "If you say so."

"Can you help me carry him to a bed?" Alice asked.

"Um. Sure," Henry replied. They couldn't exactly leave him there.

Henry grabbed the man beneath the arms, and his head lolled backward. With the efficiency of a nurse, Alice grabbed Livingston's legs behind the knees, and together they heaved him up.

Carting him down the hallway, Henry was surprised that such a small, wiry man was so awkwardly heavy to lug around. Henry kicked the door open behind him, and they took Livingston into the room he'd once shared with his wife.

"On three?" Alice asked.

Henry nodded, and they swung the unconscious man onto the bed, where he sprawled and bounced on the mattress.

"I have no intention of changing him into pajamas and tucking him in," Henry said.

Alice wiped her hands on one another. "Don't bother. He'll be up and around soon enough, ready to go back to spewing nonsense. For now, he won't even notice."

They backed out of the room. As Henry shut the door, Livingston let out a snore and Alice couldn't hold back a grin.

"I don't know what to do about him, Alice," Henry said, suddenly serious. "He's out of control."

"I wish there was something I could do to help," Alice said.

"Yeah. But we know what your dad would say about wishes," Henry said with half a smile.

CHAPTER TWENTY-NINE

Eve's mouth was pulled into a thin line as she tried to concentrate on the steps Caroline had shown her, working the old loom. The experience of creating something with her own hands—something that could be touched, felt, given as a gift to another, some physical sign that would show that she existed—was compelling.

But Alice was in the house with Henry, and Eve found it hard to keep her mind from wandering there.

As if thoughts of Alice had conjured her into being, the door to the shed creaked, and there she stood.

"Hiya, Eve," Alice said. "I don't want to bother you. I just wanted to say hello and let you know I left some plates in the oven for you and Henry."

Eve studied the woman. She was gracious and giving, but more than that, she knew Henry in a way that Eve never would. She'd known him since he was a child, watched him grow into the man he'd become. For Eve, Henry had become a part of her, and she could feel that growing stronger by the day. She couldn't imagine life without him. Didn't want to imagine it.

But Alice was easy with him, able to talk and laugh, so sure of her place in the world and in the hearts of the people who loved her. Eve wanted that. She envied that.

"Thank you," she said quietly. It wasn't Alice's fault, but the envy didn't seem to care.

"Oh, this is lovely," Alice said, moving to touch a finger to the woven piece of fabric on Caroline's loom. "You did this?" she asked.

Eve bit her bottom lip, and the jealousy wilted under the appreciation.

"It's for Henry," she said with a slight smile.

Alice sent her an admiring glance. "It's amazing," she said.

Eve felt a flush creeping up her cheeks as the emotions inside of her clashed with one another. Looking around, her eyes landed on the bucket of pink bougainvillea blossoms she'd collected to dye the wool, and she jumped from her stool, grasped the bucket, and fled for the door of the small, crowded shed.

Alice followed her out into the sunlight, but it was better, somehow, not to be closed in with the other woman.

Eve walked to where the water faucet attached to the side of the shed and set the bucket on the ground. It wasn't heavy, not really, but she stretched and rubbed a hand along her lower back, pushing away at an ache. She'd been bent over the loom for hours, and her body felt stiff and creaky.

She turned on the spigot, and the crisp, cool water flowed over the blooms in the bucket, darkening them. A breeze kicked up, and it felt good to be out in the midst of the day after the dimly lit darkness of the shed. Eve turned her face and body into the wind and closed her eyes, drinking in the sensations caressing her skin.

When she opened her eyes, she was smiling.

She caught sight of Alice's face, and the other woman was not. Alice had gone as pale as fresh-churned milk, and she was staring at Eve like she'd seen her own nightmares come to life.

"Alice?" Eve asked, taking a step toward her.

Alice put a hand over her mouth, like she was going to be sick at any moment, and backed away, shaking her head. She turned and nearly ran back toward the house and Henry.

Eve watched her go, her brows drawn together. Then she looked down at herself, where the wind had outlined and molded the loose dress she was wearing around her form.

She sucked in a breath, and for a moment it felt as if her heart had stopped beating.

Her secret was no longer hers alone.

CHAPTER THIRTY

Henry had practical matters on his mind when the front door flew open and Alice reentered the house, riding a cloud of indignation. He'd been hired to build a shed on the other side of town, and he was supposed to start tomorrow, but with all the uncertainty that went along with having two severed fingers delivered to your door, he was loath to leave Eve alone for that amount of time. She'd just have to come with him, he thought.

"Alice?" he asked, concerned. Her face was a wide canvas that had brush strokes of pain and betrayal slashed all over it.

"How could you?" she cried. "You let me pour my heart out to you, go on and on about a baby, and the whole time you never thought—"

She broke off her words on a sharp intake of breath, and Henry could see she was fighting back tears.

"Alice, what's happened? Why are you so upset?" He crossed the room and put his hands on her forearms, and leaned down to look her in the eyes. She was trembling, he realized with a shock.

She threw her arms up, breaking the connection and taking a step back. This time when she faced him, it was disgust instead of betrayal he saw in her face. And Henry had the distinct impression that disgust was directed at him.

"How long, Henry? How long was she here before you started sleeping with her?"

It was his turn to take a step back.

"Excuse me?" he asked.

"I know how you two feel about each other. I'd have to be an idiot not to see it, and I'm not an idiot, Henry."

"Up until about five seconds ago, I would have agreed with you," Henry said, folding his arms across his chest.

Alice gave a short, bitter laugh.

"Typical. Just like a man. What were you *thinking?*" she raged.

"I don't know, Alice. But clearly you have an opinion about it, so why don't you do me a favor and fill me in. What *was* I thinking?"

"Oh, you fool! How could you be so careless? So . . . so stupid? You had your whole life in front of you, and now you've gone and—"

She threw her arms up and looked him up and down.

"That girl," Alice said, enunciating each word with a finger pointing in Henry's direction. "That girl is damaged."

"Her name is Eve," Henry said coldly.

"I know her name!" Alice shouted. "How long did *you* know her name before you jumped into bed with her?"

Henry's jaw clenched as he struggled to keep a leash on the anger that was threatening to break away from him.

"And now look what you've done! Not only have you completely disregarded her state of mind, you've really topped it off, haven't you?"

"That's enough," Henry said quietly, straining to stay calm in the face of such fury. "I don't know what you're accusing me of, Alice, but I don't like it."

"Oh, you don't like it?" she said with a harsh laugh. "You don't like it? That's rich, Henry. That's brilliant. What difference does it make if you like it or not? You're not the one who ended up pregnant, are you?"

A ringing began in Henry's ears, and he shook his head, trying to clear it out, trying like hell to rearrange the sounds that had come from Alice's mouth to create words different than the ones she'd just tossed at him like a grenade.

He squeezed his eyes shut, then opened them again, hoping to see something different than an indignant woman casting blame at his feet.

And he did see something different. He saw a woman, a friend, whose contempt was slowly draining away, replaced one drop at a time by something even worse. Pity.

"You didn't know," Alice said quietly, bringing her hand to her chin, her fingers spanning across lips that had parted in surprise.

There was a finality to those words, spoken in sympathy—a finality that left Henry feeling like the world had moved ten steps past where he was standing, and it wasn't waiting for him to catch up.

"You're wrong," he said.

"Oh, Henry," Alice said gently, shaking her head. "I'm a labor and delivery nurse. Honey, I'm not wrong. Maybe you'd better sit down."

He did as she said, his body moving of its own accord as his mind shifted into gear, struggling to catch up. Eve, in her ill-fitting hand-me-down dresses and oversized sweaters. Eve, squeamish at the sight of the meat laid out in Ms. Watson's kitchen.

He shook his head again, but once a thing is seen, it can't be unseen so easily.

Alice, too, was reaching an epiphany of her own.

"Henry, how could you not—" Her words stopped midsentence and her mouth dropped open. "Oh my God," she said quickly, gripping Henry's arm. "You didn't know because you and Eve aren't . . . You haven't . . ."

Henry's head dropped into his hands, which for Alice only confirmed her train of thought.

"God, Henry, I'm sorry. When I realized she was expecting, I just assumed. Of course you haven't. I should have realized. I'm so sorry for jumping to conclusions."

He waved away her concern. He had other things on his mind.

"I should have known," Alice babbled on. "She's only been here, what? Four months? It would have had to have happened nearly immediately, and you're not that kind of guy . . . I'm sorry, I'll shut up. I'm just making things worse."

Henry raised his head and looked square into Alice's face, her own so full of sympathy and helplessness.

"What are we gonna do, Alice?"

She opened her mouth, but no sound came out for a time.

"I don't know," she said finally. "I really don't. But I do know one thing. The fact that you asked that question, instead of asking what is *she* gonna do, says a whole lot about what kind of man you are, Henry. Caroline would be proud of you."

Henry gave a short laugh. "Yeah, sure she would."

"She would," Alice tried to reassure him. "You could still join the military, you know."

"I can't, Alice," he said.

He didn't tell her he'd been struggling with that very question for months. Even if he could convince Eve to marry him, he'd realized, she was hardly in a place where she could adjust to the ever-changing realities of being a military spouse. She could barely adjust to *this* life, which was about as removed from the rest of humanity as you could get.

"That's not going to work, Alice. Not in a million years. Eve can't handle being a military wife. Hell, I couldn't handle it! Because she'd have to marry me, you know. And what about basic training? What do I do? Leave her here with Livingston? That's never gonna work."

Henry stood, pacing the room like an animal stuck in a cage. That was how he felt—caged.

He ignored Alice's careful study of his reactions. He didn't care that she was seeing them raw as they washed over him. The hard fact was, he was losing a lifelong dream, one he'd held close when things had gotten bad. One he'd depended on as a shining light far off in the distance, drawing him toward a future away from here, a doorway to the rest of his life.

And the hell of it was, that door had already started swinging closed, from the moment he'd pulled Eve from the river and breathed life back into her. His life. He simply hadn't faced that yet.

But the stark realities of Eve's pregnancy slammed that door shut with a bang that echoed through every part of him.

"You know," Alice said, her voice tinged with a practicality that Henry wasn't ready to appreciate. "We're getting ahead of ourselves. Right now, we need to focus on Eve and the baby and making sure they get the care they need. After that, everything will work out. It always does."

"Does it, Alice? Does it really? Or is that something we say to make ourselves feel better?"

The resignation in Henry's voice was clear. Alice didn't miss it.

Neither did Eve, who was standing just outside the still-open front door. Henry's harsh words rang inside of her, reverberating through all the cracks and dark corners.

CHAPTER

THIRTY-ONE

Henry walked the path that his mother's feet had walked before him so many times. Through the pines, deep into the darkness of the swamp beyond. He searched blindly for the serenity that Mama always seemed to find in this place, and after a time, a kind of calm acceptance did seem to settle around him.

When he came to the old hunting shack hiding in the back of the woods, he stopped and stared. The seemingly abandoned shack was perched in the distance, rising from the fog like a watchful bird of prey.

Henry didn't admit to many people, hardly even to himself, that this place had featured prominently in most of his nightmares as a child. Del and Mari, sensing his weakness, as older siblings are so adept at doing, had filled his head with gruesome fireside stories about a cannibalistic swamp witch who wore the finger bones of children around her neck. At six years old, Henry had been a skeptical soul, but young enough that those seeds of terror had taken root in his imagination anyway.

He wondered if the ground around the shack was still littered with the chicken bones that Del and Mari had planted there, setting the scene to wring the maximum amount of fear from their young stepbrother.

It was Mari who lured him in, teasing him to come closer and closer.

"Swamp witches sleep during the day, Henry," Mari had whispered. "Come on, don't be such a crybaby."

Even at twelve, Mari was full of mystery, and she held him in thrall then, just as she'd done since the twins and their father had come into his life.

Del was easy, a boy like any other, content to treat Henry with the complacent disregard of an average older brother. As long as Henry did as Del said, and steered clear when Del didn't want him around, they rocked along just fine.

It was Mari who wove her spell on Henry, and she knew it. Mari wove a spell on them all, with her mercurial moods—achingly kind one moment, withdrawn, even cruel, the next.

When Del had leapt from the trees he was hiding behind, decked out in rags, mud, and chicken bone jewelry, screaming like a banshee, Henry had wholeheartedly believed he was about to die. As this had been the twins' ultimate goal all along, they were delirious with glee when Henry let out a shriek that harkened back to primitive times.

What they hadn't expected was Henry, face-to-face with imminent death, instinctively launching his skinny six-year-old self at Del, arms flailing and teeth gnashing in what he truly believed was a fight for his very existence.

"Holy crap, Mari, help! Get him off me!" Del had cried, blocking Henry's wild blows.

But Mari was laughing too hard at the spectacle to be any use at all. Henry, adrenaline pumping through him, didn't register that the befuddled voice coming from the swamp witch sounded strikingly like his brother's.

Del grabbed at him, struggling to keep Henry's fists from landing, but Henry had forward momentum on his side, and the two boys tumbled backward in a tangle of limbs and elbows. They rolled down and down, straight into the waiting arms of the murky green marsh.

Del came up sputtering, with muck sliding in chunks down his face and arms. He had one hand on Henry's forehead, keeping him at arm's length as he continued to thrash.

Henry could remember the sound of Mari's laughter so clearly, like manic bells ringing on the wind.

Later that day, Mama had sat the three of them down and told them the real story of the abandoned shack. The story of a man and his son and a hunting cabin. No one knew exactly what had been going through the boy's head when he'd shot his father in his bed, then hanged himself from the beam in the front room. And no one ever would.

Henry took a good look at the shack now, with its weathered piers and rotting siding. Some places hold on to death the way used fireworks hold on to the stench of gunpowder and flames.

There was no sign of anyone there now. Not that he'd expected there to be. The people who came and went from this place might have been ghosts. Only Eve, and two bloody fingers left on his doorstep, gave any indication that the sounds that he could hear at night coming from this place weren't just in his head.

Henry found that he preferred the childhood terror of a witch that feasted on errant children to the adult terror of the truth. The witch was more straightforward, to his mind.

Henry sighed.

He'd come to terms with the loss of the army. He'd been coming around to that anyway, in his own time.

It hadn't been that hard to do once he'd compared it to the thought of parting from Eve.

That. That would have been like cutting him in half.

"She should see a doctor," Alice had said before she'd left.

"That worked out well last time," Henry had replied.

"This is different, Henry. So many things could go wrong."

"I'll talk to her," Henry said.

And he would. But first he had to get his mind right. The last thing he wanted was to show Eve the tug-of-war going on inside of him. He needed to be the strong one. He had no choice.

So Henry had walked into the woods, searching for peace, and finally found it.

The sky was growing dark when Henry stepped back out of the trees, and the house glowed warm in the distance. For a moment, he tried to see it as Eve must have seen it, when she was abandoned and alone in the woods. Scared. Hungry. It beckoned to him as it must have to her.

He was thankful it was there for them both.

When he reached the house, Henry's steps echoed on the wooden boards of the porch, and the screen door creaked as he opened it, the same pattern of sounds that had welcomed him home since he was a boy.

For once, he was mindful of what a gift home was.

"Eve," he called as he shut the front door behind him.

There was no reply.

He walked through the front room, peeked into the kitchen, then down the hallway.

There was no sign of her.

He looked in on his stepfather, another problem he still didn't have an answer for, but when he found him sleeping soundly, as he'd expected, he shut the door and resolved to deal with that problem another day.

"Eve," he called again, checking the room that had once been Mari's, the one Eve slept in, alone. It was empty.

The feelings of contentment that had stirred in Henry on his walk home began to give way to the first creeping fingers of concern.

He never should have left her here alone.

With quicker steps than the ones that had brought him into the house, he left, heading for the shed. There was a light burning there—he could see it through the cracks under and around the doorway.

He wanted to breathe a sigh of relief, but it stalled in his chest. He needed to see her, put his eyes on her face, and know that she was okay before he could release that breath.

"Eve," he called, throwing open the door of the shed.

What he found was destruction.

Pieces of tubing and shards of glass jars littered the earth floor. The vast copper pots lay on their sides or upended on the ground. The stink of liquor and mash filled the air, overwhelming the small space, making his nostrils flare and bringing stinging tears to his eyes. His mother's loom, and the piece that Eve had been working on, the one that she and Mama had started together, lay in pieces, like a wild animal had torn into it.

"Eve!" Henry shouted. He turned his head from one direction to another, taking in so much devastation in such a small space.

The men from the shack. They must have come back. Eve wasn't here, they must have come back for her. He turned his back to the room, ready to rush into the woods and get her back, when the smallest movement caught his eye.

There. In the corner, curled up in the smallest ball she could make of herself, was Eve.

"Oh God, Eve, are you all right?" Henry asked, rushing to her side. "Look at me, Eve, are you okay?"

She didn't raise her head, but Henry could see her body shaking with sobs, and he could hear the choking sound coming from her as she tried to hold back the tears.

He pulled her into his arms and placed one hand over her hair as her head leaned against his chest. She was shaking. He was shaking too.

"I'm so sorry. I never should have left you here alone. I promise you, I won't let them hurt you. I won't leave you alone again. Not ever again."

If anything, Henry's reassurances made her sob harder.

"Eve, did they hurt you?" He dreaded asking the question, dreaded the answer even more. But when she shook her head no, he let out a pent-up breath. There was that, at least.

"Eve," Henry said. "Can you tell me what they looked like? How long ago they left, what direction they were going? Anything at all?"

She shook her head harder, and the crying intensified.

"It's okay now. You're safe. Everything's going to be all right."

"No, no, it's not," Eve moaned. "It's ruined. It was so perfect, and now it's broken and useless. It'll never be all right."

"Oh, Eve, I'll fix it. I can fix it. All of it," he said.

"Can you?" she asked, but the words were flat, hopeless, her distraught tears giving way to a chilling calm as she raised her head and looked at him with blank eyes.

"Of course I can. I can fix anything," he said, running his hand down her hair, trying to give her a smile she could believe in.

"Can you fix me?" she asked.

Henry tilted his head and looked at her expression more closely. Their eyes met, and as they held, he felt his chest begin to tighten. Those eyes, so rich and dark, held more than just fear of an intruder. They held much, much more than just the pain of a troubled past. They held a troubled right now.

Henry leaned back mere inches, still with his arms loosely around her. Her gaze dropped to the hands curled in tight fists against her middle.

Slowly, she unfurled her fingers and stared at her palms. Henry stared too. He couldn't break his eyes away. Those hands, they were raw and ripped. Blood dripped down from the cuts in her palms, marring the dress that had once belonged to Mari. The blood dotted and stained the fabric, pulled taut over her belly, the pregnancy so obvious now that he knew to look for it.

Henry's arms dropped away from her.

"You did this," he said in a whisper.

Eve raised her eyes again. She didn't nod, only stared at him, waiting. Waiting to see what he would do now.

Henry scrambled backward on the ground, pulling back from the devastating truth he saw in her face.

His palm landed on a broken shard of glass, but he barely felt it. His attention was on the woman in front of him, kneeling in the midst of the destruction she'd brought down on both of their heads.

He jumped to his feet, wiping his hands nervously on his jeans. He didn't want to look around at the broken pieces of his life, not again. He didn't want to see the loom that had belonged to his mother, the one he'd claimed would be so easily mended just a few moments before. He didn't want to look at the broken, scattered parts of the still that had been handed down for generations on his father's side.

Henry hadn't lied. He was good at fixing things. It was what he did. But this?

This was too much for him.

He turned away from Eve, desperate to get out of this shed with its overpowering scents and its troubles that he hadn't asked for.

In a daze, he wandered out the door, leaving it swinging free behind him.

The night greeted him, not as an old friend, as the evening had earlier, but as a fool who was in over his head. The bullfrogs calling from the swamp, the mosquitoes buzzing in his ears, the cicadas singing—it all sounded like laughter to him. Laughter at his naive words, spoken with such a loose tongue.

He could fix anything?

He couldn't fix this.

Henry found himself at the door of his truck. His hand went to the handle, and the creak of the old hinges grated against his senses as he opened the door.

The keys were hanging in the ignition, just like they usually were.

He turned the key, and the truck rumbled to life. He looked down at the gas gauge. He had three-quarters of a tank. That would get him miles from here. Miles and miles.

CHAPTER THIRTY-TWO

Eve lay on the bed with the handmade quilt thrown over the top of it. Made by hand for someone else. Someone who deserved it, and the love that it had been given with.

She ran her hand down the soft fabrics, worn thin with age and use, and wondered about the story behind them. So many stories, and just as many lives a person could lead. It came down to choices. Choices determined what shape those lives would have. Eve had come to understand that, just as she understood that, for a very long time, she'd had no choices to make.

Once, a long time ago, the woman in whose house she'd existed had seen her husband throw some scraps from his dinner to the girl. He'd said words to her that sounded almost kind.

Later, the woman had taken a strap to her.

It wasn't uncommon, but that time had been worse than ever before.

She'd taken the blows, trying not to cry out at first, but when it didn't stop, only growing more vicious, she eventually lost her well-practiced ability to swallow the noises that rose from her belly and threatened to escape her throat.

Darkness finally overtook her, and she'd surrendered to it willingly.

The girl didn't know how much time passed, how many days she spent in and out of the darkness.

She thought maybe that was the first time she'd met Death, there, in the black. Met Death, and begged him to take her away.

He'd denied her, making her choices for her, like everyone else.

With Henry, here in this place, her choices were finally her own, yet she continued to make the wrong ones.

And now there was no way to fix it.

She'd gathered together the pieces of the broken things she'd ruined in the shed. With tears in her eyes, she'd tried to salvage what she could, but in the end, the best she could do was to sweep away the glass and stack the remnants together. It could never be enough.

Henry was gone. He'd run, once he'd seen the monster she truly was.

Eve had showered, leaning her head against the tile and letting the hot water run down her body in rivulets, washing the blood from her hands, hanging limp by her sides. But no amount of water could cleanse her of who she was.

That she would take with her.

She'd leave this house in the morning, walk away from the only place she'd ever felt real and the only person who'd ever loved her.

Crying herself to sleep, she could feel the distance between her and Henry growing. She clutched her arms to her body and held herself tightly together, trying to block out the bright and pulsing sensation of her heart being ripped in half.

CHAPTER
THIRTY-THREE

Henry made it as far as Lafayette before he swung the truck onto an exit from the interstate. The Texas–Louisiana border was an hour and a half gone, but it had passed by without distinction.

He couldn't make himself turn the wheel around, but moving farther down the highway, knowing he'd eventually be forced to keep going straight and end up in the Atlantic or hang a right to Disney World, had lost any appeal.

It was late. Most of the service stations were closed, but he made out a truck stop in the distance, the neon lights advertising cigarettes and hot showers.

He turned into the parking lot, but once he was done filling the tank, he found it hard to get behind the wheel again.

There was a diner attached to the station, and Henry followed the lights.

He'd been running on autopilot since he'd left Blackwater behind. The fuzz in his head was starting to clear, but the voices he heard calling to him he wasn't ready to listen to.

As the bells on the door jingled above his head, Henry walked in and found a seat at the counter. There were plenty to choose from, with only a gnarled gnome of a man sitting at the opposite end, nursing a cup of something hot and staring at the television screen, where an impeccably groomed woman spoke in precise language about the latest rounds of bombs falling in the Middle East.

"What can I get for you?" asked a gray-haired man in a stained apron.

Henry started to answer, but before he could, the man held up a hand.

"Before you answer that, I should tell ya, the line cook got thrown in jail today, so it's just me tonight. I'd steer clear of the eggs. Never been able to get the hang of 'em."

"Take his advice, son," said the man from the other end of the bar, who spoke without taking his eyes from the icy blonde on the screen. "His eggs turn out like an old, old woman. Tough where they oughtn't be, and flabby where they ought to be firm."

"Ah, shut the hell up, Dutch," the man behind the counter called, then said to Henry, "I was you, I'd go for the club sandwich."

Henry nodded. "And some coffee, if you don't mind."

Within minutes, the man, who had a patch on his shirt that read "Apollo," set a plate in front of him. Good as his word, the club was impressive, open-faced to show off the craftsmanship that had gone into it.

Henry put the top side of the buttered bread on the mountains of meat and had to use both hands to raise the thing to his mouth.

Apollo watched him until Henry let out that first groan of satisfaction. "That's what I'm talking 'bout," Apollo said with a nod, pulling out a rag to wipe down the counter. "It's the avocado that does it, and the Frenchy bread with a name nobody can pronounce right. I do make a mighty fine sandwich, even if I gotta say so myself."

"And you only say it about two dozen times a night, dontcha," Dutch said.

"Dutch, you're trying my patience tonight. Every man's got a skill. Can't help it if the gods have blessed these old hands with a natural and innate talent."

"Talent, my ass. Being able to fry an egg, now that's a talent. You slap some shit on some bread and act like we're supposed to call you Emeril Lagasse."

"You'll have to excuse that old cuss, my friend. Known him for thirty-five years, and he ain't never had no manners to speak of at all."

"I got manners plenty, 'Pollo. I just save 'em for the ladies," Dutch said with a little wiggle of his head.

Apollo let out a big belly laugh. "Last woman that came within a mile of him was a leathery old trick looking for change for the pay phone," he said to Henry. "He grinned so big his dentures fell out, and she run the other way."

Dutch turned his head toward Henry, and a smile broke across his wrinkled, hairy face, then his teeth started moving up and down in his mouth, showing off a dexterity that you just can't get with real teeth.

"Put that mess away," Apollo told him with a shake of his head. "Man's trying to eat here."

Dutch sent Henry a sly wink, then turned his attention back to the newscaster.

"Where you headed to?" Apollo asked as he grabbed a broom.

Henry didn't know what to say to that. "I don't really know. Nowhere, I guess."

The other man raised a brow at him. "Nowhere, huh? A man going nowhere's usually intent on leaving somewhere behind, in my experience. Where you from?"

"Texas," Henry said.

Apollo nodded, like that was the answer he'd expected.

"You got a Texas look about you. See lots of Texans come through here. Usually headed down to New Orleans, looking to get up to some trouble."

"Not looking for any trouble," Henry said with a shake of his head.

"Yeah, you got that look on you too. Like trouble done got your number down by heart."

Henry sighed and pushed the half-empty plate away from him. The food was sitting like a ball of lead in his belly.

"Trouble of the female persuasion?" Apollo asked.

"There any other kind?" Dutch threw in.

Henry didn't say anything. He didn't need to.

"Sometimes, when you're young, you know, it's not always easy to recognize the value of a good, steady woman. They're like fine wine. Need to be savored. Appreciated. She a good woman?"

Henry had been trying to hide from thoughts of Eve for hours, but the question brought her to his mind, fresh and clear as if she were standing in front of him.

"Not exactly," Henry said.

Apollo gave a low whistle, leaning on his broom.

"Well, then. That's a whole other story, ain't it. I had me a 'not exactly' good woman once too."

Henry saw the two men exchange a look that said more to him about their friendship than their insults ever could.

"Long time ago now. I love my wife, brother. I do," Apollo said with a shake of his head. "Best thing that ever happened to me, no doubt about it."

"You got that right, man," Dutch said.

"But I gotta tell you, friend. You'll never appreciate the daylight till you've walked on the dark side of the night, without even the stars to show you the way."

"You're so full of shit, Apollo." Dutch didn't sound like he was joking this time.

"No," the man said, shaking his head. "No, I ain't. You say what you want, Dutch. Probably all true anyway, but damn . . ." He had a far-off look in his eyes, and Henry could see he was a long way away from this Louisiana diner, with his dirty apron and a broom in his hand.

"That woman was lightning. Nothing on God's green earth can make a man feel as alive as the love of a bad woman."

"Did you hit your head on something back in that kitchen? One of those iron skillets fall on top of you?"

Apollo ignored his friend. He looked at Henry out of old eyes that showed a spark of the young man he must have been once.

"I tell you, it got bad, son. Real bad, in the end. But I never regretted it. Don't get me wrong, I don't want it back. My Linda and me, we got a good thing going. Been going for a lot of years now, and I wouldn't trade it for nothing in the world. But I still remember the smell of lightning. Yes, sir, I do. That's a smell you don't ever forget."

Dutch swiveled his stool to face Henry.

"Take a piece of advice, boy. Don't listen to that shit. That woman nearly put him in the ground." The old man fished in his pocket, pulled out some wrinkled bills, and slapped them on the counter. "You got a woman like that at home, a crazy one? There's only one thing to do, and that's get in your car and get as far gone as the road'll take you."

Apollo shook his head. "Dutch, you never did get it. There's no shaking loose of that. Doesn't matter where you go, once she's in you, that's where she's gonna stay. It's like a virus. Nothing to do about it but hope you're still kicking once it runs its course."

Dutch shook his head. "You're a dumbass, 'Pollo. Don't listen to him, Texas. You saddle up your ride, and you ride like hell in the other direction."

Dutch looked at Apollo with a face on him like an old schoolteacher's, almost prim in its disapproval. "Give Linda my best, will you," he said.

"Your best? What the hell she want with your best? She's got *my* best, fool," Apollo said to his friend's retreating back, but Dutch just lifted a middle finger over his shoulder as the bells over the door signaled his exit.

"He's right, you know," the older man said. "Probably, you should keep on keeping on. Smart thing to do. You a smart one, boy?"

"That's a damn good question," Henry muttered.

CHAPTER
THIRTY-FOUR

The moon hung low and fat in the sky as Henry pulled the truck into the drive.

He'd made his decision, and he'd stand by it.

He'd stand by Eve. For better or worse . . . if she'd have him.

Letting himself into the quiet house, he saw that only the grandfather clock marked the passage of time. Everything else was as he'd left it. The only thing changed was him.

On light feet, Henry made his way down the hallway. He pushed slightly on the door to Eve's room, as Henry had come to think of it, and it swung silently on its well-worn hinges.

She was lying on the bed, facing away from him. She was on top of the quilt, like she'd fallen there and couldn't bring herself to go any farther.

Henry had spent the hours of the long drive home debating the best course forward. Because they would move forward. And they would do it together. He'd chosen his path. He only hoped he could convince her to travel it with him.

Gently, not wishing to disturb her, he took a throw from the back of a chair in the corner and shook it out. He pulled it across her slight frame, which somehow seemed more fragile in sleep.

Eve turned her head and looked at him with eyes that were clouded. Not with sleep, but with sadness and with worry.

"You came back," she whispered.

"I'm so sorry, Eve," he whispered back, his heart in his words. "I told you I wouldn't leave you alone, and then I ran. I can't take it back, but I hope you'll believe me when I say it won't happen again."

Eve sat up in the bed, then put a hand on Henry's cheek.

"I'm not good for you."

Henry met her eyes in the dim room, the moonlight through the window casting shadows across her face. "No, you're not," he said, shaking his head. "But that doesn't make any difference. Eve, you *are* me. You're the parts of me that matter."

"I should leave," she said.

"Then go," he said, his voice stripped to the raw underbelly of truth. "But you'll be taking the heart that beats inside of me. How long do you think I'll last without it?"

When she pulled him to her, he could feel the wet tears on her cheeks dampen his face.

"Marry me, Eve," he whispered in her ear.

She tightened her hold, laying her head against his chest. Surely she could hear his blood pumping through his veins.

"No," she said.

Then she kissed him.

He lost himself in her touch, lost all sense of himself as a separate being. Surrendering to it, he knew, this was their truth. This was their world, in the dark, together, with only the moon as witness.

CHAPTER

THIRTY-FIVE

The days that followed turned into weeks, then slowly slid into months. Henry spent the time doing what he'd always done. He fixed things as best he could.

His mother's loom was the first and easiest to repair. Eve resisted when he presented her with the finished contraption.

"I can't," she said.

"You can," he told her simply. "Mama meant for you to have it. Use it."

And after a time, she did. He found comfort in having her nearby, working the shuttle, weaving the colors neatly through and around one another, lost in her guarded thoughts.

Turning his attention to his father's pot still was a trickier business, but he'd learned the ins and outs of distilling a long time ago. He had his dad's old journals for reference, but he'd been doing this since he was eleven and found he rarely needed the reference to get the setup running again.

This was where Henry found the most intimate connection to a father he'd never had a chance to know. Times were different for Henry than they had been for Weston Martell. Henry didn't have too many worries about the local law, given that the products he still provided were an open and well-established secret. Del and Brady certainly weren't going to give him a hard time, and Sheriff McKinney himself was one of Henry's best customers.

But he found the pull of the alchemical, secretive process a throwback to the wilder days his father and grandfather before him would have lived. Thoughts of the men who'd come before, the men he'd never had the chance to know, floated through his head as he set up the thumper and the worm and applied the oatmeal paste to the seal.

He wondered what his father would have thought about Eve. From the remnants of tattered memories the folks around him had offered up, Henry believed Weston had a more capricious streak than he ever would. He'd like to think his father would have understood the need to go his own way, in the face of rationality. Or maybe that was just wishful thinking.

Lord knew, his stepfather wasn't as sanguine. The pressure was building by the day. They couldn't keep Eve's pregnancy hidden much longer. In spite of the fact that Livingston was gone more days than he was home and Eve was careful to steer clear of him when he was, he was bound to take notice eventually. Livingston had transformed into more of a Bible-pushing, gospel-shouting loony than ever before, wielding his religion and his judgment like a sledgehammer, but he wasn't a fool, even now.

Henry knew a confrontation was coming. A baby out of wedlock? In the man's own backyard? It very well might be the impetus that pushed his stepfather over the edge. Henry knew his mother's wishes when it came to Livingston, but he wasn't sure he'd be able to honor those if push came to shove. If—or when—things came to a head, there was a very good chance that Livingston would have to go.

He'd made his decision, and he hadn't wavered. He would stand by Eve, and the baby that was coming, whether Livingston liked it or not.

But he still wished there was another way. One that didn't include tossing his stepfather out of the home he'd considered his own for nearly twenty years.

And Henry's worries didn't end there. Eve still refused to see a doctor, much to Alice's frustration. Alice had brought vitamins, insisting that Eve at least take care of herself, if she couldn't be talked into seeing an obstetrician.

"The heartbeat's strong, at least," Alice had said, putting her stethoscope away after her last visit. "But I can't say it enough. You *need* to see a doctor, Eve. There are so many things that could go wrong."

But Eve remained firmly entrenched. She'd only allowed Alice to examine her after Henry had insisted, again and again. But she refused to entertain the idea of a physician.

Her stubbornness left both Henry and Alice in a perpetual state of anxiety.

And these concerns were heightened by the ever-looming threat of the people who owned the shack in the marsh. Henry wanted to believe they were done with them, their message sent and received, leaving everyone free to go their own way. But that kind of optimism stank of a naïveté that Henry had never been real comfortable with.

With everything on his mind simmering like a stew in a pressure cooker, it was with a sense of resignation rather than surprise that he watched the stranger walk up the drive.

He observed the man, unseen, from the shadows thrown by the doorway of the shed. Wiping his hands on a shop cloth, he steeled himself to meet whatever new issue the man's boots were bringing to their door.

"Hey there, mister," Henry called, catching the stranger off guard.

Glancing around, the man spotted Henry as he stepped out of the shadows.

"Didn't see you there," he mumbled.

"Can I help you with something?" Henry asked, straight to the point, as he walked toward the visitor.

The man was grimy, looked like it'd been a while since he'd seen soap and water. But Henry didn't exactly smell like a rose, so he didn't hold that against him.

"I sure do hope so, friend," the man said. Something about his tone set Henry's jaw on edge. It was as oily as his hair.

"I'm not your friend, friend," Henry said lightly, tucking the shop rag into his back pocket.

"Course not. Meant no offense," the man said, ducking his head and sending a sly smile in Henry's direction.

"None taken," Henry said. "What's your business here, stranger?"

"Well, now, it's funny you ask," the man said.

Henry didn't see much funny about it, but he'd found that keeping quiet was usually the best way to get people to fill up the space with words of their own.

"I'm looking for somebody. Somebody I been told might have found her way out this direction." The man looked furtively around Henry, peering at the house and the shed with rheumy eyes, perhaps thinking he might find what he sought hiding in plain sight.

"That so?" Henry asked.

"Hmm," the man murmured. "A girl. 'Bout so tall," he said, gesturing with his hand to a place in the sky that presumably Eve would fit beneath. "Dark hair. Kinda shy." He punctuated the last part with a wink that made his leathery, wrinkled skin contort on his skull. Henry felt like a copperhead had just climbed up his back.

"Shy, you say?" Henry said. "This girl got a name?"

"Well, now you mention it, that's a funny thing, it is."

Henry had the feeling he and this man didn't share the same sense of humor.

"Known her nearly her whole life, I have, but she ain't never been right. Her mama neither, for that matter. Never did know if she even bothered to give the girl a name. Always called her 'girl,' she did. Least when she was around. Sort of stuck, it did."

"Sorry, pal. I don't know any girls without a name."

He did know one named Evangeline who was currently behind those walls the man was staring at so closely, resting—she tired easily these days—and that was exactly where Henry hoped she'd stay until he could get rid of this sleaze.

The man squinted at Henry, clearly doubting his words. After a moment, he broke into a smile that showed off his crooked, yellowed teeth and held out a hand in Henry's direction.

Knowing full well that he hadn't convinced the man that he didn't have the girl he was looking for, Henry wondered how long it would take him to regroup and return, once he'd sent him on his way. Maybe under the cover of darkness next time.

Playing along with the charade, Henry moved to shake the stranger's hand. His handshake was sweaty and unpleasant, but that wasn't what caused Henry to tighten his grip on the other man's wrist, turning it so that he could get a good look.

It was the sense that something wasn't right with the hand that had touched his own. And his senses weren't wrong.

The hand that he was looking at was dirty and stained. The hand of a working man or a vagrant—Henry couldn't be sure which. It also had only three fingers, sitting next to two puckered, skin-covered nubs where the pinkie and ring fingers used to be.

"I don't have your girl," Henry said, staring down at the man's hand. "But I've come across something else that belongs to you."

The stranger pulled his hand away, tucking it back into his pocket and looking around furtively. Not like he was searching for something this time, unless it was a way out of there. But Henry wasn't done with him yet.

"I got a feeling there's a story behind those missing fingers," he said, staring intently at the man.

"I'd imagine there's all kinds of stories in the world, friend," said the man, dodging the question.

"True enough. But the one I'm interested in is how you came to be separated from your digits."

The man tried to look nonchalant, but the single step he took back gave away his discomfort.

"And why would I be sharing such a grisly tale with you?" he asked.

"Seems to me, we're both in possession of information of the sort that might be useful to the other."

"Information about my girl?" The discomfort had fled, and the man's eyes sparked with a greed that turned Henry's stomach.

"About *a* girl. Somehow, I doubt she was ever yours."

Henry could see the calculation in the man's eyes as he weighed his options. Truth be told, Henry didn't want anything to do with the stranger, but he needed to know what he was up against.

"What do you want to know?" the other man asked, squinting up at Henry beneath bushy gray eyebrows.

"Everything."

"And what do I get in return?"

"You tell me your story, and if it's worth the price of admission, I'll tell you where the girl is. Although she doesn't like to be called that anymore."

"How do I know you're a man of your word?"

"I guess that's a chance you're gonna have to take," Henry said. "Or not. That road'll take you out just as easy as it brought you in."

The man barely hesitated.

"All right. All right, then. Don't see no harm in it. But talking's thirsty work, you hear what I'm saying?"

Henry glanced up at the house. Nothing was moving, no sign that there was anyone around for miles except for the two of them.

That was just fine.

"Yeah, I hear you loud and clear." Maybe the man thought Henry was going to invite him in to share a cold beer in the front parlor, but he thought wrong.

He pointed to his old blue truck pulled up next to the shed. "That'll do just fine."

The stranger sent a glance of his own toward the house, but he played along.

They walked together to the truck, and Henry let down the tailgate with a bang.

"You're welcome to one of those jars over there," he said, pointing to the crates of moonshine stacked in the back.

"Yeah?" the man said, raising a ponderous eyebrow.

"Help yourself."

"Don't mind if I do, and thank you kindly, friend."

The man had unscrewed the top of one of the jars, breaking the seal on the whiskey. Henry watched him take a swig and waited for the inevitable gasp.

"Whew, boy!" the man said, wiping his mouth on the back of his dirty sleeve. "That stuff's got some kick to it."

Wiping tears from the corners of his eyes, the man spoke again when he got his breath back.

"Name's Augustine," he said. "Folks mostly call me Gus."

He took another gulp of the fiery liquid and twisted his face up, shaking his head back and forth as he did. The stuff Henry'd given him was rotgut, the cheap whiskey he sold to King for the customers that were slow to pay their tabs, but that didn't seem to bother the man in the least.

"Hey, this stuff isn't gonna make me go blind, is it?" Gus asked, once he'd found his voice again.

"Guess we'll find out," Henry said.

Gus turned his head sharply, but Henry's face stayed blank. Finally, Gus's face made that slow morph into his sly smile.

"You fooling on me," he said. "That's funny. You got a sense of humor. I like that, friend."

"I already told you once, I'm not your friend."

"Ah, come on now. We're sharing a drink, ain't we?"

Gus was the only one drinking, but rather than point that out, Henry nodded toward the man's hand, which was gripping the mason jar just fine, even with three fingers.

"Tell me about the hand."

"Not one for small talk, then. Hey, I can respect that."

Gus was stalling, Henry could tell. Probably sorting through versions of the truth to find the one he felt most likely to get him what he was after.

But Henry was nothing if not patient.

"All started with the girl, I suppose," Gus said, taking another drink from his jar. Watching the man wet his lips, then place them along the rim of the glass, Henry made a note to make sure that one got sanitized twice before it was used again.

"Rita, see—my old lady—she never got on with that sister of hers. Her name was Maeve, but she called herself Starr. Ain't that something? Starr. Two *r*'s at the end. Like that extra *r* made her a high-class hooker instead of just another whore in a dirt-poor border town."

"What town are we speaking of?" Henry asked, noting the slippery way Gus's words had started to bump into one another.

"That ain't important to the story, I don't suppose," Gus said, with a look that cut sideways at Henry.

With a nod to acknowledge the block, Henry signaled him to continue.

"My Rita, see, she's a good, God-fearing woman, and that's why, see. Why, according to her anyway. I always figured it was pure old jealousy. 'Cause Maeve—Starr—she's the one got the looks in the family." Gus took another swig from the jar. "Religion seems to come easier to the ugly girls. You ever notice that?"

"Why, what?" Henry asked.

Gus's face contorted, and one eye squinted at Henry. Henry realized he'd lost the man.

"You said 'that was why,' speaking about your wife and her sister," Henry went on slowly. "Why, what?"

The cloud cleared from the other man's face.

"Why she hated her, of course. Hated her with a deep-down kind of mean that she saved just for Maeve. At least, until Maeve left her girl with us. Then she hated the girl."

"Your sister-in-law left her daughter with you and your wife?"

Gus nodded. "Girl was young. I don't know, six or seven. Maeve'd hooked up with some flashy grifter, looking for a meal ticket. No use for a kid underfoot. Truth be told, Maeve had no business with a kid in the first damn place. Used to keep her locked in the closet when she was entertaining. And that's a fact I can attest to, you know what I mean?"

Gus sent a wink in his direction, and Henry's hands twitched, yearning to ball themselves into fists and smash into this man. Either the liquor had started to do its job, or Gus was stunningly unobservant, because he took no notice of the flex of Henry's jaw.

"I heard some talk 'round town that Maeve didn't always lock the girl up, though. Sometimes she brought her out, let her do a little entertaining of her own. I don't know that's true, but I can't say I was shocked to hear it. Maeve, now. That woman'd do just about anything for a fix. If you could snort it or shove it in your veins, Maeve'd sell her soul to the devil, then take out a second mortgage on it."

Henry felt a sick rage waking inside of him.

"You'd think the girl'd have it better, once her mama decided to skip town. She didn't stay gone for long, though, Maeve. Wasn't two years later, she showed up again, back at tricks. By that time, she must have forgotten she ever had a girl. Never bothered to come and get her, leastways."

Gus shook his head.

"Never did figure out why Maeve left her at Rita's door. That woman," Gus said, gesturing with the jar and sloshing whiskey on his boots, "that one's got a mean streak down to the bone, she does. They say women are the softer sex. You know that?"

Gus made a hawking sound deep in his throat and leaned over to spit in the dirt.

"Whoever says that ain't never met my Rita, that's all I got to say about that."

Gus must have finally taken notice of the violence welling up behind Henry's eyes, because he started backpedaling.

"I tried my best to do right by the girl. I swear to you I did. I'm probably the closest thing she's ever had to a friend. Why, there was times I was even able to distract Rita when she was in one of her moods, taking it out on the girl and all."

Gus's eyes opened wide, but Henry wasn't buying the bullshit he was selling.

"The fact the girl didn't starve to death alone, why, that was all on me. I made sure she was fed. Ain't nobody else could say that. That was all me."

"How long?" Henry asked quietly.

Grasping on the change of subject, Gus shook his head.

"I don't know, she's probably with us twelve, fourteen years now. Right up till I got her out of there."

Gus nodded sharply, trying to convince Henry and maybe himself that he'd been some sort of fairy godparent to an abused, neglected child.

"That's right. It was me, see. You gotta give credit where it's due. I didn't have to pay the girl's way, you know. Believe me, I was real tempted to put it in my pocket and go on whistling Dixie, with none the wiser, but that just didn't seem right, you know."

Henry shook his head, exasperated with the man and his winding way of skirting around the heart of a matter.

"What the hell are you talking about?"

"The money!" Gus said.

"What money?"

"From the settlement," Gus said slowly, like Henry was a child who wasn't paying attention in class.

"When Maeve went and got herself killed. The sombitch who did her, turned out he was a cop. They said it was a accident, but everybody knew old Officer Brinkley, and he was dirty as a port-o-john shitter. Something fishy about that whole deal, I always said. And I think they knew it too, which is why they paid out like they did."

There were plenty of questions clamoring inside of Henry's head to be answered, but the liquor had loosened up Gus's tongue, and Henry let the man ramble.

"Course, the people who cut the check didn't have no idea Maeve had a kid. Far as I know, the girl never set foot in a schoolroom in her life. Probably wasn't even born in a hospital, knowing Maeve. Spent most of her life locked in closets or basements, getting used up and beaten on."

Henry could feel a tic starting behind his left eye.

"Made that big damn check out to Rita, they did. And you'd think that'd be a fine thing, now, wouldn't you? Having a wife who's got a pay-day land in her lap like that. But what does that old bitch do? Claims we ain't *for real* married! You believe that?"

The sheer offense of it was written all over Gus's face, but luckily Henry wasn't required to respond at this point.

"'*What the hell?*' I said. '*You never heard of common-law, Rita?*' I mean, goddamn, I only been faithfully by the woman's side for nigh on twenty years. You try sleeping in the bed next to a cold, mean-ass, ugly woman for two decades, see how you like it! And she wants to go and tell me we ain't *for real* married."

"Would you get to the point?" Henry said through clenched teeth.

"I'm getting there, chief, I'm getting there. Well, I's so damn mad, the only thing I could think to do was take away the woman's favorite toy. See how she liked that, you know."

Gus took another long swig from the jar, which was mostly empty by this time, and leaned in close. Henry couldn't tell if the stench off his breath was from the teeth or the rotten core of the monster that lurked under the guise of a human being.

"It was easy, man. So easy. Just a signature on a check, and nobody bothering to ask any questions. Hell, I don't know what I was so nervous about. And I'm walking away with cold, hard cash. Cash that, by rights, should have been half mine anyway."

Gus tossed the glass jar, empty now, carelessly into the truck behind him.

"Went and got that girl out of the basement, and I took her to some people I know."

"What people?" Henry asked with deadly intent.

"People it's best not to say too much about. Let's just say they deal in exports and imports. And let's just say you're looking to get exported from one side of the border and imported to another. Well, now, these are the people to see. But it's gonna cost you. Sure enough it is. They're not running a charity over there."

"You're talking about smuggling illegals into the States? Human trafficking?"

If Henry thought this story couldn't get any more twisted, he was very wrong.

"That's one way to put it, I suppose. But we was already in the States, so it was more like relocation than smuggling. They even knocked some off the price, since I worked with them before. Running trucks down the interstate over to Louisiana or Florida. Easy work for easy money. Can't hardly beat that."

"You sold your niece to human traffickers at a fucking discount?"

Realizing he'd said way, way too much, Gus began to backtrack again.

"I didn't sell her! I paid her fare for her! They provide a service, see. I was doing the girl a favor, friend. I swear to you. These guys, people pay them to help 'em get to a better life! I was helping her! I didn't have to do it. I could have put that money in a G-string somewhere and got my knob polished for weeks! But I was thinking of the girl!"

"Sure you were. You're quite the hero, aren't you, Gus?"

"That's right, I *am* a goddamn hero! All that girl had to do was what she was told, and she'd have been just fine. But what does she do? She's got to go and cut a man up with a stolen knife! I swear to God, I'd have been better off if I'd have never set eyes on that crazy-ass family."

"You're probably right, Gus. So I gotta ask. What in the hell are you doing here? This girl's so much trouble, why would you want to find her?"

"They know where I live, don't they?! The girl's run off on them, so it's fine for her, but me?" Gus raised his hand toward Henry's face and grotesquely wiggled the nubs where two of his fingers had once been.

"So you're looking to what? Get revenge? Deliver her back to them so *they* can get revenge? You gonna try and take two of her fingers and sew them onto your hand?"

Some sense of self-preservation must have broken through the other man's haze of anger, because his eyes grew large and pleading.

"No! No. I just want to do right by the girl. I can't hardly go back home, even if Rita hadn't thrown me out. But if I gotta make a new place for myself in this old world, I figure I should find the girl and take responsibility for her well-being. That's all."

Henry stared down at his palms, keeping his thoughts to himself.

"Intentions as pure as the driven snow, right, Gus?"

"Of course, friend. I'm her uncle. She belongs with me."

Henry gave a short bark of laughter. "I doubt she'd see it that way."

"I'm the only thing in the world that girl's got, and I mean to do right by her."

"Then what brings you here?"

Gus opened his mouth, then thought better of whatever answer he was about to give, reconsidering his words.

"You say you're not working with the traffickers, just looking out for the girl, so you must have had some reason for believing she'd be around here."

"Well, I been here before, see. When I was working with them in the past. This is one of their stops, they got a place over there in the marsh."

"Yeah, I got that part. But surely they have a lot of places you might have tried. What brings you *here*, to *my* door?"

Gus stuttered. "I . . . I'm just . . . going down the line. This seemed as good a place as any, seeing how they like this spot so much. They got the local law on the payroll, so they usually stop here when they have a run, knowing they don't have to worry."

"You know an awful lot about their operation for somebody who claims he's not working with them."

"I was just guessing, friend."

Henry nodded, rubbing his thumb across the calluses on the other palm.

"Uh-huh. I guess you expect me to take your word for that?"

"You calling me a liar?"

"Yeah, Gus. That's exactly what I'm calling you."

Gus straightened his spine and started to sputter, but Henry'd had enough.

He stood up and pulled the other man off his tailgate. Gus stumbled with the suddenness of the move combined with the effects of the rotgut whiskey.

"You get on down this road now, or I'll toss you in the back of this truck and drive you to the edge of town and dump you out."

"We had a deal!" Gus yelled. "I know you've got that girl. You think I'm just gonna listen to some jumped-up little shit tell me what to do?"

"Yes," Henry said. "Yes, I do. Because it's in your best interests, Gus. And if there's one thing I think you care about, it's your best interests. You go, and you keep going. Forget everything you ever thought you knew about your niece and don't ever come back here, or I swear to God, I'll be hauling you out of here tied to the back of my truck next time."

"You don't understand!" Gus said, pleading now. "They'll find me. I have to get that girl back!"

"Well, I'll tell you, Gus, I don't know what you expect me to do about that. I've never seen your girl before in my life."

"You're a goddamn liar!" Gus shouted, losing his smarmy façade at last and pushing his way into Henry's face. "I know she's here. You got her in there, keeping her to yourself, I know it!"

"What you know and don't know is not my problem," Henry said in a low voice, stepping into Gus's outraged face with enough force to make the man stumble backward. "Now, I'm done talking to you. Get down the road, Gus, before I take you down it myself."

Gus made a visible effort to pull himself together, but Henry could see he was a seething cesspool of rage beneath that sloppily stitched-together mask of control.

"All right, then," Gus said, taking a deep breath. "I can see I'm not welcome, but I'm telling you now, I'm coming back for that girl. She's mine, you hear me? Mine, and I mean to have her back."

"Yeah?" Henry asked. "Well, good luck with that. *Friend*."

CHAPTER THIRTY-SIX

Henry pushed through the door into the Sheriff's Department riding a wave of anger he'd rarely known. His mood hadn't been helped by the layer of panic that had overtaken him when he'd gone back into the house and found Eve missing.

His pulse had picked up speed, but time had slowed as he'd searched every room and come up empty-handed. It wasn't until he'd forced himself to stand still and listen to the heartbeat of the old house that he'd zeroed in on the closed door leading to the closet in the bedroom.

There he'd found her, curled in on herself, rocking back and forth. She wasn't crying. She wasn't making any sound at all. It was a mystery how he'd known to look there. But when he knelt in front of her and took her into his arms, she was shaking like a million tiny earthquakes were happening inside of her.

"Del!" Henry now called across the expanse of the room, not caring that he was causing a scene. There was only Gladys to witness it, and she must have recognized the signs of a family argument looming, because she looked intently down at the computer screen in front of her and pretended not to notice.

The door to Sheriff McKinney's office was closed, as usual. He was most likely sleeping off a hangover from the night before. No sign of Brady.

But it didn't matter, because his brother was the one Henry was looking for.

As Del looked up from the paperwork on his desk, Henry saw that he had bags under his eyes. If the situation had been different, he might have sympathized. He couldn't imagine the stress of what Del and Alice were dealing with.

But the situation wasn't different.

"You need to tell me what the hell's going on with you, Del," Henry said once he'd reached his brother's desk.

"What's your problem, Henry?" Del sighed, leaning back in his chair like the last thing he wanted to deal with was another issue.

"I think the real question is what's *your* problem, brother."

"I don't have time for games today."

"Yeah? I suggest you make time. Or do I need to slip you a little cash to get you to pay attention?"

Del's face froze, then settled into hard lines.

"Excuse me?" he said slowly.

"You heard me. Do I need to pay off Brady too? You in on this together, like you two do everything?"

Del stood so quickly that the chair slid across the floor with a screech. He pushed his way into Henry's face, but if he was expecting his younger brother to back down, he was mistaken. Chest to chest, the two stared at one another, each daring the other to back down first.

"How much are they paying you to look the other way while they buy and sell human beings like cattle?" Henry spit out in a disgusted whisper.

Del's eyes widened. In that moment, Henry knew he wasn't wrong. The surprise and guilt were written there on Del's face. He recovered quickly, forcing his expression into a mask, but it was too late.

"How long, Del? How long have you been on the take?" Henry asked. He'd never had any illusions about the sort of man his brother was. Del's intelligence landed somewhere just below average, at best, and he had a short temper at times, but Henry would have never pegged him as crooked. He was surprisingly disappointed in him.

Del grabbed Henry by the upper arm and looked around to see if anyone had overheard Henry's damning words, but Gladys still had her head buried in her computer screen. Whether she'd been able to make out their heated conversation was anyone's guess, but she was trying very hard to look like she was minding her own business.

Henry wished he were in a position to do the same.

"Come on," Del said, nodding toward the door, then heading that way.

Henry stayed where he was for a moment, watching his brother walk away from him. Del's hair was starting to thin in the back. Henry had never noticed that before, and suddenly Del seemed very old. Ancient, in fact.

Del turned to see why Henry wasn't following him, then jerked his head impatiently.

"You want to talk about this or not?" he said. "Gladys, I'm gonna buy my brother a cup of coffee at the diner. I've got my radio."

"Sure thing, Del," Gladys said, busying herself with the files on her desk and giving the deputy an overly sunny smile.

Knowing it was the only way to get answers, answers he needed to keep Eve safe, Henry sighed and followed his brother. He wasn't sure he was ready to hear what Del had to say, but there was really no other way.

The sun was blinding, and Del pulled on the aviator sunglasses that he'd favored since he was eleven and they'd watched *Top Gun* together. It was an affectation that Henry had always thought ridiculous, but that was Del. He wondered that he was surprised by any of this.

"Get in the truck, Henry," Del said, opening the driver's door to the brown-and-white SUV with the bar of lights running across the top.

They drove to the diner in silence. Del was either gathering his thoughts or debating ways to manipulate the truth. Either way, all Henry could do was wait.

At a booth in the diner, Del ordered coffee. The waitress, a blonde named Becky whom Henry had gone to school with, smiled at him, showing off a deep dimple in her left cheek, but he took little notice.

"Same for me, Becky. Thanks," he murmured.

Del picked at a fingernail, avoiding Henry's eyes while they waited on Becky to bring two white mugs and pour the steaming black coffee.

Once she was gone, Del couldn't avoid the subject any longer. "You don't understand what it's like, Henry," he said, shaking his head and avoiding his brother's eyes.

"Then why don't you tell me."

Del sighed. "I don't even want kids," he said, leaning back in the booth and looking Henry in the face for the first time since they'd sat down. "You believe that? I mean, I don't have anything against them, but I don't know how to be a father. I mean, damn. Look at the example I have."

Henry raised an eyebrow at the whining tone in Del's voice, but he kept his peace.

"It's Alice. She's got it in her head, and once she's set on something . . . shit. I just figure she'll be a good enough mother to make up for it."

Del took a spoon and stirred his coffee, in spite of the fact that he took it black and it didn't need to be stirred.

"The IVF treatments. You're taking money under the table to pay for the treatments," Henry said.

Del went on, like Henry hadn't spoken. "She left me once, a few years back. You know that?" He looked up at Henry. "No, I guess you wouldn't. She was only gone for two days. Went and stayed with her mom in Alabama."

That surprised Henry. No one had ever said. Del stared out the window at the street beyond.

"Longest two damn days of my life. I walked around the house in my underwear, wandering from room to room, wondering what the hell I was supposed to do. Hell, if you'd have asked me before that if I loved my wife, I'd have shrugged. But somewhere along the line, Alice's husband became the only thing I knew how to be."

Henry folded his arms. "Look, Del, it's not that I don't sympathize. But do you know what those people are *doing?*"

Del shook his head and leaned over the table. "It's not as bad as you make it sound, Henry. Those people, the ones they're shuffling around, they're looking for a better life. Mexico's bad now, man. With the drug cartels and the poverty. All I'm doing is looking the other way, giving them a chance for something better here in the States."

Henry didn't know who Del was trying to convince. Did he really believe that?

"So, what? You think you're being some sort of humanitarian? Eve is terrified of these people, Del!"

"And she's right to be! She attacked Marcus with a knife! Why do you think I was so against Caroline taking that girl in in the first place?"

"Marcus? Are you kidding me right now? You're on a first-name basis with these pieces of shit?"

"It's not like that, Henry," Del said.

"Let me tell you what it's like," Henry said. "It's women and children. Women and children held prisoner by armed men who treat them like cattle."

The look on Eve's face when she'd broken down and told Henry what it was like to be pulled from one hell and thrust into another was one he couldn't erase. She'd described the cries of the babies, clinging to their mothers. The girls, no more than children themselves, who'd huddled together in fear as they'd been herded from the backs of darkened trucks to the insides of darkened rooms.

And the men with the guns. The ones who'd taken what they wanted when the mood struck.

Trying and failing to tamp down the rage that seethed inside at Eve's words and the images they'd left behind, Henry wondered if Del was really that much of a fool. If he really believed that these people were going to be delivered to some sort of American promised land, then left to live happily ever after, or if he knew, deep down, as Henry did, that there was no such thing as happily ever after.

"Why do you think that is, Del? Why no men?"

Del's face was troubled, and Henry watched him struggle with the truth. The truth that must have been there all along, if only Del had been strong enough to look it in the eye.

"I don't know, man. Maybe the men are here already. And they're bringing their families across the border to be with them?"

"You think so? All of them?"

Del shook his head, anger stepping in to disguise the truth he didn't want to face. "What are you saying?"

"I'm saying it's a lot more likely, a lot more realistic, given the circumstances, that these women are being sold at the other end of this *life-changing* journey. These men, these buddies of yours, are preying on women and children in the worst way possible."

Del sputtered and a flush crept up his neck. "You can't know that, Henry. You're assuming the worst, and there's no reason to believe . . ."

"No? Don't be stupid, Del. Eve finally talked, and what she had to say was horrifying. They weren't treated like people. They were treated like goods. And not high-end goods. They were used, Del. Abused in ways I can't even begin to explain."

"Are you saying Eve . . . ?"

"Did your friend *Marcus* tell you why Eve came at him?" Henry searched his brother's face. He could see Del struggling to swallow what Henry was shoving down his throat.

"Marcus apparently liked to sample the goods," Henry said, his voice low, hitting on every word like a drum, beating it to a tempo Del couldn't ignore. Not anymore.

"And Marcus preferred them young. Not Eve. A girl, Del, a girl that couldn't have been older than eight or nine."

He didn't tell his brother about the way Eve's eyes had burned when she'd described the scene to him, or the stony hatred in her voice when she'd spit out the words. He didn't tell him how, when Eve had been forced to witness the unspeakable acts perpetrated on a child, while the others covered their eyes and turned their heads away, Eve couldn't. He didn't say to Del that while watching this child be raped in the most brutal of ways, Eve had felt every blow, every unwanted touch, had swallowed every scream that the little girl had given. Because that little girl, she *was* Eve, in every way that mattered. And Eve was her.

"And do you know what he said, before a girl with no name attacked him with a stolen knife, hidden in the folds of her dirty clothes? He told her, he told them all, *'Get used to it. Consider it practice, because where you're going, there'll be a lot more of this. No point being shy about it.'*"

Del's face had gone slack and pale, and Henry hoped he felt as sick as Henry felt inside. He deserved to.

"And you. You're protecting monsters for cash. How do you think Alice would feel about *that*, Del?"

CHAPTER
THIRTY-SEVEN

Jonah sucked on a lemon drop. Aunt Helen wasn't with him today, and that was fine. He was just coming into town for candy. He usually came alone when she didn't need supplies. She'd told him to keep an eye out for Mr. Doucet, the loud man who lived with Henry, and he tried to do as she asked, when he remembered.

He hadn't remembered at first, but when he saw Mr. Doucet in the street, it reminded him, so Jonah was watching him, just like he'd been asked.

Jonah didn't know how long he was supposed to watch him, but he didn't mind.

Jonah thought maybe the man needed a friend. And just as he was thinking so, there came a man to speak with Mr. Doucet. It was a man that Jonah didn't recognize, but he thought maybe they could be friends, seeing how no one else wanted to be friends with Mr. Doucet.

The lemon drop was tart and sweet, and Jonah thought about getting out another one, since this one was almost gone, but he didn't want to waste them, so he sucked on the sliver and he watched the two men, hoping they'd make friends.

At first, he thought that might be just what would happen, since Mr. Doucet got real quiet, listening to the man, who looked friendly even though he was missing a couple of fingers on his hand. Maybe

Mr. Doucet would stop yelling at people in town if he had someone to talk to. Aunt Helen would be happy about that.

But then, as Jonah watched, Mr. Doucet started getting real mad, yelling again, pushing the man.

"Sinners, the lot of you! Infecting our town and paving the way for the devil, you are! Be gone with you, and don't come back here, or the might of the Lord will smite you down, it will!"

Jonah shook his head. That was no way to treat a friend. Then Mr. Doucet shoved the man hard in the chest, and he stumbled backward. The stranger spoke again, low so Jonah couldn't make out the words, but he'd lost the friendly look on his face.

"Be gone, I said to you! The Lord didn't suffer snakes in his midst, and neither will I," Mr. Doucet screamed in the man's face.

The newcomer glanced around to see if anyone was paying any attention, then whispered words again that made Mr. Doucet even angrier than before. Jonah had to wonder that the man needed a friend even more than Mr. Doucet did, if he was willing to stand and take such words in his face and still press on. Jonah might have told him he was fighting a losing battle, something his aunt liked to say, if he'd bothered to ask him, but most times, people didn't bother to ask Jonah what he thought. And that was fine too.

But even Jonah was shocked, sucking the lemon drop into the back of his throat on a gasp, when Mr. Doucet raised a hand and struck the man, open palmed, across the face. He'd hit him hard enough that the man with three fingers on one of his hands nearly fell to the ground.

And when he looked up, holding a hand to his cheek, there was a dark, hating look on his face. Most of the folks Jonah knew wouldn't take a slap like that without giving back better than they'd got, but the man didn't raise a hand. Only hissed words at Mr. Doucet that made Jonah think of a wizard in the movies, casting a spell to do bad things to folks.

"I said be gone, sinner! And I won't say it again! My house is cleansed of the devil, and I won't be letting him in the door on the word of his minions. The might and the light of Jesus will protect my doorstep. Be gone, I say again, before I strike you down!"

Jonah wasn't the only person watching the ruckus the two men were making in the street. Tinker himself had come out from behind his counter and walked over to stand next to Jonah, and Jonah could see others gathering up and down the street.

"Like a carnival sideshow," Tinker said, smoothing his large gray mustache as he spoke. "Doucet's done lost his mind," he murmured.

"Behold, there are sinners in our midst, and beware!" Mr. Doucet was shouting to the gathering crowd. "Mark this man's face, a harbinger of evil, he is. Skulking in the woods, and dealing in infamy. Drugs, prostitutes, darkness, and sin for sale, right under our noses. Push it out, good people, push it out, and cleanse our town of these evil pastimes. For if you don't, the Lord will see the darkness you let into your heart, and into your homes."

Jonah had seen the way people mostly paid no mind to the words Mr. Doucet spoke. He felt a kind of kinship with the man because of it, in spite of his loud, ugly ways. People mostly paid no mind to Jonah either. But this time, folks were whispering to one another, asking about the other man, the one backing away from Mr. Doucet and his angry words like a cockroach that's had a light shined into its corner.

The man scurried away, looking down at his feet while people whispered, but Jonah didn't miss the mean on his face when he looked back over his shoulder at Mr. Doucet, who was still going on about the devil walking among them.

It was too bad, Jonah thought. Too bad they couldn't have been friends.

CHAPTER

THIRTY-EIGHT

The veil of normalcy was thin and ragged, but Henry and Eve held it tight against their huddled shoulders, trying to find their way.

Henry brought Eve along when he went to a job across town. He'd been hired to build a pergola and couldn't afford to pass on the work. He was beginning to realize that their needs would change dramatically once the baby was born, an inevitability that Eve refused to discuss.

Neither was he willing to leave her alone for any extended period of time, so she'd brought the books that Henry had picked up from the library and settled into a lawn chair in the client's backyard while Henry had measured, sawed, and nailed. The books were colorful and bright, simple pictures and strings of letters designed to enthrall children while they learned the basics of reading.

Henry recalled the initial shock he'd felt, realizing that Eve couldn't read. He'd been teaching her how to cook, working from his mother's old recipe books, when he'd seen the blank puzzlement on her face at the sight of his mother's neat cursive penmanship. His shock soon gave way to sadness.

He'd shifted gears, and their lessons had gone from how to sear a steak to how to recognize the letters of the alphabet. Eve was a surprisingly quick study for someone who'd never been in a classroom.

Henry's heart beat faster each time she fought her way to the end of a word, sounding it out as she went, then looked up at him on the ladder, real laughter in her voice. It was a simple kind of joy. And addicting.

The wind picked up in the afternoon, cooling off the day and giving them the first hints of the storm heading their way, but they paid it no mind.

Evening was falling as he drove the truck back home. He was sweaty and tired—but content. Eve sat next to him holding the books tightly in her lap, next to her ever-growing belly, her face calm and clear. Hopeful. At least, that's what Henry saw. What he chose to see.

He was casting sidelong glances in her direction, not paying as much attention to the road as he should, so he didn't see his stepfather until he was almost on top of him. Livingston was gesticulating wildly and talking to himself, ranting, as he walked down the gravel road that led home with the wind whipping the leaves around his feet, herding them this way and that in a wild sort of dance.

Henry slowed the truck to Livingston's pace, which never faltered.

"Sinners. Sinners, I say!" he said to Henry, shaking his fist with a wild look in his eyes as he continued to trudge toward home.

"Hop in, Livingston," Henry said as the first fat droplets of rain began to fall here and there, an opening act for what was about to come.

His stepfather ignored him, mumbling under his breath. His diatribes had gotten more vehement, and more disturbing, during the weeks and months since Mama had died, and Henry had been secretly grateful that Livingston spent so much time away from the house, some nights stumbling home in the small hours of the morning. Many days, he didn't come home at all.

Seeing the state of him now, though, Henry felt a wave of shame that he couldn't ignore. His mother would be appalled that he'd allowed this to continue. Livingston was wasting away before their eyes. His skin sagged, and his clothes were dirty and hanging from his frame. He'd always been wiry, but he looked skeletal now.

Henry wondered when he'd last had a real meal.

Trying to ignore the clamor of words in his head that he knew his mother would have thrown his way, Henry put the truck in park right there in the middle of the road. It wasn't likely to be in anyone's way, since no one traveled down there unless they were heading to the house.

He opened the door and jogged to catch up with his stepfather, who was so caught up in his own circular sort of hell that he had nothing to spare for Henry.

Henry laid a hand on Livingston's shoulder.

"Livingston," he said. "Stop."

Throwing off the hand, and the kindness that came with it, Livingston turned to Henry.

"What do you want, boy?" he demanded, facing his stepson.

Henry stepped back, reeling from the decimated face in front of him. Grief had melted away most of the humanity that Livingston had possessed, leaving little behind. A mechanical man with a suit of skin hanging off him, powered by a smoking, burning passion.

"Let me give you a ride," Henry said softly, trying to soothe a man who wouldn't be soothed.

"I don't need a ride! Jesus walked, and if it's good enough for him, it's good enough for me, by God! Forty days and nights in the desert, and he had his answers. And I will too. I will have *answers*, boy!"

"Livingston, you've got to stop this," Henry pleaded quietly.

"Stop what, boy?" Livingston asked, his words sharp as knives. Henry knew he was waiting to pounce on whatever he said next, to skewer it on his spear of self-righteous indignation.

"This has got to end," Henry reiterated.

His stepfather's eyes narrowed to slits. "I'll stop when the Lord comes down and speaks to me directly, son. And not before then. When his only begotten son was crucified for the sins of humanity, God didn't stop it. And I won't stop now. Not because some snot-nosed little shit has found himself some opinions. Now, you get on my side or get out of my way, boy. I'll not be stopped."

The insults meant nothing to Henry, but his stepfather's refusal to let go of his zealous persecution of anyone who didn't measure up to the standards of Livingston Doucet—and that encompassed every person he'd ever met—left Henry fuming with frustration.

"Mama wouldn't have wanted this," he called to Livingston's retreating back. "Not in a million years. She'd be horrified, and frankly, she'd be ashamed of you. And you know it."

It was the only ace Henry had in his hand, and one he'd hesitated to play. Invoking his mother's name felt wrong somehow. Manipulative, in a way that Caroline Doucet had never been. But desperation forced him to throw those cards on the table.

The punch to the jaw shouldn't have been as powerful as it was. Henry'd seen it coming, had made a conscious decision to let it land, but the hatred and grief behind it had lent it a force that Livingston's bony limbs didn't seem capable of.

Stumbling backward, Henry nearly went down.

As it was, he had to bend over and lean his hands against his knees, shaking his head to get his bearings back.

When he looked up into his stepfather's face, he had to accept that a winning hand made no difference to a man who was no longer playing by the rules.

He'd never seen such concentrated, undiluted grief. There was no fighting against that. Henry knew then, no matter his faults, no matter his crazy, that the one true thing that defined Livingston Doucet was his love for his wife. Her death had only hardened that love, forged it in the fires of a hell of his own making.

Livingston advanced on Henry again, and Henry let him come. His only hope was that if his stepfather couldn't purge his grief in the normal way, then this would help him down that road. It was the only thing Henry had to give.

The next punch caught him in the eye. It was almost as powerful as the first, and it took an act of will for Henry not to raise his hand and hit back. Not to raise a hand even in his own defense.

He didn't do it for love of Livingston. He might have been the only father that Henry had ever known, but there had never been love between them, and that was a fact. What use had the man for another son? He had his own to screw up, and he'd done a fine job at that.

The third blow found a home against Henry's rib cage, but Livingston was losing steam. It was still more than he should have been able to give, but not as much as he'd have liked to.

Henry let it land for love of his mother. For her love of this old, broken man and the person she always believed he could be. She was wrong, in the end, but that didn't change anything.

Henry was prepared for the next fist to land. A few more punches thrown, and Livingston would collapse in the dirt at his feet, his hatred spent, and Henry would pick him up and walk him home. He'd feed him, if he could. He'd help him stumble to the bed he'd shared with the love of his life. He'd care for him in the only way he could. In the way his mother would have wanted.

But he never had the chance.

Henry had heard people say that time slows down in those moments when life hurtles into death. But it wasn't true. Not entirely.

In the seconds it took for the hammer—Henry's hammer, with his father's initials carved into the handle—to come crashing down on the back of Livingston's head, time raced past in a blinding flash, so fast it happened.

It was in the moments after, with Livingston crumpling to the ground at Henry's feet, the manic look on his face contorting strangely, with the dull thud of metal meeting flesh and bone reverberating in Henry's mind, that time seemed to stop.

As Livingston slowly fell to the ground, it was like a curtain falling away, revealing Eve, standing directly behind where his stepfather had just been. The hammer, gripped tightly in her hand, slowly came down by her side. There was a spray of red across her face, as calm now as it had been just minutes before, in that haze of contentment that Henry had reveled in.

Henry's mouth was hanging wide, gaping at the impossibility of what had just happened. The world was buzzing around him, but he couldn't hear it. He could only watch as Livingston fell, first to his knees, then forward, his body flopping like a bag of potatoes against Henry's lower legs.

Seeing the wound on the back of his stepfather's head as his dead weight pressed against him sent a wave of revulsion through Henry. He stumbled backward and away, in a rush of overwhelming panic.

Slowly, his wide, unblinking eyes rose to Eve. He opened his mouth to speak, but the words weren't there.

His attention was pulled back to the man lying between them in the dirt when Livingston gave a garbled moan. Henry watched in shock as his body twitched, then his arms came in and he tried to rise, looking like nothing so much as Frankenstein's monster trying to come to life.

Henry dropped to his knees in the dirt.

"Oh God, we have to help him, oh Jesus Christ, what—"

His words broke off as a spray of blood came at his face, punctuated by the sound of another bone-shattering blow from his father's hammer.

Henry fell backward into the dampening dirt, and all he could hear was the rush of blood in his veins.

Eve had hit him again.

"Stop! Stop! Jesus, Eve, stop!" Henry cried as she raised her arm again. He threw himself toward her, stopping her arm from coming down a third time.

His arms were around her. He stared into her eyes, both of their faces marked with the deep-red truth of what she'd just done.

"Eve," he cried, standing between her and the man she'd just murdered, putting his hands gently on both of her cheeks and forcing her to look at him. "Oh God, Eve, why? Why?!"

Her face was a mask of still waters, the abysmal depths of which Henry knew he'd never truly understood. He pulled her close, and her arms fell to her sides, the hammer dropping to the dirt at their feet. He clung to her while his mind raced and his heart pounded.

"He shouldn't have hit you," she said with her face pressed against his chest, right where his heart was. Her voice was devoid of emotion.

The rain, which had been hanging back, waiting to make its entrance, let loose upon them, drenching the two people huddled together in the middle of a lonely road.

What had she done? Dear God, what had she done?

CHAPTER
THIRTY-NINE

Jonah was watching his favorite movie about the boy wizard and his friends when the storm took out the power. Aunt Helen started cussing, but that was okay. Jonah hadn't done anything to make the power sputter, then cut out completely, so the cussing wasn't aimed at him.

"Go see if you can dig up the matches in the drawer, Jonah. I'll get the lanterns," Aunt Helen said, heaving herself out of the old, dilapidated sofa that had soft dented spots where they usually sat to watch the television. The dent where Jonah sat was bigger, but Aunt Helen's had been there longer, and she always had to put a hand on the arm of the couch and wiggle her way to the front to pull herself up.

It was dark in the kitchen, but Jonah had the place mostly memorized, and he knew which drawer to go to. He didn't even trip over anything along the way.

He had the matches in his hand and was following the sounds of his aunt's cursing when he heard, over the howling of the wind, the familiar tolling of the bell in the tree at the edge of the marsh.

He stopped and turned toward the front of the house, and Aunt Helen's words broke off mid-cuss.

"Maybe it's Henry," Jonah said hopefully. "Maybe he could help with the 'lectric."

Aunt Helen took the box of matches from Jonah's hands.

"The boy's got talents, but I don't think even Henry can help with that, Jonah. Why don't you take the boat over and see who's come calling at this hour, and in a storm no less."

"I can wear my yellow rain slicker," Jonah said, smiling at the prospect.

"That's a good idea. You go fish it out of the closet, I'll light some lanterns for the front porch."

"Okay." Jonah liked the chance to wear his rain slicker. It was bulky and sometimes sweaty inside, but the pitter-pat of the raindrops bouncing off the rubber surface made him happy.

He listened to the rain beat off the slicker all the way across the swamp. He pushed the hood back, because it was hard for him to see where he was headed in the dark with it hanging down on his face, so his hair was slick and wet when he slid the boat up on the opposite bank, but that was okay.

Henry and Eve were waiting for him, and they were slick and wet too. They weren't wearing rain slickers.

"Sorry to get you out in this mess, Jonah," Henry said over the murmur of raindrops hitting the surface of the marsh around them.

"Ah, I don't mind. I ain't gonna melt," Jonah said, smiling at the pair.

Henry helped Eve step into the boat, then pushed off from the shore, wading into the water and stepping in himself. Jonah got them turned around and followed the lights that Aunt Helen had burning to show the way home.

Aunt Helen herself was waiting for them out on the porch. Jonah wished he'd thought to bring a flashlight to shine the way on the ground, so Henry and Eve could see up the steps, but he hadn't thought of it.

They made it up to the porch just fine, all the same.

"Henry Martell," Aunt Helen said, handing over towels to both Henry and Eve to dry themselves under the shelter of the porch. "Awful odd time for a social call," she said. Normally, Aunt Helen was pleased as punch to see Henry, but she sounded different tonight. Jonah thought she sounded like something was weighing on her. Come to that, Henry had a like-minded look on his face. Jonah thought maybe there was more going on here than he was seeing, but he didn't fuss about it.

He shook himself out of the rain slicker instead and set it over the rail of the porch to drip.

"Ms. Watson, I've come to ask a favor," Henry said, his voice dead serious. "Can Eve stay here with you for a while? Not for long," he added. "Just for tonight. I got some things to take care of, and I don't want to leave her by herself."

Aunt Helen took a good long look at Henry standing there on the porch, her eyes lingering on the bruise that was swelling over his eye. Then she looked over at the silent girl who was standing next to him, her long dark hair plastered to her head.

"I've known you your whole life, Henry, and you never once asked me for a favor. Done quite a few for me over the years, but never asked for a single one in return."

She crossed her arms, her head tilted to one side while she took in the sight of the ragged pair in front of her.

"I'll not turn you down now. But I've got to ask, because I'm too nosy not to, and because you look like you've seen some trouble: What's going on?"

Henry glanced down at Eve, and Jonah didn't understand the look that passed between them. He fished in his pocket for one of his last lemon drops. The wrapper crinkled, and when he popped it in his mouth and looked back at everyone, they were all looking his way.

"What?" he asked, the word garbled around the hard candy.

Aunt Helen shook her head at him, then looked back to their visitors.

"Eve, darling, can you do something for me? Can you sit out here and keep Jonah company for a bit?"

Henry and Eve shared another glance, and Henry nodded in her direction.

Then Aunt Helen took Henry by the arm and led him inside the darkened house, taking one of the lanterns to light their way. Jonah was glad she'd left the other, and he was glad of the company. Eve was easy company. She didn't talk much, and she never got ugly with him if he didn't say the right things, like some people did.

"'Lectric's out," he said to Eve, taking a seat on the old porch swing.

She held the towel around her shoulders and took a seat next to him. The old swing creaked under their combined weight, but Jonah didn't worry about it falling. Henry had been the one to secure it to the beam above their heads, and Henry did a real good job at that sort of thing.

"I don't mind," Eve said quietly.

"That's good," Jonah replied.

Together, they sat in silence, swinging and listening to the rain come down on the roof, watching the bugs fly at the glass of the lantern over and over again. Occasionally one flew too close to the flame, and Jonah felt a pang of sympathy for it.

The thought never occurred to Jonah that Henry and his aunt might have gone inside to keep what they were saying to themselves. If it had, he'd have told Aunt Helen she ought to shut the window that opened onto the porch from the front room.

As it was, their voices tended to carry, bringing words to Jonah's ears that he didn't know weren't intended for him. Some of those words slid off, but some of them stuck. He didn't consider whether that was a good or a bad thing—it just was—so he swung next to his friend Eve, who didn't feel the need to talk. And that was okay with him.

CHAPTER FORTY

"I don't want to get you mixed up in this, Ms. Watson," Henry said.

"That's enough of that. I'm old enough to decide for myself what I'll get mixed up in and what I won't. You just tell me what's got you tied in knots and let me make my own decisions."

Henry shook his head. "It's not that simple. I can't tell you. It could get you in a world of trouble if I do. Please. Just let Eve stay here, just for a few hours," he pleaded.

Helen Sue held the lantern up to take a closer look at Henry's face.

"I've already said that's fine. I'm not gonna go back on my word. But you need to tell me what's going on."

Henry had known he was taking a risk coming here, putting Ms. Watson and Jonah in the middle of this, but he'd been desperate. He was desperate still.

"I can't leave her alone, and the things I've got to do . . . I can't take her with me. Please, Ms. Watson."

"Son, I can see by the look on your face that you're in something over your head. Your mama was a fine woman, and I considered her a friend. I consider *you* a friend. I'm not about to let you leave here and wade back into whatever it is on your own. Now, you tell me what's going on, before I have to start getting mean."

"I . . . I can't . . ." Henry's voice caught and he was overwhelmed by the sounds and images in his head. The crunch of the hammer against Livingston's skull. The thud his body had made when Henry had loaded it up in the back of his truck in a panic and driven it home. The second thud, as bad or worse than the first, when he'd pushed it onto an old blanket laid out on the ground after he'd arrived.

The image of Livingston falling, then trying to rise again, with a hole in the back of his skull. The sight of the body-shaped parcel that was leaning against the wall of the shed at his house, with boxes and crates stacked up against it.

Henry put his face in his hands and tried to block it out, but it was impossible. He scrubbed the heels of his palms against his cheeks, knowing he didn't have time for this. He didn't have time to lose it. Eve's future, and his own, depended on him holding it together, right here, right now.

But to pull this off, he was going to have to take some calculated risks. And in the end, didn't Ms. Watson deserve the opportunity to throw them out? He felt certain that Eve wasn't a threat to Helen Sue or to Jonah, but did he really have the right to leave her here alone with them, ignorant of what she was capable of, and take that chance?

Henry squared his shoulders and looked up into the earnest and worried eyes that were studying him.

"Livingston is dead," he said slowly, saying the words out loud for the first time, and hopefully the last, in a voice that was stronger than he expected. "Eve killed him. We got into a fight, and Eve killed him with my father's hammer."

The slight bulge of Ms. Watson's eyes was the only indication that she'd heard and understood what he'd said, but it was enough.

"I have to get rid of him. I've turned over every possibility, searching for some other way, but all of them end with either Eve in prison, or me."

Henry stood and ran a hand through his wet hair in frustration. "And I'd gladly go. I'm as responsible for what's happened as she is. More, really. But if I go to prison, what happens to Eve? What happens to the baby? She's not right, Ms. Watson. She's not right in the head, and I can't leave her. I'm all she's got. I'm all she's ever had."

"Oh, Henry. Oh, my boy," Ms. Watson said, dropping down onto the arm of the sofa behind her.

"If you don't want her here, I understand. I've got no right to ask."

A fearsome look came over the older woman's face. "Is that girl dangerous to Jonah, Henry? You tell me the truth now."

Henry shook his head. "No. I mean . . . No. I wouldn't have brought her here if I thought she could hurt either one of you, but she *is* a murderer. There's no getting around that."

The weight of his stepfather's body was too recent in his arms for Henry to forget that.

"You said you got into a fight?"

"Of sorts. Livingston punched me. I said something about Mama, and what she'd have to say about his bullshit, then he hit me, and I let him. Then he hit me again, and I let him. I shouldn't have."

Henry stood and paced, thinking useless thoughts about what he should have done differently.

"I never considered Eve seeing it, how she might react. I just wanted to give him a way to get rid of all that anger and grief he was carrying around. So I let him hit me."

"And Eve was protecting you?" Ms. Watson asked slowly.

He looked her in the eye.

"Yes," he said. "I didn't need protection. God knows, I didn't need or want *that* kind of protection, but yes, in her mind, she was protecting me. And now there's no going back."

The two unlikely friends stared at one another while they digested that immutable truth.

"All right," Ms. Watson said, and took a deep breath before letting it out in a slow push. "All right. Now let me tell you what we're gonna do."

While Helen Sue Watson laid out her thoughts on how to go about helping Henry and Eve get away with murder, Henry had the fleeting thought that in spite of their obvious differences, his mother and Ms. Watson weren't so different, when push came to shove.

And push had most definitely come to shove.

CHAPTER
FORTY-ONE

The night that followed crept past, carrying Henry with it. For the most part, his mind was able to stay shrouded in a misty fog of self-preservation, focusing only on the next step needed and blocking out everything else. But there were breath-stealing moments when the stark and morbid reality of exactly what he was doing punctured his defenses.

Twice, he was forced to stop the task at hand and heave up the contents of his stomach.

The first time, he was sitting in the pirogue alone, floating silently through the marsh. The rain had given way to a heavy, humid mist, and he could feel his still-damp clothes clinging to him. He'd taken the boat, loaned to him by Ms. Watson, and made his way almost a mile down the slough to where the traffickers' shack sat along the banks. Coming on the dilapidated building from the water was a perspective Henry rarely saw, and it rose up out of the marsh, menacing and strange.

This was arguably the most important variable of the entire night. If the shack was occupied, an unpredictable possibility, then the entire plan crumbled in his lap. Everything hinged on the old place being empty of everyone save the ghosts of the past, and maybe a few of the present.

Henry was glad no one was around to see his nerves get the best of him as he pushed the pole against the bottom of the marsh.

The place was dark and silent. There were no vehicles parked out front, no lights coming up the road that led out of the woods, and none of the normal noise that could be heard all the way to his own home when the place was in use.

It was empty. This first crucial box, the one Henry had absolutely no control over, could be checked off.

The relief was sickeningly palpable, and like that of a child who's eaten too much candy on Halloween, Henry's stomach began to churn. With only the bullfrogs as witness, busily croaking their disinterest, he leaned over the side of the pirogue and vomited into the marsh. Wiping his mouth with the back of his sleeve, Henry had no way to rinse the taste of bile off his tongue.

He pulled the pirogue up to the shore, very near the place where Mari and Del had tricked him so many years ago, Del rising from the marsh disguised as the swamp witch and triggering Henry's fight-or-flight instincts.

He'd fought at six, in spite of his terror. And he would fight now. He'd already tried to run but found he couldn't do it. He belonged here, with Eve. It was that simple.

Henry stepped out into the soft muck that ran along the edge of the marsh and took out of the boat the metal barrel he'd brought along. It was the barrel that Jonah used to store bait for the gators, and Henry dreaded having to open it when the time came.

Because alligators preferred rotten meat over fresh. Oh, they'd take the fresh if they had the chance, but their habit was to push it underwater somewhere and let it rot, then come back for it later.

If you wanted to really get a gator's attention, the putrid stench of rotten meat was your best bet.

But that could wait. At least for the moment. Henry would never make it through the now if he focused too closely on what was waiting ahead. Instead, he set the barrel, still thankfully sealed, on the bank and pushed the boat back away from the shore.

The night was passing, and he had many things to do before he could sleep.

CHAPTER FORTY-TWO

As he passed by in the borrowed boat, Henry saw the light shining in the distance from Ms. Watson's lantern hanging from a nail on her porch. He could make out the shadow of a lone figure standing watch. Helen Sue Watson herself, he supposed, correctly.

He hoped that Jonah was sleeping the sleep of the innocent somewhere inside the darkened house, beneath his rocket ship blanket.

And Eve. He suspected Eve wasn't sleeping and wouldn't until he returned for her. He only hoped the demons that lived inside of her gave her some peace as she watched the hours tick past.

He'd brought a flashlight with him, though he hadn't turned it on up to this point. But he did so now, flashing it on and off twice in the direction of the Watson house. The signal they'd decided on earlier.

Henry wasn't headed back there. Not yet. But his heart stayed with them even as he continued on.

He pulled the flat-bottomed boat along the shore where Jonah usually left it when he went into town and found his truck where he'd parked it earlier. He twisted the key in the vehicle's ignition, and the familiar feel of the truck coming to life below him was reassuring, in spite of the noise it spewed into the quiet night.

It was a toehold back to solid ground, something Henry desperately needed.

Turning the truck around and making the mile-long drive back to his house, Henry kept his mind purposefully empty, focusing only on the circular beams of the headlights bouncing along the ground in front of him.

When those beacons came to the end of his drive, he pulled the truck up to the shed, brightening the doorway with washed-out light. He caught the two gleaming eyes of a raccoon frozen in the beams before it scuttled away.

Leaving the truck running and the lights burning, Henry stepped out and pulled the door to the shed wide with a creak, allowing the truck headlights to shine in.

And there in the corner, just where they'd left him, poorly hidden behind several crates of homemade liquor, was the body of the man that Henry had most often mentally referred to as *not my father*.

He probed his feelings on the matter for a split second, double-checking to see if Livingston's brutal death had changed them, but he still found it impossible to think of the man any other way. There were some things that even murder couldn't erase, it would seem.

Still, as he moved the crates out of the way and squatted in front of Livingston's prone form, he couldn't help but feel a deep and abiding sense of regret for the spark that had been extinguished when his life had ended.

He'd never have the chance to hold a grandchild. He'd never have the opportunity to tell his real son that he was sorry for the pain his grief had brought down upon their heads, or that he was proud of the man that he'd become. He'd never have the chance to make things right.

There was an infinite level of sorrow to be found in those wasted chances that would never come again.

With a sigh, Henry whispered the words "I'm so sorry." It didn't change anything, but it was a truth that he couldn't hide from.

With a heave, Henry picked up the body of his stepfather and walked out into the night. He set down his burden just long enough to take a bag from his toolbox and fill it with what he'd need, then kill the engine and the lights on his truck.

With the bag slung over one shoulder, and the bundle containing Livingston's body across the other, under the dim light of the crescent moon hanging low in the sky, Henry made his way across the field and into the woods.

CHAPTER FORTY-THREE

Death was heavier than Henry expected. More than the sum of its parts, it would seem.

He shifted the load on his shoulder, wishing he could unknow what was wrapped inside the bundle he struggled with. He had to find a way to shake free of it—the knowing. If he didn't, it would keep adding weight, pressing his feet farther into the ground, pushing until he sank below the surface of the earth and finally disappeared altogether.

The shack loomed ahead, balanced precariously on aged, water-marked piers, jockeying for a piece of the night sky among the stately cypress that dripped Spanish moss—a struggle it was always going to lose.

Forcing one foot in front of the other, Henry moved toward the rickety steps. He pictured himself sloughing off his doubts, his horror, and his regrets in a trail of moldy bread crumbs behind him.

Henry knew what he had to do. Wishing otherwise served no purpose. That would only fill him up, leaving no room for the strength he needed to dig deep and find somewhere, somehow.

The steps creaked beneath his feet, giving a voice to the night that stood witness to his actions. A reminder, in case he'd forgotten.

As if he could forget.

The door, which hung crookedly on its hinges, swung wide as he pushed it with his foot, revealing a mostly empty space. Moonlight shone through the windows, save for the dark lines of the iron bars installed over the cracked, dirty glass. The place greeted him, and his heavy load, with the resignation of a bookie who knows desperation when he sees it, or a drug dealer who can spot a junkie at a mile. The place knew the score.

Henry could smell it, clogging his nostrils—the thick stench that fear leaves behind. It was rolling off him, mingling with what was already there.

Tonight would be different, but no less the same.

Dropping the bundle on the floor with a thud that echoed through the bare room, Henry took a moment to catch his breath.

A mistake.

Unbidden, thoughts of his mother crowded in. He didn't want her here, but he was powerless to stop her. The smile lines around her eyes crinkled as she sent him that look, the one that said she knew what he was thinking. The wink she'd toss his way when she slid the last pancake onto his plate at breakfast.

Henry squeezed his eyes shut.

"There's no other way, Mama," he whispered to no one, wondering if she'd understand if she were there.

Putting a thing off never made it easier, Henry heard his mother whisper in his mind, something she'd said to him countless times.

Wishful thinking, maybe, but it was the closest thing to absolution he was going to find.

It would have to do.

Grasping the corner of the blanket at his feet, he pulled, rolling out the body cocooned within, flipping it until it broke free and sprawled, lifeless and indignant, in front of him.

Steeling himself, he reached into the bag slung over his shoulder and removed the tools he'd need, setting them neatly in a row.

There was no going back. It was too late for that.

His only hope, the one he clung to during the long nightmare that followed, was that these atrocious acts he was committing had a purpose. That they fanned a distant flame of flickering light at the end of a deep tunnel.

Or so he wanted to believe.

So it was necessary to believe, as he was faced with the remains of his stepfather's body that he'd taken apart, piece by piece. Trying his damnedest to tamp down the roiling horror in his mind, Henry kept on with the task at hand, until the job in front of him was done.

He didn't notice the tears streaming down his cheeks, mixing with the blood and gore. The place was a mess, and so was he, but he wasn't done yet.

After retrieving the crumpled blanket from the corner, Henry put the parts that had once been a man back on the blanket. Tying the corners together in a knot and removing the immediate visual of what he'd done should have made things easier, but he was beyond that point.

Nothing would make this any easier.

His body ached nearly as badly as his soul as he heaved the bundle over his shoulder.

The loose weight of it nearly took him down, but he stood straight and walked toward the front door of the shack, his feet casting shadows in the light of the flashlight that he'd laid upon the floor what seemed like a lifetime ago.

Making his way through the dark of the night, Henry took the steps down onto the ground and turned to walk along the side of the shack, heading for Jonah's rusty metal barrel.

Dropping the bundle at his feet, Henry pried the lid off of the barrel and stumbled backward at the stench that came up and assaulted him.

Coughing and moving away from the stinking thing to find some cleaner air, Henry pulled in a deep, deep breath and held it as he moved back toward it.

Kneeling and lifting the blanket and its contents, Henry planned to push the thing in its entirety into the container, but his knot gave way, and pieces began to tumble out. Most of them fell inside with a sickening cacophony, bouncing off the sides and the bottom of the metal barrel with a noise that Henry would never be able to scrub from his memory. He would wake in the night, sweat-drenched, with a scream on his lips, as the sounds echoed against the walls of his mind through all the time he had left to live.

But it was the severed foot of his stepfather that fell outside of the container, lying there on the ground, that sent Henry to the brink of sanity.

His stomach revolted and he turned to vomit again, but this time there was nothing left inside. Dry heaving there, next to the marsh, his hands on his knees while sweat and tears mixed with the blood on his face, Henry heard himself whispering into the dark.

"Our Father, who art in heaven," he began, his chest heaving under the crushing weight of what he'd done. "Hallowed be thy name."

He felt another wave of nausea come upon him but fought it back.

"Thy kingdom come," he gasped, struggling to hold the tattered remnants of himself together. "Thy will be done."

He could feel the presence of his mother, and he imagined her warmth enveloping him, holding him close to her, in spite of everything, her tears mixing with his own.

"On earth as it is in heaven."

Forcing himself to stand and face his crimes, Henry turned and retrieved Livingston's foot, and placed it in the barrel along with the rest of him.

"Give us this day our daily bread," he murmured, stripping first out of his work gloves, then pulling the ruined shirt off his body. He tossed them into the top of the barrel. "And forgive us our trespasses, as we forgive those who trespass against us."

Henry continued to remove his clothing, and the humid night air kissed his skin.

"And lead us not into temptation," he said, raising his head to look at the stars for the briefest of moments. "But deliver us from evil."

Standing there, naked as the day he was born, Henry wondered if he'd ever feel clean again.

He placed the rest of his clothing in the metal container, then replaced the lid. They weren't done with one another yet—not by a long shot—but it was time for Henry to move on.

Because there was no going back.

On bare feet, he returned to the shack and gathered the tools he'd brought, careful to touch nothing but the things he was taking away, now that his gloves had been discarded.

As he walked back through the woods in the direction he'd come, naked and bathed in moonlight, the rest of the Lord's Prayer played across his tongue.

"For thine is the kingdom, and the power, and the glory."

He caught sight of his home, the home of his father and his grandfather, standing tall in the distance, the home he hoped to share with Eve and the baby that was on the way.

"Forever. Amen."

CHAPTER
FORTY-FOUR

By the time Henry had showered away the physical signs of the night's work, which was almost but not quite complete, he could feel the hours of darkness slipping through his fingers.

Dressed in clean, dry clothing, he caught sight of himself in the bathroom mirror, the starkness in his eyes as jarring as the bruises Livingston had left behind. He wondered briefly if this was going to work. Wouldn't Del be able to read the guilt on his face? Or Alice, with her feminine eyes that were vastly more perceptive than her husband's?

Shaking off the thought, he set his mind to what he had left to do. It was critical that he pay attention, canvassing the details again and again, searching for the smallest ones, hoping to catch them all.

With a plastic trash bag in hand, he gathered up the clothing that Eve had changed out of before he'd taken her to Ms. Watson's, all the way down to the worn sandals she had been wearing.

The loose gray cardigan that she wore nearly every day was ruined, of course, as was the oversized dress that had helped to hide her pregnancy from Livingston.

But there was no need to hide her growing belly now. Other secrets had stepped in to take its place.

With a last look around the house, Henry had done all he could do there.

Taking the bag, he left the house, shutting the door behind him with the desperate hope that when he came home again, with Eve this time, they'd be able to start over.

As he walked to his truck, Henry realized there was one final piece of the playing field that had to be dealt with. Reaching into the bed of the truck, he took his father's hammer from where he'd thrown it in his haste to get Livingston off the side of the road.

He ran a thumb across the initials on the handle and dropped it into the bag.

The truck was still parked next to the shed, so Henry uncoiled the hose from where it hung along the exterior wall, and proceeded to spray the dust and mud and blood from the bed.

That done, he shut off the water, rolled the hose, and replaced it, wanting nothing more than to put the world back to rights.

The darkness of the night was lessening, diluted by the first signs of the sun creeping around the edge of the world, when Henry took the garbage bag in hand and walked back to the shack in the woods.

He thought he was prepared this time for the stench that greeted him when he removed the lid of the barrel. He was wrong. His eyes began to water and sting as his nose objected to the attack on his senses, but he managed not to dry heave in the grass, at least.

He placed the bag on top of the barrel's contents. He had to shove to get it all to fit, but finally it did, and he managed to tighten the lever of the lock ring closure around the lid, securing it for now.

He wondered that he'd bothered to shower at all, since he could feel the stink clinging to his skin and his clothes. He knelt down by the marsh and rinsed his hands in the green water, knowing all the while it would do no good.

When he was done, Henry picked up a dead branch from where it had fallen sometime, with no one to witness its descent. Branch in hand, he examined the ground at his feet. It was unfortunate that the rain had made the surface of the earth so soft, and looking at his tracks, Henry could see each step he'd taken branded into the ground.

Using the branch, he scrubbed and swirled the damp, muddy earth, hoping to obscure what he felt was a road map leading to the answers to questions that would inevitably be asked. Answers that would lead back to him, then in turn to Eve, if he wasn't careful.

When he was done, he tossed the branch off into the woods, hoping it would decay and take its secrets with it.

Working in reverse, Henry backtracked to his house. He didn't go inside, but stepped up into his truck again, turned the ignition, and headed back to where Jonah's boat waited for him.

On the marsh once again, he passed by the Watson house in the distance. He didn't know if Ms. Watson still waited and watched; it was difficult to tell in the mist that had begun to settle around the cypress swamp, with the gray light of dawn trying its best to penetrate the depths. But he had a feeling she was there, so he flashed the light twice again in the direction of the house, just in case.

He made his way across the water, silent save for the lapping against the sides of the boat. There was a splash in the distance, and Henry caught the movement from the corner of his eye.

An alligator. Maybe Ol' Brutal, out for a morning swim. The gators didn't bother him. He knew they'd mind their business, as long as he minded his.

Dawn was almost fully broken as Henry pulled the pirogue up to the shore next to the shack, and a sense of urgency was growing in him with the brightening of the day. He stepped out into the edge of the marsh and pulled the boat up to where the barrel stood waiting for him.

He balanced the barrel along an edge, the bottom rim pressed into the soft ground, and walked it, tipping it from side to side as he went, to the boat. He had to dig his fingers into the ground to catch the bottom and lift it into the pirogue, but in it went.

Glancing behind him, he saw the mess he'd made in the mud. Knowing what had caused it made it easy for Henry to imagine someone else being able to work out the night's events, so again, he found a branch and set to work muddying up his tracks.

Tossing the stick he'd used into the water behind him, Henry took a last glance. He could think of nothing else. He was used up, spent in a way that he'd never been before, his mind empty.

Once he'd pushed the boat, heavier now with its load, away from the shore, Henry stepped in as it floated on top of the water. Using the pole to push along the bottom of the marsh, he drifted away from the shack.

He didn't bother to look back. There was nothing there he wanted to see.

The light had fully taken hold of the day by the time Henry made it back to the pier that jutted out from the Watson house, which materialized from the fog as he drew the pirogue close.

He heard footsteps making their way down the pier and looked up to see Ms. Watson, looking nearly as tired as Henry felt, walking toward him.

"I won't ask how things went. I can see enough by your face," she said, holding her arms tightly across her middle.

"I still think it's a bad idea to tie the barrel off here. You're taking a risk that's not yours to take."

"And my own decision to make," she said lightly. "We've been over this. No one will think to look here, and it's the safest way to move forward."

"Burying him would have been enough," Henry said.

She walked to the edge of the pier, where a rope was tied to the corner post. Leaning over, she took it and threw it to Henry.

"Tie that barrel off and sink it down in the water, Henry Martell. Just like we talked about. That barrel's always been there. We've used it to store the gator bait since God was a boy, and that's where it's gonna stay."

The sound of footsteps came from the house. They were heavy, too heavy for Eve.

Henry pushed away any hesitation and removed the bungs on the lid.

He tied the free end of the rope around the barrel and dropped it into the water with a splash. Pushing down on it, Henry let the swamp flow in through the two small round openings. The water would soak the contents of the barrel and pull it down under the surface, where, if all went as planned, it would stay until Henry retrieved it.

If all didn't go as planned, well . . . Henry tried not to think about the hell that would come crashing down on all of them. For the moment, he concentrated on getting the job done before Jonah had a chance to ask too many questions.

"I'm gonna go make that boy some breakfast," Ms. Watson said, glancing back up to the house. "You're welcome to join us, when you're done."

Henry shook his head.

"No offense, but I don't think I could stomach anything."

She nodded and turned to head back up the pier, but she stopped and turned around to face Henry halfway there.

"Yesterday and last night might well have been the worst day and night you'll ever have the misfortune of enduring, Henry."

He met her eyes, saw the strength and the sympathy and the loyalty there. He'd done nothing to deserve her kindness. A patched roof couldn't compare to the gift she was giving him now, just knowing that when the chips were down, he had someone on his side. He and Eve both did. Whether they deserved it or not.

"Then again, the bad can always sneak up on us," she said. "But I know, in my bones, you'll get through it, Henry Martell. You did what you had to do. Don't you forget that."

Henry was so tired.

"I'll try," he said.

With the mist floating around her, she nodded again, then she was gone.

But it wasn't forgetting Henry was worried about. It was forgiveness.

Henry replaced the bungs on the barrel, then looked up and saw a small figure with long dark hair standing at the edge of the porch, watching him.

Forgiveness for them all, he thought.

CHAPTER

FORTY-FIVE

It was late afternoon by the time Henry woke, slowly fighting his way back to consciousness through the fog of strange dreams full of fears and regrets. They clutched at him, pulling and clawing at his feet, but he shoved them back down, reaching for the clarity of wakefulness.

The sun streaming through the windows was wrong. That wasn't morning sun. For the briefest of moments, Henry existed in a place where yesterday hadn't happened. Where the night before was only the dregs of a leftover nightmare.

Then reality crashed in with all the noise and clanging of a ten-penny brass band.

He remembered the boat ride back to his truck, Jonah chatting happily while he and Eve remained silent, so many unanswered questions between them.

He remembered taking a second shower, the hot water sluicing down his body as he tried in vain to wash away the long, long night. And falling into the bed. Eve lay next to him, and he held her close, feeling the life growing between them.

Henry had felt at that moment that he'd never sleep again. He dreaded closing his eyes, dreaded more the possibility that that moment, there alone together, might have been the most precious gift he'd ever received, and it could be taken from him in the space of a heartbeat.

But exhaustion can't be fought forever, and eventually Henry's eyelids surrendered. He'd slept.

Now, he'd have to face whatever the rest of the day might bring.

He heard the murmur of voices from somewhere in the house, and his throat clenched involuntarily. His thoughts raced as he wondered who it could be. Perhaps he'd have to face the consequences of his actions sooner than he'd anticipated.

Throwing back the covers, he rose from the bed. If that was the case, then so be it. He wouldn't cower in fear.

Henry threw on some clothes and went to find out who and what was waiting for him.

His relief was palpable when he saw Alice with her stethoscope, listening to whatever messages the baby inside of Eve was willing to share.

Alice barely glanced in Henry's direction when she heard him come into the room. Gingerly she removed the buds of the stethoscope from her ears, her attention on Eve.

"Sounds good," she said. "But I still can't stress enough that you should see a doctor," she added sternly.

Eve didn't meet her eyes as she sat up and pulled her shirt down to cover her stomach.

"No doctors," she said quietly.

Alice sighed and stood, the set of her jaw saying clearly what she thought about that.

"Eve said you were sleeping," she said to Henry, giving in and changing the tired subject as she put her instruments away. "You feeling okay?" She spoke without looking up.

"Yeah. Just up late last night."

Images flashed behind his eyes, so he squeezed them closed and turned away before Alice saw what he saw.

"Hey, man," Del said from the doorway that stood open to the front porch.

Henry's head snapped up. He hadn't known Del was there. He felt panic try to take hold but clamped it in a vise.

"Hey," Henry said. His voice sounded off to his own ears, but Del didn't seem to notice.

His brother was shifting his weight from one foot to the other, his hands deep in his pockets. Henry looked closer. Del was nervous. He looked like he'd pulled an all-nighter himself, judging by the dark circles under his eyes.

"Dad around?" he asked, glancing off toward something in the distance. Henry got the feeling he was avoiding meeting his gaze.

Guilt, Henry supposed. Guilt came in all shapes and sizes.

"Haven't seen him," Henry said, trying for nonchalance and failing miserably. Del still didn't notice, just nodded and looked down at his shoes.

"You got a minute, Henry? I wanted to talk to you," Del said. He looked as uncomfortable as Henry had ever seen him, and Henry realized that Del was trying to be circumspect around Alice. His wife didn't miss much, though, and sent a puzzled frown in Del's direction.

"Sure," Henry said, jumping at the chance to escape from Alice's suspicious gaze. Del stepped away from the doorway, and Henry joined him on the porch.

"Need to feed the chickens," Henry mumbled, continuing down the steps and away from the women in the house.

"That's a helluva shiner, buddy," Del said. "What happened?"

Henry saw again the storm of grief and rage in Livingston's face as he threw the punch, remembered the feel of it as it landed.

"Accident," Henry said, nearly choking on the word. "Clumsy with some lumber on a job."

Del nodded distractedly, uninterested in the specifics. He clearly had something on his mind. "Hey, about what we talked about before? About those men?" Del said.

Henry grabbed the bucket from the side of the shed and filled it with feed, keeping his hands busy.

"I just wanted you to know, I'm gonna take care of it."

"Take care of it how, Del?"

But his brother continued on like he hadn't heard the question. Henry thought maybe he'd practiced what he was going to say and didn't want to deviate for fear of losing his place.

"I been thinking about it, about what you said. I've known you a long damn time, Henry, and you're a son of a bitch sometimes, but you've never been a liar."

"Why would I lie, Del? Why would Eve?"

"That's my point. So I wanted you to know. I wanted to tell you myself, it's gonna stop."

Henry set the bucket down and leaned against the post, looking at his brother clearly for the first time since he'd arrived.

"I don't have all the details worked out yet, but it's gonna end."

"You're talking about the pay-offs?" Henry asked, just to be sure they were on the same page.

Del shook his head.

"Not just that. The whole thing. I'm gonna bring 'em down, if I can. But even if I can't, I'm gonna run them out of town. I'll burn that shack to the ground if I have to."

Del's face blazed with an almost religious fervor, and in that moment, Henry was hit by Del's resemblance to his father.

"I don't want to get Brady involved too deep, if I can manage it. But I wanted you to know. Because however this shakes down, Eve's gonna be a target."

"She already is," Henry said, lifting the bucket and heading for the chicken coop.

"Dad had a run-in yesterday in town with one of the men from the shack," Del said.

"That so?" Henry asked. He knew that already. Jonah had seen it and told Helen Sue, who'd told Henry. Jonah hadn't known who the man was, only that he was a stranger with three fingers on one of his hands, but it hadn't taken long for Henry and Ms. Watson to figure it out. But it seemed best to keep that piece of information to himself.

"What kind of run-in?"

"Somebody asking questions. Dad sent him off with his tail between his legs, but that means they're not done with her, Henry. Not done with her, and not done with you."

"You talked to your dad yesterday?" Henry asked lightly.

"Not really. He did most of the talking. Or shouting, if you want to get technical. Going on about those degenerates running loose in his woods, and what the hell I was gonna do about it." Del sighed and scratched at his head. "I just let him, because I'd been wondering the same damn thing myself."

"Why don't you just go in there and arrest them?" Henry asked. But even as he posed the question, he knew the answers would be a problem.

"Well, I could, Henry. But the truth is, I don't really fancy going to jail myself. Nobody would listen at first, if they started telling tales about paying off the local law. But Brady's not stupid, no matter what he looks like, and eventually it would occur to him that I had to get that money from someplace. A little bit of digging, and I'm sunk, brother."

"Then what exactly are you gonna do, Del?" Henry asked, truly curious.

"I'll figure it out, man," Del said. "I will. But I can't do much of anything until they come back to town. So keep your eyes open, will you? Let me know if you hear anything going on over there, or if anybody comes by asking questions, okay?"

Del had always been the type to show up late to the party. But Henry nodded all the same.

"Of course," he said.

"Not a word to Alice. I'll tell her everything, if I have to. But I don't want to lay it all on her if I don't need to." The look in Del's eye was pleading, and considering Henry was on new and intimate terms with his own set of secrets, he could empathize.

"All right. But don't go doing anything stupid," he added.

"Get Dad to call me when he shows up. I want to talk to him again, see if I can get anything else out of him."

That wasn't ever going to happen, but Henry just nodded, swallowing his own serving of guilt.

CHAPTER
FORTY-SIX

Three days and nights passed, and Henry felt each hour drag by, weighted down as he was with the knowledge of what had transpired. The barrel holding Livingston's remains may as well have been tied directly around his ankle.

It was a thin, shaky tightrope he was walking now. He'd gone to see Ms. Watson the day before, nervous that he was putting it off too long.

"Not yet, Henry. Patience, son," she'd counseled.

But their lives hung in the balance, and he found his store of patience tested to its limits.

Del hadn't said anything about his dad yet, but it was only a matter of time. Livingston had been acting peculiar lately, unpredictable. But it was still out of character for him to fall off the face of the earth for so long. If Del didn't take notice soon, it would be up to Henry to raise the alarm. It didn't make any sense that he wouldn't.

But first, he needed to finish the job he'd started.

Tonight, he thought. *It has to be tonight. I can't wait any longer.*

He was decided.

The phone in his pocket vibrated, shaking Henry out of his thoughts. His brows drew together when he saw who was calling. Henry hoped like hell he hadn't just hung himself on his own rope.

"Del," he said, answering the phone.

"Henry, we need to talk."

Henry sighed. "Yeah. We do."

"I've decided I'm gonna get in touch with the state police," Del went on. "Turn this whole thing over to them and let the chips fall where they're gonna fall."

"I thought you didn't want to involve anyone else?" Henry asked.

"Yeah, well, if the state boys come in and pick them up, it's out of my hands. These guys, the traffickers, they're gonna know there's nothing to gain by adding bribery of a law enforcement officer to their charges."

There was a pause.

"You don't sound entirely convinced," Henry pointed out.

"I'm not. But that's the best I've got, man. If it comes up, it'll be my word against theirs. Unless the state boys decide to dig deeper. But they won't. They won't." Del let out an unconvincing sigh. "It'll be out of my hands anyway. I just thought you needed to know."

Henry opened his mouth, then shut it again. He debated whether he was doing the right thing, but it was too late for that. It was the only thing he could do. It didn't make any sense for him not to speak up.

His time had run out.

"There's something else, Del," Henry said, his heart pounding double time in his chest. "It's important. Or it might be anyway. Might be nothing. It's about your dad."

"What about him?" Del asked, the irritation evident in every syllable.

"He hasn't come home."

"Yeah, you said he'd been keeping weird hours. Probably in town, yelling at people from that stupid-ass trash can again."

"That's the thing, Del. I was in town yesterday, and no one's seen him. Not for a couple of days. Has he been by your place?"

"No. The last time I saw him was three or four days ago. Right after he got into the argument with the stranger in the middle of town."

Henry held his tongue, letting Del digest the words that had just come out of his mouth.

"You're telling me no one's seen him since then?" Del asked slowly, the magnitude of the situation finally taking hold.

"That's what I'm saying, Del."

There was an explosive crash on the other end of the phone, and Henry imagined that whatever it was wouldn't be easily mended.

"Damn it, Henry! I'm on my way over. I'll be there in ten minutes." The line went dead.

Henry had set the wheels in motion. God help them all.

CHAPTER FORTY-SEVEN

Del stared at the bloody mess in the shack. His face had lost all color, and Henry wondered if hell was real. Because if it was, he'd surely have a place saved for putting his brother through this.

When Del had made it to Henry's house, the two had talked it over, considering the possibilities.

"Maybe he's wandered out into the swamp, gotten hurt or something," Henry had suggested, hating the lies that fell from his lips.

"Maybe," Del said, standing on the front porch with his brother. "I'll pull together a search party, but first, I think there's someplace we need to check. Come on."

Henry knew he was going to lead him to the shack in the woods. Knew it as surely as he'd ever known anything. Del couldn't ignore the fact that Livingston had gotten into a confrontation with a man who was a suspected associate of the traffickers in the woods.

Henry knew what they'd find too. But that didn't prepare him for the whoosh of air that escaped Del's lungs when he caught sight of the scene in the empty hunting cabin.

"Jesus," Henry whispered. His own shock was real. He'd last seen the place by dim flashlight. Under the unrelenting light of day, it looked so much worse.

Del took a hesitant step inside the doorway, and Henry couldn't help wondering what was going through his mind.

He moved to follow, but Del held up a hand.

"Don't," he said. "This is a crime scene."

"Jesus, Del," he said again.

"He's dead. Look at this place. They've killed him, Henry," Del said, looking up from the floor and meeting Henry's gaze. There was stark, unfiltered pain in his face. "Those sons of bitches killed him." His voice was low, shocked.

Henry saw again the body of Livingston crumpling at his feet.

"But why?" Henry asked. His voice was odd. He wasn't a practiced liar, and he'd been forced to utter more untruths in the last hour than in the rest of his life combined.

"Who the hell knows," Del said, the words leaking out of him weakly like a punctured tire. He glanced around the room, his eyes wide. "For being a nosy, belligerent asshole probably."

"There's no way to know what happened here," Henry said. "Maybe this isn't Livingston's blood. Maybe he's passed out drunk in King's place under one of the tables."

Henry sounded like he really wanted to believe that was true. Because he *did* really want to believe that was true, even when he knew it wasn't.

"For three damn days? King would have called one of us to come and get him, Henry. Don't be stupid. No," he said, shaking his head. "There's too much blood here. Somebody died, and that's a fact. And the only person who's missing is Dad. God damn it!" Del said, angry now.

Henry watched helplessly as the different emotions played havoc with his brother's expression. He didn't know what else to say, but he was spared the necessity as Del stormed past him and out the front door of the shack.

Del took his radio from the clip on his belt.

"Gladys, you there?" he asked.

"Yeah, Del. Whatcha got, hon?"

"I need you to get in touch with . . ."

Del stopped and turned, staring at the shack that stood at his back. Henry thought there might actually be tears in his eyes. Henry hadn't seen him cry since Mari had died.

"God damn it!" Del shouted, pushing away the grief and replacing it with a sharp, hot anger.

The radio crackled, then Gladys's voice came back across the line.

"I'm sorry, Del, I didn't catch that."

For a moment the radio hung limply from his hand, and Henry waited. The right thing to do was to call in the state police now, or the crime scene unit out of Cordelia—probably both. Henry knew it. Del certainly knew it too. Knightsbridge County wasn't big enough to handle this sort of thing on its own.

He held his breath.

"Del? You still there, hon?" came Gladys's voice.

Del ignored her, turning his attention to the twin tracks of the path that led out of the woods. It didn't take too much imagination for Henry to figure out that Del was following them backward in his mind, straight back to the men he was certain were responsible for this.

"Del?" Gladys's voice came again.

Henry watched his brother stand up straighter, his decision made.

"Never mind, Gladys," he said into the radio at last. "Hey, if you see Brady, send him out to Henry's place, okay?"

"Sure thing, Del," Gladys replied. Henry could hear the faint confusion in her voice.

"Del," Henry said. "What are you doing?"

His brother turned and looked him in the eye. "What I should have done months ago. I told you I'd take care of things, and I will."

Del turned and started walking back through the woods toward the house. Henry trotted to catch up.

"Del, what about . . . I thought you were bringing in the state guys. You're not just going to leave that mess out there?" Henry said, gesturing at the shack receding into the trees behind them.

"That's exactly what I'm gonna do. I told you I'd take care of this, and I am."

"But . . . but how, Del? You don't have the resources, the manpower. The state police are better equipped to handle this kind of thing, aren't they?"

Del stopped and faced Henry dead-on. His face was like concrete that had begun to set, hiding the maelstrom of emotions that ran underneath. The only thing that showed clearly was rage.

"Yeah. Yeah, they are, but this is personal now, Henry. I'm not fetching coffee for the state police while they go out and track these guys down and pick them up. I'll do it myself, by God."

Henry hadn't expected this. He didn't know what he'd expected, but it wasn't this.

"It's the least I can do," Del said, quietly. He turned away and headed back down the path.

"And then what, huh? What happens then?" Henry called to his brother's retreating back.

But Del's silence was the only answer Henry got.

CHAPTER FORTY-EIGHT

Brady and Del were arguing in the yard. Henry could hear the yelling all the way inside the house.

Apparently Henry wasn't the only one who thought Del's approach was questionable at best.

Eventually, the two men stomped their way into the house, their heated words having given way to a tense silence between them.

"Sit, both of you," Brady said to Henry and Eve.

After a glance at one another, they did as he asked, side by side on the sofa. Henry held her hand tightly, grateful there was at least one person in the room he didn't have to lie to.

Because, for the two men in uniform, he was about to have to go into a tap dance like they'd never seen.

"Tell me everything. And I mean everything," Brady said, his little black notebook flipped open in his hand, his pen poised to take down the flood of untruths Henry was about to unleash.

The lies tripped off Henry's tongue easily, though they didn't sit gently on his conscience. No, they hadn't seen Livingston in days. No, they had no idea where he stayed on the nights he didn't come home. No, they hadn't heard anything unusual in the woods, hadn't seen any signs of anyone coming or going. Everything was a shock, such a shock.

Henry knew, though, that there was one thing that still needed to be discussed, and he didn't want to do it in front of Eve.

Henry, glancing over at Eve, asked Del if they could speak outside. He didn't want to discuss her uncle in front of her, didn't want her to relive any memories that hearing his name might cause. After Del exchanged a glance with Brady, the two brothers left him questioning Eve and stepped outside, shutting the door behind them.

"Why didn't you tell me this before?" Del asked, his voice harsh and unrelenting once Henry told him about Gus's visit.

"Her uncle showing up was the reason Eve told me all that stuff about the men in the woods, Del. About the women and children, the attack. She was terrified and traumatized, and rightfully so. It seemed a lot more pertinent that you were taking money from these guys to damn well *protect* them, which is something I learned from Gus, by the way."

"Keep your voice down," Del said, glancing around.

"I thought you said you were gonna let the chips fall wherever they were gonna fall? What the hell happened to that, huh?"

"Things are a little bit different now, wouldn't you say? I think I've got bigger problems on my hands at the moment than a few bribes. Like who murdered my *father*!"

"Del, you don't even know if he was murdered," Henry said. "There was no body."

"Henry, were we seeing the same thing? Nobody loses that much blood and walks away. And if he did, where the hell is he?"

"That blood could belong to anybody. It could have been one of them. Hell, it could have been an animal," he said.

Henry had no idea why he was trying to convince Del that what he believed had happened out at the shack wasn't exactly what Henry needed him to believe. He'd orchestrated it that way, and it had worked. So what was he doing?

"It wasn't an animal!" Del yelled. He pushed out a breath and visibly struggled to keep himself under control. "It wasn't an animal.

Nobody slaughters an animal inside. And this town is awfully small, Henry. There isn't anyone else that hasn't come home. I would have damn well heard about it. Now stop. It was Dad. You know it, and I know it. Just stop."

Henry knew he should. Del was right. He clamped his jaw shut, wondering if there would ever be a time in his life when he wouldn't have to lie and whether he'd remember how to be honest when the chance came to make a true statement.

"Now tell me about Eve's uncle again. I need all the details you can remember," Del said.

So Henry told him.

By the time Del and Brady left, Henry felt like he'd been hollowed out from the inside.

But he couldn't stop now. Henry knew he had more to do.

There was a barrel waiting for him out in the swamp. And a missing man that needed to disappear for good.

CHAPTER

FORTY-NINE

"Henry, son," Ms. Watson said with a shake of her head. "I really think you're making a mistake. Wait till all this dies down, I'm begging you."

She was standing on the end of the pier. The night was thick around them when Henry stepped into the pirogue. The overhead floodlight was entertaining a swarm of bugs high above their heads and outlining the two of them in a bright circle.

"I can't wait, Ms. Watson. I'm putting you and Jonah at risk, and I won't do it anymore. I can't sleep at night knowing he's here."

"Just give it a few more days," she pleaded.

Henry shook his head.

"I need it over with. Please, just look after Eve for me while I'm gone. Please?"

She looked like she was going to argue, but when she opened her mouth to speak, the familiar sound of the bell ringing across the other side of the swamp interrupted her.

Helen Sue and Henry both turned and stared.

"Looks like we've got company. Henry, you take the boat on over and pick up whoever that is. And for goodness' sake, leave that barrel be. Nobody's going to give it a thought unless they see you messing around with it."

Cursing under his breath, Henry didn't have a choice. Taking up the pole and the flashlight, he nodded to Ms. Watson, who nodded gravely in return.

"Go on, then," she said.

So Henry did.

As he poled his way through the water, his mind skipped ahead, wondering what fresh problems awaited them on the other bank.

He saw the brown-and-white SUV first and assumed it was Del, but when the voice came out of the darkness and said, "Hey there, Henry. Didn't expect to see you here," Henry realized he'd jumped to conclusions.

"Brady," Henry greeted him. He tried to keep his voice calm and collected. "This whole thing with Livingston has upset Eve. We came by to visit for a while, get a sense of normal back." Henry heard his words and knew they didn't make much sense. The tilt of Brady's brow and the scrutiny in his face said they didn't make much sense to him either.

"Normal, huh? I don't know how much of that you're gonna find out here with Aunt Helen and Jonah, but to each his own, I suppose."

Henry breathed a sigh as Brady let it go and stepped into the boat.

"What brings you by?" Henry asked, trying to shift the focus off of his own questionable motives.

"Del filled me in on the visit from Eve's uncle." Brady shook his head. "I told him this is a job for the state boys. If those folks out there are really smuggling people across the border, this is bigger than we can handle. But he's got his heels dug in, Henry. I think this thing with his dad has really messed up his head."

Henry didn't know what to say to that, but Brady didn't seem to expect an answer.

"But then Del's been acting odd for a while now. Have you noticed?" he continued.

Henry was grateful for the shadows that hid his face, and he kept his eyes on the marsh gliding around the boat.

"Maybe. I just chalked it up to the stress about Alice and the IVF treatments."

"Hmm," Brady murmured. "Yeah, I get that. But I don't know. I can't help thinking there's more going on than I can get a handle on."

"You think Del has something to do with all this?" Henry asked, truly taken aback. "I know he and Livingston didn't always see eye to eye, but Brady, that's crazy."

"No, man. I know. I just feel like there's something he's not saying. I've known Del a long time, and I can tell when he's got something heavy on his mind."

"Well, you'd probably know better than me. He's my brother, but that's the way he's always treated me. Like a kid brother. Not exactly a friend, not exactly not. You see what I'm saying?"

"Yeah. Yeah, I do. But I'm worried about him. Just do me a favor, Henry. You'll let me know if there's anything . . . I don't know. Anything weird that I should know. Will you do that?"

Henry was touched by the concern and worry he could hear in Brady's voice. He could see the ripples of what they'd done spreading faster and farther than he'd ever imagined. The lies were like stones dropping in his stomach, weighing him down.

"Sure, Brady," Henry lied.

"Anyway, I thought I'd have a word with Jonah about what he saw in town the other day."

"You mean the run-in with Eve's uncle?" Henry asked.

"I asked around town, trying to get a handle on what went down. Tinker told me he'd caught the tail end of it. Said Jonah might be able to tell me more, that he'd been watching too."

Small towns have a lot of eyes. Something Henry knew he would do well not to forget.

"I don't know how much you're gonna get out of Jonah, man."

Brady chuckled. "Believe me, I know. But sometimes he sees more than he realizes."

They could just make out the Watson house in the distance, and Henry could see figures outlined on the porch.

"I hate what happened to my brother, Henry," Brady said quietly. "I live with that every day of my life."

Henry had never heard Brady talk about that day so long ago. He only knew the vaguest details about the accident that had left Jonah with a mind that didn't get any older.

"Mari and me, we were to blame, you know. We just wanted to spend some time alone. We were seventeen. In love. Or we thought we were. What the hell does a seventeen-year-old know about love? But it was exciting as hell. The sneaking around so her dad didn't find out. Mari liked it. Hell, Mari loved it. Looking back, I think maybe she loved the sneaking around more than she loved me."

Brady looked up at Henry, seeming embarrassed at the truths he'd let slip out. "I'm sorry, you don't want to hear this."

"It's fine," Henry said. "Nobody talks about her. Not really. And I think about her a lot."

"I forget sometimes that you lost her too. She loved you, you know. Maybe more than Del, and he was her twin. Hell, maybe more than anybody. She used to say you were an old soul, like she was."

Henry knew the love he'd had for Mari, that he still had, but he'd never heard anyone put into words that it had been returned. It was something he'd never known if he'd imagined, made up in his head because he wanted so badly for it to be true, or if their bond had been real.

"Thank you," Henry whispered. "Thank you for that, Brady."

"Water under the bridge now." Brady shrugged, then looked up toward the house where his brother lived. "I've wished a million times I could go back to that day, make things different. Jonah was being a pest, following us around. We started tossing things into the river, telling him to go get them, just to get him out of our hair for a little while. But he wouldn't stay gone long enough, so we started throwing things farther. Mari made that last throw, and she looked like a goddess under the afternoon sun. I watched her wind up and fling that rock like she was standing on a baseball mound, her lip caught between her teeth. How she laughed when Jonah went racing after it like a dopey golden retriever. God, she was beautiful."

Brady shook his head.

"I couldn't keep my hands off her. And she loved that too. Loved the power she had over me. Over everybody."

He turned and looked Henry in the eye, and Henry saw a depth to Brady that he'd never suspected.

"That's what we were doing when Jonah got tangled up under the water and couldn't make it up. We were kissing, celebrating it. In the knowledge that we shouldn't be. Her dad, he'd have lost it if he'd known about us. But that just added to the excitement, you know."

Henry watched the emotions play over Brady's face, the sorrow and the love and the guilt.

"Jonah was blue by the time we got him out of the water. He wasn't breathing. I left her there, doing CPR. I don't even know if she knew how to do CPR, Henry. She'd probably only seen it done in the movies. And I left her there with my little brother while I ran off to get help."

The boat bobbed toward the side of the pier while the two men walked through the past.

"When I got back, Jonah was breathing, but he was unconscious. He stayed in a coma for three weeks. It's a miracle he lived at all. Mari did that. She saved his life."

Brady looked away from Henry's eyes, staring off into the swamp.

"But when he woke up, he was never the same." Brady sighed. "And neither was she."

CHAPTER FIFTY

Jonah didn't have a lot to add to what Brady already knew, but he duti-fully repeated what he'd seen, all the same.

"Mr. Doucet, he didn't treat the man very good. He was never gonna make a friend, treating folks that way."

Brady nodded, snapping his little black notebook closed with a sigh.

"You're right about that, Jonah," he said to his brother.

"So did I do good?" Jonah asked happily, looking back and forth between the faces turned in his direction.

"You did real good. Real good, Jonah," Ms. Watson told her nephew, patting his hand.

Brady rose and tucked the notebook into his pocket.

"I'll get out of your hair, Aunt Helen. I'm sorry to bother you so late. This thing has got us all twisted up."

"It's not a problem, Brady. You're welcome here anytime at all. You know that."

"Thank you, Aunt Helen," Brady said, leaning over to kiss the cheek of the woman who'd been a surrogate mother to him.

"Jonah misses you," she said, with a tilt to her head. "I miss you too, come to that."

He gave her a sad smile.

"When this mess is over, I'll come out and spend some time. I promise. Jonah, you and me. We'll go out fishing. Maybe catch a gator or two. What do you think?"

Jonah's face lit up and Henry had to smile.

"That'd be real good, Brady. There's a couple I been watching down at the south end of the slough."

"I know you know what you're doing, Jonah," Brady said. "But remember to be careful out there on your own, okay?"

Jonah waved him off. "Oh, I know that, Brady."

"Especially with Ol' Brutal. That big guy's ancient, and he's not scared of anybody, including you."

Jonah nodded. "I steer clear of Brutal," he said. "Like Aunt Helen says, we got us a understanding. I just toss him a good meal every now and then, and he leaves us be."

Brady nodded and moved toward the door. Jonah followed.

"Matter of fact, I bet that old boy's not gonna be needing another meal for at least a month or more, not after today."

"Oh yeah?" Brady asked, the distraction in his voice giving away the fact that his mind was already on other things.

"Yeah. I fed him a meal this afternoon like he ain't never seen. Emptied out the whole bait barrel for him."

Henry's stomach dropped to the floor, and stayed there writhing. He couldn't seem to catch his breath. His wide eyes slammed into Helen Sue's behind the brothers' backs. He glanced back at Eve, who sat characteristically silent on the sofa, but her face was serene.

"That's good, Jonah. That's real good. Keep him happy, and he'll mind his business," Brady said.

"I'll take you on over back to your truck," Jonah said as they walked out onto the porch.

"That's okay, Jonah, I can take him back," Henry interjected. He didn't know if Jonah had anything else to say about what he'd been feeding that giant gator that afternoon, but Henry didn't want to take the chance.

"Okay, then," Jonah said, acquiescing. "I'll just play checkers with Eve, then. See ya later, Brady."

"You take care, Jonah. Aunt Helen." Brady leaned over and gave his aunt another peck on the cheek, and she mumbled her good-byes as she tried to organize her face in an expression that didn't give away her shock.

Brady was quiet on the return trip across the swamp. Contemplative. Henry was grateful for the silence.

"You watch yourself, Henry," Brady said before he stepped out of the pirogue. "There's something going on out here in these woods. Something bad, and I can't seem to catch hold of it. Things people aren't saying."

"I'll do that, Brady," Henry replied.

"Be sure you do. You've got that girl back there to protect now, and a baby on the way. Bad things can happen in a flash, Henry. Bad things that can't be made right."

CHAPTER FIFTY-ONE

Del had been watching, waiting.

He was patient.

And his patience had paid off. He stared at the man across the tiny table in the tiny room. It could loosely be called an interrogation room, though its most common use was someplace for Gladys to eat her lunch. But today, it had been commandeered for its intended purpose.

Del knew this was the guy. The two missing fingers gave him away. Del thought he recognized him anyway, with his ferret features partially hidden by a bushy mustache. He'd never dealt directly with the man—he was a lackey, a gofer boy—but Del thought he remembered him hanging around the fringes of the operation. Of course, he'd had all ten of his fingers then.

"I told you, I don't know anything about that crazy old man. I just asked him if he'd seen my niece, that was all!"

"What made you think he knew anything about that? The men you work for sent you, didn't they?"

"No! No, I told you already, I haven't had anything to do with those guys since they decided I didn't need all my fingers. I was just trying to do the right thing, man. That girl's in trouble, and I wanted to get her gone from around here!"

"So you're being a Good Samaritan, are you? You sticking with that story?"

"I'm telling you, man. I don't know nothing about nothing!"

"Why'd they take your fingers, Gus?" Brady asked in a calmer voice than did Del, who was standing with his palms down on the table in front of him.

"Because of the girl," Gus spit out, disgusted. "I brought her to them, and they thought I should have warned them she was dangerous. That's all."

"Then they just let you go? Let you take a few days off to warn her? Give you the chance to snatch her out of here before they came back to get her?"

Gus's eyes rolled around in his head, his gaze looking for someplace to land other than on the two men in uniform sitting in front of him.

"I . . . I guess so. Man, I don't know what they were thinking. I hadn't really done nothing, you know. I guess they figured I'd paid enough."

"How'd you know to ask the old man about the girl?" Del demanded, pulling Gus back to the topic he wanted answers to the most.

"I was down at the beer joint. Just hanging out, trying to decide what to do next. I asked around. That's all. I mean, I could have just left her here, let her deal with them on her own. Hell, I should have. That's what I get for having a soft heart, though."

"Yeah, you seem like a real humanitarian, Gus," Brady said.

Gus's brows drew together. "I don't know what that means."

"Always putting other people's needs in front of your own."

The slimy little man's eyes lit up with understanding. "That's right! That's what I am, a hu-mani . . . whatever that word was you said. I was thinking of the girl. I should have been gone days ago, but I couldn't just leave the girl on her own."

"Tell me about the smuggling. What do you know about the operation?"

"Nothing, I'm telling you," Gus said with a frustrated sigh. "I just run errands, do what I'm told to do. Take this truck here, pick up that person there. Stuff like that. I'm just as surprised as you are to find out what they've been up to."

Gus sent a sidelong glance at Brady. Del wasn't kidding himself; he knew Gus was aware that he'd known all along what they were up to—the gist of it, at least—but if Gus wanted to put on a show for Brady's benefit, he'd play along. Del had more important questions on his mind.

"I bet it pissed you off when the old man knocked the crap out of you in front of the whole damn town, didn't it?"

"I didn't do anything!" Gus yelled back at Del. "I told you already. I hooked up with a woman, Janine, down at the bar. We've been partying ever since. She's been with me the whole time, man. I couldn't get rid of her if I'd wanted to, once she saw I had a little money in my pocket. I've got an alibi, I'm telling you. Just ask her!"

"An alibi for what, Gus?" Brady asked mildly.

Word had spread around town that Livingston had disappeared into the wind. Not many folks seemed sorry to see him go, but Del and Brady had managed to keep the macabre discovery at the shack a well-guarded secret.

Gus wouldn't know how important an alibi would be, unless he'd been involved in whatever had taken place. Del was convinced he knew more than he was saying.

"For whatever it is you're trying to pin on me!" Gus cried. "Whatever it is, I didn't do nothing!"

"And where'd you get a little money, Gus?" Brady asked, cleaning his nails with a pocketknife.

"Ah, man, come on. I told you everything I know, which is nothing. You got no call to hold me here. I know my rights!"

Brady sighed and pushed back from his chair. "Can I talk to you outside?" he said to his partner and friend.

Del followed Brady out of the room, shutting the door on the now satisfied-looking Gus, who'd leaned back in his chair and crossed his arms.

"He's right. We can't hold him," Brady said, shaking his head at Del, who was still staring at Gus through the window to the small room. "We've got nothing, and the hooker that was with him has got him alibied anyway. She's out front, waiting till we let him out. She's sticking to her story, and there's a whole lot of nothing we can do about it."

"He knows something," Del said, jabbing a finger at the closed door. "You know it, and I know it."

"What I know doesn't make a bit of difference. We've got nothing. Now cut him loose."

Del looked like he was going to argue.

"Cut him loose, or I will," Brady said, turning to walk back to his desk.

Del opened the door so hard that it slammed against the wall with a bang. He advanced on Gus, and leaned across the table to force the man to meet his eyes. He whispered to him in a low, violent voice, "It's not gonna matter, Gus. You don't have to say anything at all. Because I'm going to put the word out that you sang like a bird. And when it gets back to your buddies that you flipped on them, because it will, where do you think it'll be safe to run to? You won't be able to go back home, that's for sure."

Gus leaned back in his chair, real fear evident on his face. "You . . . you can't do that," he stuttered. "You're gonna get me killed, man. You're gonna get me killed!"

Del simply walked out the door, leaving it swinging wide behind him as he called over his shoulder.

"You're free to go."

CHAPTER

FIFTY-TWO

The feelings inside of Eve were strange and unfamiliar. Even with months to get used to the idea that another life was growing inside of her, she tried not to think about the future. A baby.

She'd never had a future to think of before and didn't know how to wrap her mind around it.

Henry's face changed whenever he put his hands on her belly. He looked at her with such light in his eyes, and she craved that, even as she worried it couldn't last. No one had ever looked at her that way.

More than that, she couldn't help feeling there'd been no *her* to look at before Henry had seen her. Eve had been formed from nothing beneath his gaze.

And now everything was changing.

Her stomach had been tightening uncomfortably throughout the day. Her lower back was aching more than usual, and twice she'd had to sit down and squeeze her eyes shut against spasms of pain that rocked her body.

But she kept her silence. It was her only weapon against the changes coming, and she clung to it tightly.

Weeks and weeks had passed since she'd hit the old man, and stopped him from hurting Henry. She could see the tension in Henry sometimes, as he stared across the field toward the woods and the shack.

She knew he worried about what might come for them through those woods one day. Knew he struggled with what she'd done and what he'd been forced to do because of it.

But she couldn't find remorse for the death of the angry little man. He was a bad man. Eve would no longer be hurt by bad men. She'd sooner die.

And hurting Henry was the same as hurting her.

So she couldn't regret what she'd done, and she didn't dwell on it. Instead, she continued to learn to read, the books made for children opening up sweet make-believe worlds about childhoods she didn't understand, where puppies and butterflies mattered more than hunger or pain. Their silly simplicity made her smile.

She continued to become if not whole, then new, under Henry's care.

When the sound of car doors slamming interrupted her concentration on the picture book in front of her, she rose and went to the door.

It was Alice and Del.

"Eve, honey," Alice said. "I hope you don't mind. Del's got it in his head that he wants to take his brother out for a beer, and I thought I'd stay with you while they go out. I know Henry doesn't like leaving you alone out here, and I have to say, I agree with him, considering." She nodded toward Eve's stomach, which protruded in front of her.

"Is Henry around?" Del asked gruffly from behind his wife. The differences between the man he'd become in the last few months and the easy, open man he'd been before were hard not to see. Del's edges were sharper now, his face gaunter and his movements jerky. He was a man fighting off demons.

Eve knew the signs.

"He's out at the still," Eve said in a low voice. She'd never been completely comfortable around Henry's brother.

Del nodded and walked off in the direction of the shed.

"I swear, that man," Alice said, watching him go with a shake of her head. "Something's changed in him, since his dad . . . Well, you don't want to hear about that."

Alice shook off her musings and dropped her bag on the floor beside the door. "I hope I'm not interrupting anything," she said, glancing around.

"I was just reading. Or trying to," Eve answered. She'd become more used to Alice over the last few months. She hadn't been sure what to think of her at first, but she'd come to understand. Alice was good. In the way Caroline had been. In the way Henry was.

"Good," Alice said, echoing Eve's thoughts. "That's good. I want to see you resting as much as you can. Keeping your feet up. Has the swelling still been bothering you?"

"No," Eve said. "I feel fine." She didn't want an examination right now. She worried that Alice would be able to tell that things were happening, changing, in spite of everything Eve was doing to stop it.

"Okay," Alice said, blowing out a breath and looking around. "What about food? Are you hungry?"

She wasn't, but Eve thought it might give Alice something to concentrate on other than her. She could feel her stomach tightening even as she spoke.

"I am kind of hungry," she said apologetically. "I have the things to make a stew, but I haven't done it yet."

Alice's face brightened.

"Oh, good. I can do that. You sit, enjoy your book. I'll just be in the kitchen."

Eve breathed a sigh of relief.

Alice's words floated out of the kitchen. She was still chatting with Eve from the other room. Eve forced her voice to maintain what she hoped was a normal rhythm in reply, even as she bent over with her eyes shut tight, clutching at her belly.

The pains were getting stronger now. Eve felt her safe, pretty world with Henry slipping from her fingers. She wasn't ready. She wasn't ready for anything to change.

The pain loosened its grip, and Eve gasped, pulling in deep breaths and wiping her brow. She'd barely had time to compose her face before the front door opened.

"Eve, Del's insisting I go into town with him," Henry said. He looked irritated and distracted, and Eve was glad. "Will you be okay if I'm gone for a little while? Alice is going to stay, but if you need me for anything, all you have to do is call, and I'll come right back home."

"Henry, she's going to be fine," Del said from behind him. "You're fine, aren't you?" he shot at Eve.

She wasn't fine, but the last thing she wanted was to say that in front of Henry or his brother.

"Of course," she said, keeping her voice light. "Go. It's no problem."

Henry must have noticed something off in her voice, because he looked at her more closely than she was comfortable with.

"You heard her, come on, man," Del said, placing a hand on Henry's arm.

"Okay, okay," Henry said, glancing back at his brother. "Calm down, Del. Alice, we're heading into town. Call me if you need me, okay?"

"You got it, Henry," Alice said, stepping up to the doorway that led to the kitchen, wiping her hands on a dishrag. "She's in good hands. Don't worry, okay?"

"Thanks, Alice," he said, and leaned down to give Eve a kiss on the cheek.

She smiled her best *everything's fine* smile at him. It must have worked, because he and Del left. She let out a pent-up breath.

"This will take a little while to get ready, Eve. Do you want me to make you a sandwich or something until then? It's no trouble," Alice said.

"No, thank you," Eve replied. "I think I'll go take a bath and maybe lie down for a while. I'm pretty tired."

"Sure," Alice said. "Don't worry about me, I'll just make myself at home."

Eve forced one more fake smile onto her face. She was getting good at the fake smiles. "Okay, then."

She rose and made her way down the hallway. She almost made it into the bathroom before another wave of pain gripped her middle and stole her breath and all her fake smiles with it.

CHAPTER
FIFTY-THREE

Henry was thinking about Eve as Del's SUV bumped along the back roads that led away from Henry's house. There was no way to know exactly when her due date was without the advice of an obstetrician, but Alice thought it must be close—within a few weeks—and Henry had a nagging feeling he should have stayed home.

Lost in his thoughts, he didn't immediately notice when Del turned the vehicle in a direction that didn't lead to town.

"Wait, I thought we were going to King's," Henry said, when Del pulled the SUV to a stop.

They had come to the marsh that led to the Watson house, but Henry didn't see Jonah's boat. Just the murky green water that was Livingston's final resting place. Henry would never be able to see this part of the swamp again without wondering about his stepfather. Had Brutal really taken care of all the evidence, or were there pieces of Livingston still hiding, waiting to be found?

He'd never be sure.

"It's time," Del said, glancing over at his brother. His face was dark, set in granite. Not the face of a man with plans to blow off a little steam at the local bar.

"Time for what?" Henry asked cautiously.

"Time to face the music."

He knows, Henry thought in a blinding flash of panic, laced with the smallest thread of relief. *It's over now. He knows.*

Del nodded toward the glove compartment of the SUV, indicating Henry should open it.

Henry slowly reached his hand out to the latch, sure, for the briefest moment, that when he did, his stepfather's severed foot would come tumbling out into his lap, all the evidence Del needed to cement his fate.

The image was so powerful that Henry was momentarily confused when he opened the latch and saw nothing but old yellowed papers and a small black case.

"What am I looking for?" Henry asked hesitantly.

"In the case," Del said.

Henry picked it up slowly, feeling its heft. Whatever was in there, it wasn't Livingston's foot.

But his relief was short-lived. When he unzipped the case, the light caught on the barrel of a small black pistol, snuggled into the foam that lined the case.

"What the hell is this?" Henry asked.

"It's untraceable. I bought it from a dealer in Cordelia. The serial number's been filed," Del said, staring out the window in front of him.

"For what?" Henry asked. It wasn't that he was unfamiliar with guns, but the back-alley dealing that Del had gone through to get this one stank of plans Henry didn't want to be involved in.

"They're back," Del said simply. "Six weeks and no sign, but my snitch on the other side of town says they're back tonight. It's time to get justice for Dad. I owe him that. We owe him that."

Henry stared at Del's determined profile, then down at the gun in his lap. He stayed silent for a moment, absorbing the surreal path that had brought them both to this point.

"Have you lost your mind?" Henry asked slowly. "Why the hell don't you just call in the state police and go arrest them?"

"And then what? They go to jail for murder and human trafficking?"

Henry's eyes widened. "Yeah," he said. What the hell else was Del hoping for? Considering the gun sitting in his lap like a snake about to strike, Henry had a sinking suspicion that he knew the answer to that.

"That's not good enough, Henry," Del spit at him. "That old man was a son of a bitch, and a crazy one at that. But he was my father!"

Del threw open the door to the truck and stepped out. Henry had no choice but to do the same. Henry watched, speechless, as his brother dragged a small aluminum boat from the brush along the side of the road.

"Del, what in the . . . This is crazy! You can't just go over there with guns blazing and expect to . . . to . . . What exactly *do* you expect? Some sort of revenge?"

"Yes, Henry, I do. I want to know what happened to my father, and I don't intend to let the state police get in my way. They'll just make a deal, a trade-off to shut down the trafficking, and that's not good enough. I need to know what happened to Dad. Now, either you're with me or you're not, but I'm going."

Del pushed the boat into the water and stepped in.

"Damn it, Del. Wait," Henry said. "I said wait! You're not going over there by yourself."

Del used an oar to hold the boat, and Henry stepped in with him.

"This is insane. You're going to get yourself killed," Henry said in a harsh whisper. They were a mile or more from the shack still, but he couldn't help the urge to keep his voice low.

Del didn't reply, just sank the oar into the water and pushed them one step closer to his goal.

Henry realized he was still holding the opened case with the gun in his hands, and he didn't even think before he tossed it deep into the swamp with a splash.

"What the hell did you do that for?" Del demanded.

"You're a cop, for God's sake," Henry said, leaning into Del's face. "I never thought you were a very good one, to be honest, and taking money from those guys didn't exactly prove me wrong, but right now I need you to remember that you're a police officer! Whatever you're planning to do, you need to do the right way."

Del stared at Henry, who could see the fire burning behind his brother's eyes. His words were clearly falling on deaf ears. When had Del become so unhinged? Was it the moment he'd walked into the shack? Was Henry ultimately to blame for this?

"Where's Brady?" Henry demanded. "You didn't tell him, did you? Damn it, Del!"

Henry fished his phone out of his pocket, scrolling to find Brady's number, but he never had a chance to make the call. Del snatched the phone from his hand and tossed it into the marsh, to sink in the same way the gun had.

"What the hell?" Henry demanded.

"No. We do this my way," he snarled.

"Your way? What are you, Dirty Harry?"

"Henry, if I'd have known you were going to be such a whiny little girl about this, I'd have left you at home. Now, you can follow me and do what I say, or you can stay in the damn boat. I don't really give a shit."

Del was whispering now. Henry should have known they were pulling close to the shore by the way Del was keeping his voice low and hard, but he was facing his brother, trying to find the words to tell him that he shouldn't do this. He shouldn't put his life at risk, because those men, whatever they were guilty of, and Henry was sure it was plenty, hadn't killed Livingston.

He had to tell him. This had never been the plan. Del was supposed to have Brady with him, a team of state police, and take down the men who'd been trading on the weakest members of the human race. The people who most needed help.

He wasn't supposed to put his life on the line to try and get revenge single-handedly, like some sort of action hero in a low-budget movie.

Henry stared at Del, considering and hastily rejecting strings of words that would give the truth to his brother and still manage to protect Eve. The only way to do that was to put himself in the line of fire, and although he was willing, Henry wasn't entirely convinced that Del would *believe* him. Del had often accused him of being soft, a mama's boy. Henry had accepted the ribbing silently, never denying the claim, which would have somehow felt like a betrayal of his mother.

Instead, he'd recognized, even as a child, that Caroline Martell Doucet was the strongest person he'd ever known or ever would.

Mama, help me, he thought. *Help me do the right thing for everybody. What do I do?*

But Mama was gone.

And Henry had stumbled so far down this darkened path that he didn't know if even his mother's light could lead him out.

Henry had opened his mouth to speak, although he still didn't know what he was going to say, when he felt the boat bump into the shore behind him. The jolt nearly knocked him into the water, it came so unexpectedly.

Then Del was pulling them to the edge, stepping out onto the shore.

"Del!" Henry whispered.

His brother made a violent motion across his throat in Henry's direction, clearly telling him to shut the hell up. He pointed in the direction of the shack, from which, even at this distance, Henry could hear the faint murmur of footsteps crossing the old floorboards. A dim light shone through the barred windows.

Del crouched and disappeared through the trees. Henry was left with no choice but to follow.

It's all slipping out of my hands, Henry thought in horror.

He scrambled after Del, needing to catch him before he did anything rash. Maybe, just maybe, his presence could keep Del inside the shaky paper walls of sanity, but there was no guarantee.

He could make out his brother in the distance, a dark figure moving through the same trees they'd haunted as children, when their biggest concern had been making it home in time for dinner. Henry wondered how things had gotten to this point.

Suddenly, Del stopped, turning back to Henry and holding a finger up to his lips for silence, then crouching down in the darkened brush.

Henry heard whistling coming through the trees. A man was coming toward them, no realization at all what he was walking into.

The man stopped, just feet from where Del stayed still and silent, waiting in the woods.

It was so quiet that Henry could hear the zip as the man unfastened his trousers, and the telltale little jump a man makes before he takes a leak.

Jesus, Henry thought.

The sound of a stream of piss hitting the ground at the man's feet mingled with his out-of-tune whistle.

Henry realized what Del was going to do just moments before he did it. Henry stood to speak, to warn the man, to stop it all before it got any worse, but Del was closer. His brother rose from his hiding spot and clutched the man from behind, pulling his large forearm tight across his neck in a choke hold.

"Del, stop," Henry whispered. "What are you doing?"

But Del ignored him.

"Hey there, Gus. Fancy seeing you here. Quite the coincidence, wouldn't you say?" Del asked with a vicious yank on the man's neck that pulled his feet temporarily off the ground.

Gus didn't reply, couldn't reply. He could do nothing but grab at the hand across his neck, gasping for air.

"Del, let him breathe!" Henry whispered again.

"I'm going to loosen my hold, and you, Gus, are going to answer my questions. Aren't you?"

Henry could see Gus nod emphatically. Slowly, Del lowered the other man's feet to the ground and allowed the air to flow back into his lungs.

"How many men are inside? And don't even try to lie to me."

"Four," Gus rasped, not even attempting to equivocate while he rubbed at his neck. "Four men."

"Armed?" Del asked sharply.

Gus gave a nod.

"How many women and children?" Henry asked him.

Gus turned, startled. He hadn't realized Henry was there.

"I . . . I don't know," Gus said, glancing back and forth between the two men. "A dozen maybe. Four or five kids. Look, man, I'm just here to get a line on what they have planned for my niece. I'm not . . . It's not what it looks like."

"Is that so?" Del asked. "That's good, Gus. Because what it looks like is you've come running back to your employers. I'd hate to think that was the case. That would mean you're going down with them."

"Hey, man, I don't . . . I'll do anything you want. Just say the word."

"Which one of you killed the old man, Gus? Was it you?" Del demanded.

"*Killed?* I never killed nobody! I told you, I don't know nothing 'bout nothing!"

Del's temper was stumbling down a slippery slope. He grabbed Gus by the shirtfront and pulled him up into his face.

"You're lying."

"I . . . I'm not, man. I swear, I don't know anything!"

Del stared into Gus's eyes in the dark.

"He's telling the truth, Del," Henry said, moving slowly toward the two of them. He had to tell him. He had to tell him now, before Del did something he couldn't take back.

"Yeah. Listen to what he's saying, Del. I'm telling the truth! I got an alibi!"

"And that," Del said, with a shake, "is the only reason I'm gonna give you a chance right now, Gus. I'm gonna let you go, and you can walk out of here a free man. Don't turn around, don't look back. Walk away."

Gus went quiet and still, glancing between the two men. Del let go of him and stepped back. Henry breathed a sigh of relief.

The three of them teetered on the edge of a blade while each stood motionless, waiting to see which side of the knife they were going to fall on.

Then Gus ran. Henry realized with horror that he was running back toward the shack, tripping events into motion that Henry was much, much too late to stop.

"Cops! The cops are here!" Gus was shouting, running for his life, literally.

Henry took off running after him, hoping to knock him to the ground and shut him up before he could draw any more attention, but he pulled up short when a gunshot broke through the night.

Gus fell.

Henry turned back to his brother in shock.

He hadn't seen Del draw his weapon, and the words that were there on the tip of his tongue got tangled and lost. *He didn't do it, nothing to do with it. It was me, me and Eve.*

But it was too late. The gunshot rang through the woods like the starting bell at the dog races. Shouts came from the shack, and the sounds of people moving quickly.

Henry ran to Gus, who was sprawled on the ground just yards ahead of him. He rolled him over, and blood gurgled from an exit wound in his chest.

"Why didn't you go, you idiot!" Henry shouted, putting pressure on the wound. "All you had to do was walk away. Damn it!"

But there were no last words, only the spasms of a dying man, as his eyes rolled back in his head. More blood, so much blood. He coughed a red spray out of his mouth.

Once again, Henry found himself with blood on his hands.

But he didn't have time to dwell on it. Del grabbed him from behind, propelling him forward and below the floor of the shack that was raised up on piers.

Henry could barely hear the shouting voices mixing with the screams of women from above them over the sound his blood was making in his veins.

"Why, Del? You killed him! You fucking killed him!"

"Shut up," Del said in a harsh voice, his gun still in his hand. "He was lying, Henry. I gave him a chance. He should have taken it."

"He didn't do it!" Henry yelled.

"It doesn't matter," Del spit out, raising the gun and watching the steps that came down from the shack in front of them. "He had his chance."

There was more shuffling, screams, and footsteps from above, then the sounds of men shouting.

"Stay here," Del said. "Stay down." He looked at Henry with a vague sense of disgust. "You shouldn't have thrown the gun away, Henry," he said. Then he was gone, disappearing into the darkness of the woods that enclosed them.

"Del!" Henry called in a low whisper, but it was too late. No one was listening.

Henry was alone, standing beneath the raised shack, leaning against one of the piers and trying to catch his breath. He could see nothing except the steps that led down to the ground from the porch above him, nothing except the trees through the gaps in the boards. But he knew he wasn't alone. Not really.

From above him there were the stifled sounds of fear. And around him, somewhere blended within the woods, Henry knew his brother waited and watched, feeding on his anger.

A male voice called out from above.

"I heard a rumor, compadre, that our police friend had changed his loyalties," the voice said. "I thought to myself, no, not our friend. He's been bought and paid for, good American currency. But I see I must have been mistaken."

Henry saw feet step down onto the top step above him. Bare feet, too small and skinny to belong to the voice.

The feet of a child.

"There seems to be some sort of miscommunication here. One I'm sure we could get straightened out, if you'd like to step out and talk this over, man to man. No need to get anyone else involved."

There was a whimper and the sound of crying coming from somewhere above the too-small feet.

It was a little girl. They'd sent out a little girl. As a shield?

"I've got a few friends here with me, compadre. But you know, friends are a funny thing. There are always more where they came from. I don't mind losing a few."

The muffled crying increased, along with a muted feminine scream.

"What about you?"

Henry held his breath, but Del didn't step out of the woods. Didn't make a sound.

"I'm done playing around," the voice came again, harder and louder this time. "Come out now, and we'll talk this over like men. Don't come out, and the girl dies."

Henry didn't hesitate.

"Wait!" he shouted, moving out from the shelter beneath the shack with his hands up. "I'm coming out. Don't hurt her."

He glanced up into the glare of several flashlights pointing in his direction, held by men with guns spread out across the porch. He could see three of them and assumed there was at least one more inside.

The girl was standing front and center, visibly trembling.

255

There was a man standing behind her, one hand placed upon her shoulder, almost gently. His face was young, fresher than Henry had expected, if he'd thought to expect anything at all. The man had a slight smile upon his face.

"And who are you, may I ask?" he asked in a surprisingly congenial way.

"Nobody," Henry said. "Nobody who matters. A neighbor."

"Ah." The man nodded in recognition. "The neighbor who's taken in one of our girls. That neighbor?"

Henry nodded, looking into the face of the terrified child.

"Well, that is interesting. And what brings you here, neighbor? Looking for another girl to take home? Because that'd cost you this time. The last one was free. Damaged goods, you might say. But I'm not in the habit of giving away the merchandise."

Henry's stomach turned. "Let her go. Let them all go."

The man looked at Henry in surprise and let out a laugh. His face didn't look so fresh anymore.

"Let her go, he says," the man mocked. "What do you think of that, Marcus?" He glanced back at the porch toward one of the men with a gun.

Marcus said nothing, but his gun remained pointed straight at Henry.

Fresh Face looked back at Henry, an amused smile playing across his lips. "See, neighbor, unless you're a leprechaun with a pot of gold hidden behind you, I don't think that's going to happen. And you don't look like a leprechaun to me."

The other man tilted his head and studied Henry. "Why'd you come here? I'm guessing that gunshot was for Gus, since he hasn't shown his stupid face. Is he dead?" he asked curiously.

Henry nodded. There were a few grumbles from the men on the porch, and they shifted their feet, glancing toward one another, but they were clearly taking their cues from the man standing behind the little girl.

"That's too bad, neighbor," the man said, shaking his head, although he didn't sound like he really gave a damn either way.

"Gus was worthless. Worse than that, he was reckless. I took his fingers in payment for the damage his girl did to Marcus's face, because she was his. But that should have been the end of it. The girl wasn't going to talk. Not after I sent her my little care package."

"That was you?" Henry asked, stalling for time. Where the hell was Del?

The man grinned. "You liked that? Eloquent, I thought. And effective. But that idiot Gus wouldn't let it go. Wanted payback. Now his recklessness has brought you to my door, and I'm stuck in a position I don't really like to be in."

The man shifted from one foot to the other, and although Henry got the impression that he enjoyed hearing himself speak, he knew he was running out of time.

"I suppose you did me a favor, taking a liability off my hands. Still, I'm left in a quandary. See, somebody made a mess in my little vacation cabin here," he said, waving his gun in the direction of the shack behind him. "And I don't like messes. Gus swore up and down it wasn't him, and he knows better than to lie to me. I'd take more than his fingers for lying to me."

The man tightened his hold on the little girl's shoulder and pushed her forward a bit. She stumbled down the remaining steps, and the man followed, keeping her centered in front of him. They approached Henry together, until they stood in front of him on the ground, just beyond his reach.

Close enough that he saw the way the girl shuddered in fear. Close enough that he saw the cold calculation in the man's eyes.

"But then, I've heard some strange rumors floating around. Something about a local going missing. That Gus got questioned about it. That he rolled over on me, to save his own skin."

The man's voice was distracted, and Henry watched him peer into the trees behind where he was standing, checking, he was sure, to see if Henry was really alone.

And Henry had never felt more alone in his life.

"That's not the case, though. I'm a pretty good judge of character, and Gus didn't have any. He came running back to me straightaway, because he was more scared of me than them."

The man grinned at Henry and ran a hand softly down the girl's arm. "With good reason."

Out of the corner of his eye, Henry saw something moving within the bank of trees, to the left of the shack and toward the marsh. He tried to keep his face passive, but the man must have heard movement or seen a flicker in his eyes. He turned his head.

Henry felt a sense of déjà vu overtake him, layering his childhood nightmares over the current one he was living. Coming toward them was the swamp witch that had been lying dormant in the shallow, muddy grave where Henry had banished it when he was six years old.

And the witch had his brother's eyes, burning with hatred and pain.

Covered in mud and muck that blurred the edges of the wooded darkness around him with his own, Del didn't ask any questions. He didn't say anything at all. He slowly raised his hand and fired the gun.

The fresh-faced man fell slowly, the wound to his head jerking him backward.

The little girl screamed.

Henry watched it all in stunned disbelief.

There was shouting and the running feet of the men above them on the porch. There were screams of terrified women and children from inside the shack.

Del never hurried his pace, or so it seemed to Henry, who stood immobile with shock.

His brother walked slowly up the steps of the shack. Henry wasn't sure what kept those men from firing their weapons. Maybe it was the strange and unexpected sight of what appeared to be a monster. But in his heart, Henry thought they were more spooked by the slow, steady cadence of Del's feet coming toward them. He didn't hurry. Not in the way a man would—the way a man *should*—when he was walking toward the black barrels pointing in his direction. He walked like a thing that couldn't be killed, like an avenging ghost who had no fear of the death that bullets could deliver.

Then Del raised his arm and shot again. Once, then twice. The man on the right fell, never firing his weapon. His flashlight, his body, and his gun rattled against the weathered boards of the porch.

The last man standing, the one on the left, backed away when Del turned toward him. Henry didn't know exactly what thoughts must have been going through the fugitive's head, but he had a good idea when the man dropped his gun and ran to the railing of the porch, raising his leg to leap over the side.

Henry flinched when Del's gun went off again, shooting the man in the back.

With a start, Henry realized that the little girl standing just feet away from him, the little girl who'd just watched three men murdered before her eyes, the blood of one of them marring her face and arms, was screaming, running toward the shack.

"Mama! Mama!" she shrieked.

The little girl didn't plan to become the epicenter of what would happen next, as she barreled through the empty space separating her from the only person who mattered in her small world. She sought nothing more and nothing less than the safety of her mother's arms.

Henry sprinted after her as she threw herself up the steps. Del also turned in her direction, the vengeful anger still on his face. At the same moment that the child reached the top of the steps, the door of the shack flew back on its rusty hinges, and another man emerged from the darkened doorway.

Without any of the purpose that Del had possessed when firing his gun, the man in the doorway was driven only by fear. Fear for his freedom. Fear for his life.

The only certainty that Henry had upon seeing the fear in the man's eyes, and the large black gun in his hands, was that none of them were safe.

Del, seeing what Henry was seeing, came to that realization in the same moment that the man raised his weapon to pull the trigger, no thought or care about who was on the receiving end.

With a horrified expression as he saw the little girl, Del turned and dove toward the man just as Henry overtook the child, catching her at the waist and swinging her around behind him.

"Mama! Mama!" she continued to shriek. She fought against Henry's hold with everything she had, but he held fast, crouching down and covering as much of her body as he could with his own.

Henry squeezed his eyes shut at the sound of gunfire shattering the night yet again. He could hear shouting, more screams, and the unmistakable sound of a body hitting the floor, all within a matter of seconds.

Henry didn't want to look behind him. Didn't know if he had the strength. Each misstep that had brought him to this place replayed in his mind in an unending loop.

Please, God, he's my brother, and I'm the one to blame. Not him. It was me, Henry thought, as he turned to see what fate had in store.

The man with the gun was sprawled in the doorway of the shack, his gun flung to the side of him.

And there was Del, sliding in a muck-covered heap down the edge of the wall. For a moment, Henry thought he was catching his breath, overcome by the carnage of the last few minutes. He desperately wanted that to be the case.

Distracted, he loosened his hold on the little girl just enough that she slipped from his grasp. Still on his knees, Henry reached out for her, not knowing if it was safe, but she was gone, running back to her mother, while he was left with less than nothing in his hands.

He climbed up from his prone position and ran toward his brother.

A momentary glance inside the shack showed him a dozen cowering, terrified women huddled together in a back corner, several with children in their arms, most covering their faces. Each one looked up at him, met his eyes, and he tasted their fear. Was he their savior or another monster, come to take them to a fresh kind of hell?

He couldn't answer the questions in their eyes, and he didn't have time to try. Once he'd seen that there were no more men hiding in the shack, with guns or without, he turned his attention to Del.

Kneeling by Del's side, he looked his brother in the eyes. There was a film of pain there that told Henry it wasn't shock or exhaustion that had brought him down.

Del was gripping his stomach with both hands. There was blood seeping between his fingers.

"Show me," Henry said harshly, but Del ignored him.

"The girl?" Del asked.

"She's fine," Henry replied. "Scared, but she's fine."

Del nodded. "Tell Alice—" His face twisted in pain, and he took in a sharp breath. "Tell her—"

"Tell her yourself," Henry said, pulling Del's arm away from his middle and wrapping it around his neck. With a heave, he stood. Del was a bigger man than he was, always had been, but Henry didn't stumble.

"I can't, Henry," Del said with a gasp, still holding his free hand to his stomach.

"You can," Henry said angrily. "You will."

He half walked, half dragged his brother to the edge of the porch. The steps splayed out in front of them, laughing at Henry's attempt to move a man who outweighed him by fifty pounds and was practically dead weight.

Tightening his grip on his brother, Henry made it down the first step, then the second, before Del's feet gave way beneath him. For a moment, Henry believed they were both going to tumble down the steps under his weight, then, without warning, the load was lightened.

Henry glanced up to see a dark-haired woman slide herself beneath Del's other arm, taking part of his weight on her own shoulders. He might have been mistaken, but he had a feeling that this was the mother of the little girl who'd been used as a human shield and somehow survived. The woman said nothing, simply nodded to Henry, then focused on helping him get Del down the steps.

Somehow, they managed. Del's feet were dragging beneath him by this time, but they didn't stop.

"That way," Henry said, turning and heading unerringly toward home.

Henry had never counted the number of steps between the house he'd grown up in and the shack through the woods by the marsh, though he must have made the trip a hundred thousand times, in his youth and as an adult. Perhaps his mother had known.

At the moment, it felt like a billion, and each one a mountain to climb.

Del didn't speak. Henry glanced over at his brother when his head lolled forward on his neck, and within moments, the weight in Henry's arms seemed to triple. Del was unconscious. *Unconscious, or dead,* he thought.

The forward momentum of Del's weight was too much, and Henry stumbled. Del went down onto the dark and wooded path, taking Henry and the woman with him.

"No, no, no," Henry chanted in a low voice. "You're not going to die right here. Not here. Not like this."

He rolled his brother onto his back, shocked at the white glow coming from his skin. Henry wanted to check his pulse, make sure they were carrying a wounded man and not a dead one, but he couldn't. He told himself he didn't have the time to waste checking, but the truth was he was too afraid of what he'd find.

They still had so far to go.

Grabbing his brother beneath the arms, with his back now faced toward home, and Alice and Eve, Henry grunted and gave another desperate and mighty heave, lifting Del's upper body from the ground. He'd drag him home if he had to.

But he didn't have to.

With shock and wonderment, Henry saw that he and the woman who'd helped him weren't alone. All of the women from the shack, and the children as well, were following them silently on their trek through the woods, away from the marsh and the dead men they were leaving in their wake.

No less than five other women had stepped up to join the one who'd been helping already. They took Del's legs and torso in their hands, and they shared the load with Henry as he lifted his brother off the ground.

With awe and gratitude clogging his throat, Henry could do no more than nod shortly as the women worked in concert with him, carrying the unmoving body of his brother back home.

The remainder of the walk through the woods was interminable, made more so by Henry's growing sense that time was running out.

When he could make out the lights of the house in the distance, Henry had to stop himself from breaking into a run. Still, he quickened his step, and the women followed suit.

Together as one, they carried Del through the field, toward the burning lights beckoning them to home and safety.

When Henry and the women reached the boards of the porch steps, he opened his mouth to shout Alice's name. But the sound that came from inside the home tore the words from his throat. Screams. There were screams coming from inside.

Setting Del on the porch in a panic, Henry threw open the front door, forcing himself to face whatever was waiting inside. Had one of the men from the shack escaped, made his way here, even as Henry had carried his brother home?

Alice didn't look up from where she knelt on a blanket on the floor. Her face was set in hard and determined lines, echoing the expression on Del's face as he had walked into the line of fire.

"Henry, I tried to call you," Alice said in a distracted, reproachful voice. He finally registered that the figure lying on the floor just in front of where Alice knelt was Eve. She was panting and sweating, and her knees were raised in his sister-in-law's direction.

"Alice, it's Del . . . ," Henry said, dizzy with the weight of the needs converging upon him at once.

"I tried to call Del too. What were you two thinking, not answering—"

She lifted her eyes, meeting Henry's gaze, and her words broke off. He couldn't begin to imagine what he must look like, covered in blood and mud and fear.

"It's Del, Alice," Henry said. "He needs you. He needs you now."

For just a moment, she was speechless. Then it must have registered that given the current circumstances, only life or death would cause Henry to pull her away at this particular moment.

She rose and she ran past Henry onto the porch. "Where? What? Oh God . . . Del," she breathed, catching sight of her wounded husband lying on the ground, ringed by a group of women and children she'd never seen before.

"Oh. Oh," she said with shock and fear in her voice. But only for a moment. Because she had no more than that to spare.

With determination, she placed her hands on Del's midsection and ripped apart the shirt he wore, laying open the bullet wound for all to see.

It was surprisingly small considering the damage it had done.

"Call 911, Henry. Call them now," Alice said in a voice made of steel. "I should have done it already. Eve insisted. Insisted no doctors. Shouldn't have listened," Alice was mumbling to herself.

She glanced up at Henry, who hadn't moved.

"Now!" she yelled, leaning down to put pressure on her husband's wound.

Del groaned, and she whipped her head back to him.

"God, Del, what have you done to yourself?" she asked in a voice that was calm yet reproachful.

"Alice," he whispered.

"I'm here. Henry's calling for the ambulance. You hang in there, you're gonna be fine."

Henry ran for the house phone and grabbed it from its cradle. His fingers were fumbling, and he was searching for the right buttons when he heard Alice speaking again from the porch.

"What do you mean 'no'? Don't you tell me no, Delwyn Doucet. I don't know who you think—"

She broke off, and Henry ran back toward the door, the phone still gripped in his hand.

Del was speaking again, a whisper intended only for his wife's ears, in spite of the audience that had gathered.

"Too late, love. Too late," Del said, shaking his head.

"Don't you die on me, you bastard! Don't you dare!" Alice shouted down at him.

"Really did love you, Alice," Del said, his voice so weak now, it could barely be made out. "Always were too good for me."

And he closed his eyes.

That was all. He closed his eyes, and they didn't open again. His breath went out, and it didn't come back in. A quiet, quiet death that rang through the darkness of the night, echoing all the way to the moon and back again, hitting both Alice and Henry in their cracked hearts, finally shattering them into a million broken shards.

The scream that filled the night came from every direction—Alice, mourning for the husband dead in her arms, and at the same time, Henry realized, Eve, screaming as another life was coming into the world. The screams did a dance around one another, weaving, tangling together and becoming one.

Turning away from Alice's grief, he saw Eve on the floor, straining at the pain ripping through her.

He ran in her direction. He had no idea what to do, but he knew, as surely as he'd ever known anything to be true in his life, that he couldn't and wouldn't pull Alice away from Del right now.

She didn't deserve this, she'd done nothing to deserve it, but now that it was here, he knew only that these moments with her husband, as his life left his body, were precious and sacred.

"Eve," Henry said on a breath, skidding to a halt and kneeling in front of her. "Look at me, breathe," he said. Her eyes opened and he saw panic, pure and simple.

"Henry," she gasped. "I can't. It hurts, Henry. It hurts!"

And with hardly a breath to spare, another contraction ripped through her body. Eve's muscles tensed, her shoulders rising from the floor. She opened her mouth and let out a scream that put a voice on all the horror and pain of the weeks and months past and encapsulated the rage and the violence of the night that had descended upon them.

Henry glanced down, saw the crown of the baby's head, and he had the terrifying realization that there was no one else. The first hands this child would feel would be his own, whether he was ready for the crushing weight of that responsibility or not.

"Almost there, Eve," he said, trying to soothe her. She was a cornered animal with nowhere to run. Her eyes gave away her fear. All he could do was his best.

"Breathe, Eve. Take a big breath, then one more big push. As hard as you can. The baby's almost here. It's almost over."

"I can't," she panted, shaking her head, looking around the room with wild eyes, searching for a way to escape. "I can't. I can't. I can't," she said, over and over again.

"You can," he said firmly.

Henry looked up into the eyes of the woman who'd helped him carry his brother home. She was kneeling behind Eve, setting Eve's head in her lap, wiping the sweat from her forehead.

"One more push, Eve," Henry said. "Just one more."

Another woman took Eve's right hand, and Henry saw Eve's face register confusion before the pain began to overcome everything. A third woman took her left hand. The women whispered and crooned. Henry could hear some English, some Spanish, and he thanked God they were there.

There was no more time.

"Deep breath," Henry said as the contraction wound up the final pitch inside of Eve. "Now push!" he yelled as her body tensed a final time.

The veins rose in her reddened face, the muscles in her neck strained, and she gripped the hands of the strangers who surrounded her like her very life depended on those connections. But Henry didn't see that.

What Henry saw were the first glorious moments of a child being brought into the world. Moments as precious as the last moments of a life. Henry saw the shoulders push their way out and into the light. He saw the rest of the bloody little body slide out of Eve behind those shoulders. He looked onto the face of a creature that he'd only vaguely imagined up until that moment, just a muted form somewhere in the distance that he couldn't make out.

But this was real. More real than anything that had come before.

Henry gazed in wonder at the baby in his arms.

"It's a boy," he whispered, awed by the miracle that had taken place right before his eyes. "Eve, you have a son," he said, stronger now, his face alight with joy.

He looked up into her face, tears in his eyes, his arms full of the weight of a new life, but her eyes were squeezed shut.

There was a figure at his side. One of the women from the shack was leaning over, clearing the baby's mouth with her finger, and the baby gave a great gasping cry.

"Eve, you have a son," he said again, laughing while the baby made his entrance known to the world.

There were laughter and tears from the women who surrounded him. Someone arrived with a blanket taken from the arm of the sofa to wrap the child in, and Henry watched in wonder.

"We need to cut the cord," he heard Alice say from a great and painful distance. "I'll get some scissors."

He looked up into Alice's face, and there was a spent but sublime calmness to her. Henry had the brief hope that perhaps, one day, she'd be all right. In the end.

And so Alice held the child, directing Henry how to clamp and cut the umbilical cord. Then she handed the bundle, so light and yet so incredibly heavy, back to Henry, motioning toward Eve.

"Eve," Henry said gently, moving up to her side as Alice saw to the rest of the job below. "Eve, would you like to hold your son?" he asked.

She opened her eyes, and what Henry saw there made him blink. It was pure and naked fear.

He smiled down at her.

"It's okay," he said. "It's fine."

"Put him in her arms, Henry," Alice said.

So he did. Eve was leaning back against one of the women, and Henry placed the baby, her son, in Eve's lap. She looked down at him, but the confusion and shock of the last few hours hadn't passed from her yet, and she seemed nothing except overwhelmed. Tears were still streaming down her silent face as she gingerly placed her hands on the child.

"Hold him, Eve," Alice directed gently. "Lift him to your chest."

Eve glanced quickly up at Alice and did as she was told. Henry knew very little about new mothers or infants, but he knew that the process he'd just witnessed had been amazing, and traumatic, and painful. For someone like Eve, who'd suffered so much in her life, the shock must have been tenfold.

That must have been the reason she looked frightened and ill at ease with the weight of her child in her arms for the first time.

Of course, that's it, Henry thought, watching her with a warm glow in his heart. It would pass.

It would pass.

CHAPTER FIFTY-FOUR

Henry sat with Alice on the steps of the porch and held her hand while they waited for Brady and the ambulance to arrive.

"They'll take him away," Alice said. "They'll take him away, and we'll have a funeral, and bury him in the ground." Her voice was dazed, the emotions swirling inside of her hidden beneath her confusion. "Henry, how? How did this happen? What happened?"

"Alice . . . I . . ." Henry thought of the newborn inside the house, felt again the weight of him in his arms, so slight, and the enormous weight of responsibility that he placed upon Henry simply by being.

But how could he lie to Alice? She deserved more than that.

Lights were coming up the drive, quickly. Bouncing along the lane. The time had come for Henry to find the words to explain what had happened. There was no going back. The truth? The lies?

The way forward was in his hands, and still, he didn't know how to untangle the right thing to do.

"He saved a little girl's life," he whispered to Alice as they watched the outside world come to them, and all that would entail.

Alice searched his face, seeking a kind of solace. Henry knew he had that one true thing he could give her. So he did.

"The little girl inside, she's about six," he said. "Del was shot while he was protecting her."

Tears began to pool in the bottom of Alice's eyes.

"Really?" she asked, her voice unsure.

Henry nodded. He didn't trust himself to speak.

Alice's chin wavered, and she squeezed his hand. The small smile she gave him sent the waiting tears streaming down her cheeks, but she didn't make a sound, only cried in silence while she held tight to the best parts of the man she called husband.

And the lights were upon them.

Brady leapt from his vehicle. The paramedics brought a stretcher.

The questions began, questions that only Henry could answer.

And he lied.

CHAPTER

FIFTY-FIVE

"What a mess. What a big damn mess," Brady said.

It was late. Everyone had begun to settle for the night. The medics had taken Del away. A crime scene unit had been called in from Cordelia to process the scene at the shack. The bodies of the men in the woods would be taken away soon, if they hadn't been already.

Brady had called the state police. Finally. They'd want to question them all again, including the women and children who were now spread around Henry's house, trying to sleep, trying not to worry about what would happen to them the next day, the next month. Trying.

"Should have called them weeks ago. I told Del, I damn well told him, but the son of a bitch wouldn't listen."

Henry sipped from the beer in his hand. Not because he wanted the drink but because he couldn't bring himself to look into Brady's eyes.

When he did, all he could see was the devastated confusion on Brady's face when he'd leaned down and lifted the sheet and seen his oldest friend's body lying dead beneath it. His breath had left him and he'd sunk to his knees beside Del.

"He was convinced. So sure those guys had killed his dad. I knew he wasn't handling things the way he should, but I thought . . . Ah, hell. I don't know what I thought," Brady continued.

Alice had answered the questions she'd been asked, though she'd had little to add in the way of explanations. After what felt like hours, she'd gone into the back room and shut the door, saying she was going to try and rest. Henry thought it more likely she wanted a private place with no questions, a place to mourn, away from the eyes that looked at her with sorrow and sympathy. There was nothing he could do for her but give her the time and space she asked for.

"You want to know the hell of it?" Brady asked, waving his beer bottle in the air. "All this bullshit—the waiting, not calling in the state boys when we should have—I knew what Del wanted. I did. I told myself he wanted to be the one to bring them in, no matter what it took. That's what he said, and I bought it. But all you had to do was look in his eyes. He wanted payback."

Brady took a long swig from his beer and slammed the empty bottle on the porch.

"And the kicker? The real kick in the ass? I'm not even convinced those guys had anything to do with Livingston's disappearance."

Every cell in Henry's body went on alert. If Brady had been looking at him, he wouldn't have been able to miss the way Henry stiffened, or the slight widening of his eyes.

But Brady wasn't looking at him. He was staring off into the trees instead.

"What makes you say that?" Henry asked, faking a calm he didn't feel. Not by a long shot.

Brady shook his head, worry pulling his features together like he'd come across a bad smell.

"I don't know. Just . . . just something Jonah said," he replied.

Henry sat up straight and stared at Brady under the glow of the porch light. But it was Brady who wouldn't meet Henry's eyes this time.

"You don't think Jonah had anything to do with it?" Henry demanded, his voice rising more than he'd planned.

Brady shook his head, casting a quick, short glance at Henry, then looking away again.

"No. No. I mean, he couldn't do something like that. Jonah? He wouldn't."

Henry wondered which one of them Brady was trying to convince.

"No," Henry said firmly. "He wouldn't."

"I know. I know," Brady said again. "It's just that . . . I should have told Del. I should have told him, and I didn't, and I can't help but wonder if I had, if things would be different. But, Henry, Jonah's my brother. If he did something . . ."

"Jonah didn't do anything, Brady! Jonah had nothing to do with this. Did he tell you he did?" Henry demanded.

"No. No, nothing like that. Just a comment, an offhand comment. You know how Jonah is. It was nothing, just foolishness."

Brady lifted his beer bottle again, then sat it back down when he remembered it was empty and leaned back on his palms with a sigh.

"I'll tell you something else, though, Henry."

Uneasy, but grateful to shift the focus of the conversation away from Jonah, Henry waited.

"Del and me, we've been side by side for twenty-five years. Neither one of us was willing to run for sheriff because we couldn't do that to the other one, so we just did the job and let the old man sleep off the booze."

Henry had no words of encouragement. He had no words left at all. He was empty right down to the bottom.

"But Del was my brother too, Henry. You know? I owe it to him to find out what happened to his dad. No matter what that means."

The unmistakable sound of a baby crying came from inside the house. Henry looked back in that direction, and by the time he turned his face again to Brady, he was rising to go.

"I've got to get out of here, Henry. Left the sheriff in charge. That's never good. You take care, okay."

And with a clap on the shoulder, he was gone.

But his words remained, running circles around Henry's mind.

What was he supposed to do *now*?

CHAPTER
FIFTY-SIX

Henry watched the night go by in silence. He couldn't sleep. Didn't even try. Eve was resting in the bed that they had shared for months; the crib that Henry had brought out of storage was set up near the foot of it, cradling the new life who'd come into the world riding a wave of sorrow and pain.

He'd woken in the night, the baby. When he cried, Henry had gone to him, not wishing to wake Eve, who slept facing the wall.

He'd bundled the baby in his arms, cooing and rocking him, making soothing noises.

It helped. It helped to hold the child and remember why he'd done the terrible things he'd done. The guilt didn't lessen, but the acceptance of it gave it a strong base to rest upon. Henry needed that base to be strong, because the guilt was there to stay.

"He's hungry," Alice whispered from the doorway.

Henry looked up into her face, which was mottled and puffy from the grief that held her in its grip. But her eyes were soft as she looked at the child.

"Should I wake her?" Henry asked, nodding to Eve.

Alice shook her head and walked toward Henry.

"Let her sleep," she said, running one fingertip across the baby's forehead while Henry bounced him gently. "It'll be a hard thing to come by in the months ahead. I brought some formula a few weeks ago, we'll get him a bottle. Come on."

Henry followed her into the kitchen as Alice cooed to the baby boy, both of them careful to step around the sleeping women and children scattered about the floors and couches.

Henry saw the woman who'd helped him carry Del was still awake. She sent him a small smile, her arms wrapped tightly around her daughter's sleeping form. Camilla, Henry remembered. She'd said her name was Camilla, at some point during the evening. Her daughter was named Mariana. She called her Mary.

Henry wished Del had had a chance to know that. That the child he'd protected was called Mary.

"Eve tried to nurse him a bit earlier," Alice said while she prepared a bottle. "Sometimes it's hard for first-time mothers, though."

Henry watched the baby's tiny little mouth open and close, testing out the taste of the world around him, his face so wrinkled and new.

"Has she chosen a name?" Alice asked.

Henry shook his head. He'd asked, but Eve had only murmured that she didn't know.

"That's okay," Alice said. She held up her arms to Henry when the bottle was ready. "May I?"

He nodded, handing the newborn over to Alice's more experienced care.

The baby took the bottle with vigor, and Alice gave a chuckle. "No worries. Something will come to her. Something just right. Won't it?" she said to the baby with a smile.

Henry watched the two of them together. Alice would have been a wonderful mother. He'd always known that, but seeing her there with another woman's child in her arms, seeing the love that she showered on him, in spite of the fact that she'd inevitably have to face the pain of giving him back, drove that home.

Family. Family was everything. And Henry knew better than most that family wasn't restricted to those who shared your blood.

"Alice, I need to go out for a while," he said.

She pulled her gaze away from the baby and looked at Henry quizzically.

"Everything's fine, I promise. Just something I need to do before tomorrow gets here."

A frown pulled her face low.

"You're not going to tell me you're going out to have a beer, then show up here with a bullet in your gut, are you?" she said harshly. "Because I've had about all of that I can handle, Henry Martell."

"No. No, I promise you, Alice. But it is important," he said softly.

"Well, it damn well better be," she shot back at him.

She put her eyes back on the baby, and some of her anger subsided, replaced by a profound sadness.

"My parents never liked Del. Thought I'd settled," she said quietly. "Truth is, I did settle. But we had Mari in common, and we liked each other well enough. It took time, Henry. Time and patience. A lot of damn patience. And I looked up one day and realized that I might actually love him."

She sat at the kitchen table with a sad sigh, and Henry could see the truth in her eyes.

"But it wasn't until he was dead at my feet that I was sure. So don't you go out and put yourself in harm's way, or I swear to God, Henry, I might have to kill you myself. You have a lot to come back to. A lot to live for. They need you here. *We* need you here."

Henry nodded. "Thank you, Alice."

There was nothing else to say.

"Go on, then. Do what you need to do. We'll be here when you get back."

So Henry did, knowing he was leaving them in good hands. The best of hands.

278

CHAPTER
FIFTY-SEVEN

"Henry, let's just calm down, okay," Ms. Watson said to him. Dawn was breaking over the day, bringing the long night to a close, but Henry didn't feel any sense of relief at watching it go. Inside, he thought the night might never end.

They were standing on the pier. Jonah had been bleary-eyed with sleep when he'd brought the pirogue over to pick Henry up at the toll of the bell. Henry'd felt sorry for waking him, and said as much, but Jonah only grinned.

"No trouble," Jonah had said with a gigantic yawn.

And Henry knew, in Jonah's mind, it wasn't.

Ms. Watson had met him at the pier in her house shoes, belting a robe over her faded nightgown. She'd sent Jonah back to the house to make himself a bowl of cereal for breakfast.

"What's happened?" she'd asked without preamble, those eyes set in her faded, wrinkled face as piercing and inscrutable as they'd ever been in her youth.

Henry had told her. He told her about Del, about Eve and the baby, about the dead men in the swamp and the lost women and children sleeping on his floor. And he told her about his conversation with Brady.

"He thinks Jonah had something to do with it! I don't know what he said to him, but I can't let Brady think Jonah's somehow to blame for this. I've got a lot of things sitting on my conscience right now, and every one of them I deserve, but I can't add that to the list, Ms. Watson. I won't."

She cautioned him to stay calm. "Brady's not going to jump to any conclusions. Not when it comes to his brother."

"But that's just it. I don't know if I can live with Brady even *thinking* Jonah might have had something to do with it. How can I stand by and say nothing and leave that hanging over their heads?"

Ms. Watson placed her hands on her hips and stared Henry down.

"Do you really think that boy has one single care about what people think? He doesn't even care what they say, as far as I can tell. Not Brady. Not anybody. Jonah lives in his own world, and as long as there's no threat to take him away from that world, I think you really need to calm down."

"You'd really let Brady think Jonah did this?"

"Brady doesn't think that! He might think maybe Jonah knows something, that maybe he saw something he shouldn't have, and he doesn't even realize it, but Brady doesn't think his brother's a killer."

Ms. Watson sounded exceedingly sure of that, and Henry wished he could share the strength of her convictions.

"So what do we do?" he asked her.

"Nothing," she said after a moment. "For the moment," she added firmly.

"But—"

She held up a hand in his direction, shaking her head.

"No. We'd just be borrowing trouble, and more trouble is exactly what we don't need. I'll talk to Jonah, see if I can figure out what it was he said that set off his brother's radar, but that's where I think we need to leave it for the moment."

Henry didn't like it. He didn't like it one bit, but he couldn't think of a reasonable alternative, short of turning himself over to Brady and spilling the whole truth. Every decent part of him was screaming at him to do just that.

"Unless you're ready to say good-bye to that girl and her baby already," Ms. Watson added, squinting her eyes up at him.

And just like that, she'd brought it back to the crux of the matter.

"God," he said, scrubbing his hands across his face. "Not if I don't have to." He raised his eyes to hers, a determination there that was a match for her own. "But I will, if it comes down to it. I won't let Jonah go down for this. Alice would take care of Eve and the baby. I'll take it all, every last drop of blame, if it looks like Jonah's in the crosshairs of this."

"Then we agree. I wouldn't expect any less," she said. "I'll get Jonah to take you back over."

And it was settled, Henry thought.

For now.

CHAPTER FIFTY-EIGHT

When Henry walked up the steps to home, it was still early, but he could hear the bustle of women moving around the house. The smell of fresh coffee hit him, and memories of his mother nearly overwhelmed him.

Not everyone was awake, but Henry could see Alice and Camilla sitting at the kitchen table. He leaned into the doorway, and his sister-in-law's relief was a living thing when she caught sight of him.

He saw her swallow hard.

"Everything okay?" she asked mildly.

"Yeah. As okay as it'll get for now anyway. Is Eve up yet?"

She shook her head. "The baby ate, then I laid him back in the crib. Not a peep from either of them for a while now."

"All right. Thank you, Alice. For everything."

"Get some rest, Henry. If you can. It's going to be a long day. There's a lot to sort out," she said with the smallest inclination of her head and a meaningful glance in Camilla's direction.

"Yeah." Henry sighed. "I suppose you're right."

Henry walked down the hallway and slowly pushed open the door to the room he shared with Eve. He didn't want to wake her or the baby if they were sleeping, just wanted to look at their faces. He needed to see their faces.

He was surprised, but relieved, to see that Eve was awake. Her back was to him and she didn't turn. She must not have heard him open the door. She was standing next to the crib, staring down at the baby.

Henry made no noise. Only stood watching, taking in the serenity of the scene, letting it soothe him. It was a balm over his open wounds.

He didn't know how long he watched. Seconds turned into minutes, but eventually the two of them drew him into the room. Walking on quiet feet behind her, he slid his arms around Eve's shoulders.

She flinched and gave a small shriek.

He smiled and kissed the top of her head.

"Didn't mean to scare you. He's beautiful, isn't he?"

She looked back down into the crib at the sleeping form of her son.

"Have you thought of a name?"

She didn't speak, but he saw her shake her head.

He hugged her from behind, closing his eyes and resting his cheek lightly upon hers. He wished for nothing more than to stay there, as they were. Just the three of them, apart from the world.

Henry didn't see that Eve never smiled as she stared down at the child. He didn't know the thoughts that ran panicked through her mind, alternately screaming and whispering to her that nothing would ever be the same.

He couldn't know that she was a woman standing on the edge of a steep and dangerous cliff.

He couldn't know.

Or he chose not to see.

CHAPTER

FIFTY-NINE

"Human trafficking is 'problematic,' they said." Brady snorted. "What kind of word is that? 'Problematic'? Politician's word, that is."

The days and weeks that had followed on the heels of the night at the shack had passed in a mundane haze of questions and paperwork and the never-ending need to hurry up and wait. Even Del's funeral had passed them by without any real sense of closure.

There were too many unanswered questions for that.

Brady and Henry were headed to the Watson house. They had a promise to keep. Jonah was waiting for them to go fishing with him.

"They're not really going to deport them, are they?" Henry asked. "After all they've been through, you'd think they could catch a break."

Brady shook his head.

"I don't know. It's been thrown around, but the guy in charge, Richardson, he's not so bad as some of the others. He gave me a card for an advocacy group that specializes in immigration situations. They provide legal help, counseling, that sort of thing. They say they might even be able to help Camilla and Mary relocate, find a more permanent living situation. A job."

"That's good news, isn't it?" Henry asked. Judging from Brady's face, he could see the deputy didn't find it particularly uplifting.

"Yeah. I suppose so. She's cooperating with the investigation as much as she can. They say that helps her chances of securing a visa."

Brady parked the SUV near the marsh and slammed the door behind him when he stepped out.

"Then what's climbed up your butt?" Henry asked as he got out of the other side of the vehicle. "You're pissed off about something."

"Iowa," Brady said with an angry yank on the bell hanging from the tree.

Henry just looked at him in confusion.

"They asked her how she felt about moving to Iowa," Brady explained, seeing the look on Henry's face.

"And this upsets you because . . . ?"

"What the hell's in Iowa? Nothing, that's what. Corn. A bunch of damn fields full of a bunch of damn corn. And Cam gets this dreamy look on her face and says, *'Wonderful. That sounds wonderful,'*" Brady mocked in a high voice.

Henry sighed. In the two months since Del's death, the dust had begun to settle back upon the sleepy town and its inhabitants, full of people living out their own small dramas and tragedies. Dust tends to do that, even after the biggest of storms.

Most of the women and children were long gone. A few had disappeared in the night, the very night that Del had died, fearing arrest and deportation. Others were taken to the families they'd been searching for when they'd paid the men to smuggle them over the border.

Only Camilla and her daughter, Mary, remained. They had no family to go to and no desire to continue running under the cover of the night. So Camilla had decided to stay, facing down whatever would come next, even if that meant deportation, with a firm resolve that Henry admired.

"Have you told her?" Henry asked, spotting Jonah heading their way, the wooden boat skimming over the top of the water.

"Told her what?" Brady asked gruffly.

"That you want her to stay?"

Henry considered Brady's face. He thought there might be the faintest signs of redness creeping up his neck. He looked like he planned to protest, but in the end, he just pushed his hands down into his pockets.

"Don't see the point," he said. "If she wants to go to Iowa, who am I to stop her? Woman's got a right to happiness, doesn't she? And if a bunch of corn makes her happy, well, I don't see how I can compete with that."

Henry shoved the tackle box he was carrying into Brady's hands and reached out to help pull Jonah's pirogue up to the shore.

"You know, Brady," Henry threw over his shoulder, "I used to think you were the smarter of the pair. You and Del. But now I realize I gave you too much credit."

"What the hell's that supposed to mean?" Brady asked, stepping into the boat.

"You heard me. Just tell the woman you care about her, you moron. What's the worst that could happen?"

Brady opened his mouth to speak, then closed it again. Henry thought he might try to argue the point, but he was glad when he didn't.

"How you doing, Jonah?" Henry asked. "I brought you some jelly beans. They're in the tackle box."

"Thank you, Henry," Jonah said. "Thank you kindly. I do like jelly beans. 'Cept for the black ones. They taste real bad. Like somebody was playing a mean trick, slipping candy into the bag that doesn't taste like candy should 'cause they thought it'd be funny or something. But I don't think it's funny."

Henry smiled at the man and his earnest face. "No, I don't suppose it is."

"Aunt Helen says we can come by and visit soon," Jonah said, in a voice that sounded like he'd been told he'd get two birthdays this year instead of one. "She says little Noah will be big enough for me to teach him to fish soon."

Henry laughed. "Well, now, it'll be a few years yet before we can do that, Jonah."

The big man's face fell at the prospect of a few years. To Jonah, that must have sounded pretty much the same as forever.

"But I can't think of a better man for the job than you, when the time comes," Henry said and watched the joy rise back up in Jonah's face.

The affinity that Jonah had shown for the baby had been a surprise to them all. Even more so, the way little Noah seemed to return the fascination. He'd quieted his fussing when Jonah had held him in his big arms. They'd looked one another in the eye, sizing each other up, then Noah had given a wet gurgle and reached out his little fist toward Jonah's face. Jonah had laughed, a sweet, soft sound for such a big man.

Henry had known he was witnessing something special.

"Well, I'll be damned," Ms. Watson had said in wonder. "If that don't beat the band."

"Is Eve feeling any better, Henry?" Jonah asked. "Only, Aunt Helen said she'd been poorly."

The innocent question brought Henry up short.

"Ah, well. She has good days and bad," Henry said faintly, his voice missing the amusement of a few moments before.

Brady's brows were drawn together when he looked at Henry.

"It might be time for you to consider other options," Brady said.

Henry bit back the retort that jumped immediately to his lips and tempered his frustration when he spoke again. Brady was only trying to help. "We *have* considered other options, Brady. If you think of any new ones, be sure to let me know, okay. We're doing the best we can. I think the medicine Dr. Atkinson put her on might be helping."

Brady only raised his eyebrows, then glanced away. Henry knew he wasn't fooling him. He wasn't fooling anybody. Not even himself.

"Why don't we try back in the slough, Jonah," Brady suggested, changing the subject.

"Some big old catfish back there," Jonah agreed, missing the heaviness of the exchange entirely.

"That sounds all right to me."

The conversation moved on, and Henry followed along as best he could, nodding and murmuring in all the right places, but the truth was, his mind was on Eve. His mind was always on Eve these days, when it wasn't on baby Noah.

Other options, Henry thought. *Like it's that easy.*

"Postpartum depression," Alice had said to him worriedly. "It can get bad, Henry. Really ugly. There are medicines that can help, but considering Eve's aversion to doctors, I don't know how we're going to make that work."

And Alice was right. It was bad.

Eventually, Alice had called in another favor, and Dr. Atkinson had visited Eve at the house again.

She wouldn't allow him to examine her, but she did manage not to start screaming and knocking things over the way she had at their first introduction.

Instead, the doctor had kept his distance across the room, and asked Eve gentle, probing questions. She wasn't particularly forthcoming with her answers, often staring at the wall and not speaking at all, but that was apparently indicative enough to cause the doctor concern.

He spoke to Henry and Alice in the kitchen, and they elaborated on Eve's downward spiral since the baby had been born.

"Obviously, it's hard to say how much of her current state of mind is due to the shock of motherhood and how much can be traced to past trauma. Ultimately, though, I suppose it doesn't matter that much. The mind is a tricky place to navigate, even for the best of us."

Henry and Alice waited while the doctor tapped his pen against the table.

"I'm going to prescribe an antidepressant. Against my better judgment," he added firmly. "Frankly, it's questionable to give medications to someone without a more thorough examination. She needs to speak to a therapist. Someone who specializes in the kind of trauma recovery she clearly needs," he chided. "But considering the circumstances, and her extreme phobia of doctors, well . . ." Dr. Atkinson sighed, looking deeply troubled. "I think it would be more irresponsible to leave her to deal with whatever she's struggling with and not make an attempt to help."

Alice breathed a sigh of relief.

"But," the doctor went on firmly, "you'll need to keep a close eye on her. This medication can have side effects, and if at any point you feel that Eve is a danger to either herself or anyone around her—particularly to her child—then you need to call for help immediately. I know you don't want to consider the idea of institutionalizing—"

"No," Henry interrupted firmly. "No, Doctor. Eve can't be locked away. I can't do that to her. I won't."

"I understand your distaste for the idea. I do," he added when Henry seemed unconvinced. "I don't think it's the best course of action either. But I can't in good conscience walk out of here without laying all the cards on the table. It's a worst-case scenario, to be certain, but one that I think you need to bear in mind."

The doctor's words echoed through Henry's mind. Most times, he was able to set them aside, but no matter how hard he tried, Henry couldn't erase them completely.

There was something deeply wrong with Eve.

On the days she managed to get out of bed, it usually wasn't until late into the evening, and she'd wander around the house like a visitor in a strange land. She barely ate. Henry often had to spoon food into her mouth, watching as she chewed and swallowed mechanically.

She'd stopped talking to him. She'd stopped everything. It was as if she'd learned for a while what it was like to live, then she'd forgotten it all with the birth of the baby. She'd retreated into a blank space somewhere in her mind where Henry couldn't follow her.

But the most devastating thing to watch was the way she'd refused to bond with, refused to even acknowledge, the child she'd grown within her body.

Henry had chosen the name Noah. When he'd put it forward for Eve to consider, she'd only walked away. But he could no longer leave the baby without a name to call his own. So Noah he'd become. Noah Weston Martell.

Noah was doing well, in spite of things. Thank God for Alice and Camilla. Even young Mary.

But Eve. Except for the time just after he was born, when Henry had placed the little life she'd created in her arms, she refused to even hold him.

When he cried, she'd look up in surprise from wherever she'd been staring, like she'd forgotten he existed. Then she'd rise and wander silently out of the room, leaving the little one to be tended to by others. Others who loved him, it was true. But they weren't his mother.

"Henry," Brady said, pulling him back to the present. "Henry, did you hear me?"

"Sorry. Did you say something?"

Jonah had stopped maneuvering the boat through the water, and they were floating in a bend. It was a quiet and secluded spot. Henry imagined it had existed here, in its present state, waiting for them for a thousand years. That it would stay untouched and just as it was once they'd gone, for a thousand years more.

"I said there's been a development. In your dad's case."

Brady was looking down at his hands, tying off his fishing line. Henry got the impression he was deliberately not meeting his eyes.

The words *not my dad* floated across Henry's mind, a long-ago echo left over from a time when the words had mattered to him.

"What does that mean? What kind of development?"

Brady focused on what he was doing and didn't immediately respond. Henry tamped down his frustration at the man. Why had he brought it up if he wasn't willing to talk about it?

"I thought you weren't involved in that anymore?" Henry asked.

According to Brady, the state police had taken over the investigation into Livingston's disappearance.

"I'm not. Not really," Brady said, standing to cast his line in the water. "The state boys are in charge now. But this one sort of fell in my lap."

Henry stared at Brady's back. "What, exactly, fell in your lap?"

Brady sighed and looked at Henry over his shoulder. He set his fishing pole in the boat and reached down to pull a beer from the small cooler between them.

"It was Jimmy Blankenship's boys," he said. "Jimmy brought them in, dragging them by the ears. Apparently they came across something out here in the swamp. Months ago now. Something they thought they'd keep to themselves. The little shits. But when Jimmy found out, he hauled their asses down to the station."

Henry could do nothing but stare. Jimmy Blankenship's boys. He knew them, a little. Or knew of them. "Little shit" was an accurate description for them both. The Blankenships didn't live far from there, maybe a few miles in the other direction. One of their favorite pastimes was to tease Jonah, taunting him in the way some boys did. Henry had run them off with a bug in their ear more than once.

"Brady. What the hell are you talking about?"

"They found something," Brady said.

"Something? What something? Quit dancing around it, would you? Spit it out."

"I didn't want to say anything until the results came back from the lab, but word's bound to get around town. They've been bragging about it."

"Just say it!" Henry barked.

"A foot!" Brady shot back at him.

Henry's breath caught, and he couldn't help a glance toward Jonah, but the big man was happily ignoring them, content to dig through the bag of jelly beans, bypassing the black ones, his fishing pole held between his knees. He gave no indication that he was listening to anything they said.

Brady followed Henry's gaze, then took a deep breath and continued in a calmer voice.

"They found a foot. Out in the swamp. Not far from here, actually."

"Livingston's?" Henry asked, his mind churning with the possibilities.

Brady shrugged. "Got to be. I mean, who else's? The little psychopaths were keeping it in a jar, watching it decompose."

Bile rose in Henry's stomach.

"The working theory is the men running the trafficking operation killed him, then disposed of him out in the swamp. Let the gators take care of the rest. I'm sorry, Henry."

He nodded, his head hanging low as he stared at the bottom of the boat. The boat Jonah had used to unwittingly do just what his brother had described.

It was his turn to avoid the other man's eyes.

"It's a crap thing to tell somebody, I know. But I thought you ought to know. In case you were, you know . . . holding out hope or something."

Henry shook his head.

"No, it's fine. Thank you for telling me, Brady," Henry said in a low voice.

"Yeah," Brady replied, clearing his throat. He seemed to be searching for something to say. "Livingston was a right old bastard, but I don't guess anyone deserves to go like that."

Henry heard the thump again of the hammer hitting his stepfather's skull, saw his body spasm on the ground at his feet.

"No," Henry said honestly. "Nobody deserves that."

Jonah was whistling, out of tune. He popped a red jelly bean into his mouth, then picked up his pole.

"Guess Ol' Brutal'd had his fill," he said, watching his line where it disappeared into the murky dark-green abyss below.

Henry and Brady both turned to stare at him, but he took no notice.

"Mr. Doucet was a little man, but still. Must have been a fine meal for the big boy, all the same. Mr. Doucet wasn't very nice, was he?"

Brady's mouth fell open as he stared at his brother. Henry willed Jonah to say nothing more.

"No," Henry whispered. "He wasn't a very nice man at all, Jonah."

Brady turned and met Henry's wide eyes. It didn't take a genius to figure out the thoughts churning behind Brady's face.

"I didn't hear that," he whispered to Henry. He moved in close and pointed a finger at Henry's chest. "*You* didn't hear that," he said, tapping the finger into his chest. "Did you?"

Henry shook his head, shocked at the hardened flash of protectiveness he could hear in Brady's voice.

"No. I didn't hear a thing," he said.

"Good," Brady said.

He turned back to his pole just as Jonah got a bite on his line.

The moment passed, and Henry was glad to see the back of it. The three men spoke of other things. Over the course of the morning, they filled the second cooler with catfish, they drank a few beers, and above all else, they didn't speak again of Livingston Doucet.

CHAPTER SIXTY

Some sense of being alone woke Henry in the night. He reached out a hand and felt Eve's side of the bed, still warm from the heat of her body.

It wasn't unusual these days for her to drag herself from bed only once the sun had long since gone down. Henry tried not to worry. He thought perhaps the solitude would do her good, help her find her way back to them, him and Noah. Or so he hoped.

Sometimes he followed her, just to set his mind at ease. She never wandered far, usually to the porch, or occasionally to the field. Several times, he'd found her sitting on the sofa in the living room in the dark, her eyes open and unblinking, staring at nothing. Nothing except the pictures in her mind.

She'd looked so lost. He longed to show her that she wasn't alone, that he was there with her, and that he always would be. Words didn't seem to sink in. He'd tried them all. So he simply held her hand and sat with her, waiting for the day when she'd emerge from the fog she was wandering in.

Alice had gone home for the night. Since Del died, she'd split her time between her own home and Henry's, knowing that he and Eve needed all the support she was willing to give. Henry was grateful.

Camilla and Mary had moved in with Alice as well, at least for the time being, though they also spent a great deal of time with Henry, Eve, and the baby. But that night, the three of them were alone in the house.

Henry had slept restlessly, bothered by dark dreams that he was glad to wake from. He stood and looked into the crib that still sat at the foot of the bed, expecting to see the baby sleeping. He was surprised to find the tiny bed empty.

Perhaps Noah had cried in the night, hungry for his bottle. But Henry didn't think so. He was a light sleeper on the best of days, and the last few months had conditioned him to wake at the slightest sound from the baby.

Henry held his breath. Noah must be with Eve. He certainly hadn't climbed out of the crib on his own. He couldn't even roll over yet.

On soft, silent feet, Henry made his way down the hallway, listening for sounds of life.

He stopped short in the entry to the living room, where he could make out the glow of lamplight falling across the floor. His mother's old rocking chair was moving, slowly rocking back and forth, the ancient rhythm of mothers around the world.

Eve was holding her son, cradling him in her arms while he made gurgling noises and looked up into the eyes of his mother. She was speaking to him, softly. Henry couldn't make out the words. He didn't want to disturb her. This was the first time he'd ever seen her hold the child voluntarily. Perhaps the medication was working, tethering her to reality.

Stepping in their direction, Henry was pulled closer to the scene. A feeling of contentment settled on him. This was why he'd done what he had. This was what he'd gone to unimaginable lengths to protect. Right here. A mother and a child, inextricably linked.

He raised his hand to place it on Eve's shoulder but hesitated. Now that he'd drawn closer, he could make out the words she was speaking to her son.

"I love him, you know," she was saying.

Noah was watching her face in fascination, enthralled by the movement of her lips.

"I do. At least, I think I do. I've never known what love was, but I think it's this. A feeling that you're so much a part of someone else that if that feeling went away, you'd wither and die like a plant with no water."

Eve lifted a hand, and Noah grasped one of her fingers in his tiny, pudgy hands.

"And the really unbelievable part is that he loves me too. I don't know why. I have nothing to give. I'm nobody, I was nothing before he found me and brought me to life. I'd be nothing again without him."

The words she spoke cut Henry to the bone. Lovely though they were, she wasn't nothing. He hadn't given her life, only given her a chance to live it. The knowledge that she felt that way was unsettling and incredibly sad.

"And see, that's the problem, little one," Eve continued. "Because things have changed. Things are broken again. My heart is broken. I see the way he looks at you, the pure love in his eyes. But for me, it's harder. You were made in pain and anger. You're a baby now, but soon you'll be a boy, then you'll grow into a man. And there are no good men. None but Henry. You have his heart now, not me, but you were made by a monster, grown in a monster, and you'll become a monster too."

Henry went cold. His heart beat faster, and his breath caught in his throat. Did Eve truly believe that this innocent child was destined to be a monster?

"You'll break his heart," she continued gently. "As you've broken mine by being born. I can't let that happen."

Henry's mind stalled as he watched Eve gently pull her finger from the baby's grasp. She reached down at her side, where a throw pillow had been stuffed between her and the side of the rocking chair.

Without pause, she raised the pillow and placed it over her son's open, smiling face.

With horror and shock clanging inside of him like air-raid sirens, Henry reached out and grasped her wrist, clamping down. Eve gave a startled gasp of surprise, her eyes whipping to his face, but his grip was like iron as he pulled her hand, which still clung to the pillow, raising it up and away from the baby's face.

Noah blinked up at him. Without looking at Eve, Henry gave him a small smile in return. He reached down with both hands and gently took the child from Eve's arms.

"Henry . . . ," Eve began, but he didn't dare look at her. His heart was racing, and anger was pumping through his muscles and his veins. It took everything he had inside of him not to reach down and shake her, scream at her, take her by the arm and toss her out the front door.

"Don't," he said sharply. He saw her flinch backward at the tone in his voice, but he found he didn't care.

With the baby in his arms, Henry walked back into the bedroom. He laid the child on the bed, then stretched out next to him.

Henry didn't know where Eve spent the rest of the night. He didn't get up again to look. Instead, he stayed by Noah's side, protected in Henry's circle of warmth and care. The baby eventually gave a great yawn, and his eyes fell shut. He slept.

But Henry didn't. He lay awake throughout the night, his eyes on the sleeping child. Eventually the sun rose and brightened the room, but inside Henry's mind, it was still very, very dark.

CHAPTER
SIXTY-ONE

Henry sipped his coffee, leaning against the counter at the kitchen sink, staring out the window. Unwittingly, he was mirroring the way his mother had started most of her days.

He could have used her guidance just then. Or simply her presence. But she was gone. Henry alone would have to untangle the mess they'd made.

Eve was ill. She was sick. Too sick for him to mend. He was going to have to accept that.

The possibilities rattled around, bumping into one another and flying in opposite directions. He could throw her out. He knew he probably should. Most people would.

And yet . . . Eve would never get the help she needed on her own. He didn't even know if she'd survive.

As Henry had inspected the broken pieces of what their life had become over the course of the long night, he'd had to face the horrifying fact that he still loved her. In spite of everything, this hadn't changed. He'd promised her he would be there, by her side, no matter what. She'd told him she was no good for him, and he was forced to admit she was right. But he'd known that. She was still part of him. He couldn't abandon her.

No more than he could put Noah in danger. And Eve was a very real danger. It was his responsibility to see the child was safe.

A hospital? The police? Both possibilities would be abandonment, albeit under a different name.

By the time Noah had woken, fussy and crying for his early-morning bottle, Henry had made some decisions. He could only hope they were the right ones.

After feeding and changing the baby, he'd gathered some of his things and taken the child to Alice's house. Noah would be safe there, until things were settled.

He'd seen no sign of Eve when he'd pulled the truck back into the drive, and again, he didn't seek her out. There would be plenty of time for them to deal with one another after he got some sleep.

Henry had lain on the couch, his mind turning over the course of action he'd decided on, but eventually exhaustion had won out.

He'd woken in the early afternoon, alone.

After a shower, he'd made a pot of coffee. But now the time had come. He'd put it off long enough.

With a clink, Henry set the empty cup in the sink and went to find the woman he still loved.

Eve was in the shed. He was almost surprised to see her there at Mama's old loom. If he'd found her there the day before, he would have been pleased, seen it as a sign that she was healing.

Today, he knew different.

"Noah is with Alice," Henry said without preamble. "He's not safe here, with you."

Eve turned toward him, her hand laid gently across the shuttle of the loom. She said nothing, but he correctly took her silence as assent.

"He can't stay here. Not with you in this state." Henry watched her face, searching, longing to see some sign that he was wrong.

She gave him not a single one.

"Why, Eve?" Henry said in a ragged voice. "Why would you do such a hateful, terrible thing? Is it so hard to love him?"

Her face clouded and she looked away from him, her eyes on the ground. Her hands tightened and loosened around the shuttle.

"I tried," she whispered. "I did. But I can't bear to look at him. To hear him cry. He comes from before, and he's stained this life with you. Every sound he makes takes me back there. I look at him and I see the men who hurt me. Over and over again. I look at him and I feel nothing inside. He reminds me . . . He reminds me of who I am."

Henry walked toward her and dropped to his knees. He turned her chin gently to face him. He desperately wanted to fix this, fix her, but he knew better than anyone. Sometimes broken can't be fixed.

"He'll never be safe with you, will he?"

There were tears in Eve's eyes when she shook her head quickly back and forth.

"No," she said with a sob.

His heart was already broken, but with her answer, he felt it shatter a little more.

He had only one more thing to try. A Hail Mary pass.

"He can't stay with Alice," Henry said. "Not forever. I've spoken with her. It would be too hard for her, after losing Del."

With a final squeeze of her hands, Henry stood, then ran his hands through his hair. "But Ms. Watson will take him. She'll take him and raise him like her own."

Henry waited to see what kind of effect his words might have on Eve. Her shoulders slumped a bit more, but other than that, she gave no indication that she couldn't hand her child over to be raised by another woman.

"Come with me," Henry said. "We'll pack his things. Collect him from Alice. You should be there."

Eve nodded, and what little hope Henry had left faded into a flicker, the smallest candle flame. All it would take was the lightest puff, and it would die, vanishing into darkness.

CHAPTER

SIXTY-TWO

When they arrived at Alice's house, Eve stayed in the truck while Henry collected Noah.

"Thank you," he said to his sister-in-law.

"Of course," she said, without hesitation, but the worry was clear in her expression.

Opening the driver's side door, Henry gently placed the baby carrier on the bench seat between him and Eve. There was a blanket thrown over the top of it, rising over the handle.

"He's sleeping," Henry said quietly, but the admonishment wasn't needed. Eve made no move toward the baby, only gripped her arms tightly around herself and stared out of the passenger-side window.

The ride across town to the marsh went by in a series of images, flashing by the windows like a silent movie. No one spoke, and the baby never made a sound. But both of them were acutely aware of him there, between them. No matter what happened next, he would always be there, always between them.

The day was beginning to fade as Henry pulled the truck over next to the bell hanging in the tree. He opened the door to step out and ring the bell but stopped and took the baby carrier by the handle, bringing Noah with him. He didn't meet Eve's eyes, but he wasn't willing to leave the child alone with her, even for a moment.

He gave the rope attached to the bell a pull, once, twice, three times. Jonah would come and collect them.

Eve stood on the other side of the truck, waiting, while Henry lifted the edge of the blanket, checking that the child still slept. He glanced at Eve, but again, her face was turned away. With a sigh, he leaned against the front of his truck and waited for the boat to arrive.

Jonah was cheery, happy to see them, as always, seemingly unaffected by the somber mood that surrounded them.

"Jonah, there's a load of stuff in the back of the truck," Henry said to him. "Could you do me a favor and unload it for me while I take Eve and Noah over? I'll be back in just a bit and help you load it into the boat. We can take it over together."

"Sure thing, Henry," Jonah said and set himself to the task.

Henry assumed that Ms. Watson hadn't told him of the plans that had been made, not yet. He was glad of that.

After they made it across the marsh, Henry led the way into the house, where Ms. Watson waited.

"I don't know how to thank you," Henry said. "I know it's a lot to take on."

She waved his thanks away, but her face was serious when she spoke. "Nonsense. A baby is a gift," she said, peering at Eve's face. "A precious, precious gift."

Eve didn't look up from the floor. Henry was overcome with the urge to shake her. To yell. *Look,* he thought. *Look at what you're doing! He's your son, how can you just leave him here? How can you do that?*

But whatever reaction Henry was hoping to see, it wasn't there.

Helen Sue Watson wasn't about to give up that easily. She stepped in front of Eve, forcing her to look up.

"Look at me, girl," she said. "I want to see your eyes when I say this."

Eve slowly lifted her head, doing as she'd been told.

Ms. Watson reached out a hand, and for just a moment, Henry thought she meant to slap the younger woman across the face.

Instead, she laid the gnarled old hand gently on Eve's cheek.

"I will raise your child while you can't. I will do that, and I'll do it gladly. But you should know, child, when you leave here tonight, that this doesn't have to be forever. My door will always be open to you and to Henry."

Eve looked away, but Ms. Watson moved her head and put her face in front of Eve's, forcing her to look at her.

"And when you're well enough, when you've got a handle on things again, remember that we're not that far away. This child will be here, waiting for you to come back and take him by the hand."

Henry had known this unbreakable woman his entire life. He thought he'd seen every facet of her imaginable, but he'd been wrong. Because he'd never seen such tenderness. It was a thing they didn't deserve, neither he nor Eve. But there it was, all the same. It was mercy. And it was forgiveness.

It brought Eve to tears.

She choked out a sob, lifting her hand to her mouth. Henry watched her struggle to hold it back, but it was like trying to catch the ocean in a sieve.

Eve collapsed onto her knees, crying into her arms.

Ms. Watson placed her hand on the back of Eve's bent head and met Henry's eyes.

This was the breakthrough he'd been hoping for, and that dim flame of hope brightened, just a little.

He dropped to his knees next to Eve and placed a hand over hers. He ran his other down her cheek, wiping at her tears.

"Eve," he said. "Eve, we don't have to do this. We don't have to leave him here. He's your son. He's my son, if you'll let him be. Eve, look at me."

She raised her tearstained face to his, and he rejoiced at the pain he saw there. Pain was real. Pain was life. Pain was love.

"It won't be easy. You'll have bad days, but I'll be there. You won't be alone. We'll get you help, we'll get you well, and we'll raise our son. Together."

Henry pulled her close and held her in his arms while she cried.

"Do you want to go home? All of us, Eve?"

Once more, Henry held his breath. Lives teetered in the balance, and the moment stretched into infinity.

Finally, finally, he felt Eve nod.

"Yes?" he asked, pulling back so that he could look at her face. "Was that a yes?"

She nodded again. "Yes," she whispered.

"Yes, then." He smiled, wiping the tears from her cheeks. "Let's go home. All of us."

He turned his face up to Ms. Watson, who was smiling down at them through her own tears.

It worked, he thought in amazement. He'd closed his eyes and thrown the Hail Mary with the final seconds ticking off the clock, and against all the odds, Eve had caught the ball in the end zone.

He laughed, hugging her tightly to him.

They were going to be okay.

Everything was going to be okay.

CHAPTER
SIXTY-THREE

Henry had embraced Ms. Watson, thanking her again before they left.

There wasn't a peep from the baby carrier as Henry carried it back down to the boat, no sign that Noah's fate had hung so tenuously by such a frayed thread.

He held Eve's hand, smiling down at her as he helped her into the pirogue, the carrier settled on the bottom of the boat between them.

Jonah had unloaded the baby's things from the back of Henry's truck unnecessarily, he thought, as he pushed the boat through the dark water that teemed with life. He heard a soft splash somewhere behind them. An alligator, dropping down into the water, looking for a meal.

Things would be better, Henry told himself. He'd get her help. He wouldn't leave her alone with Noah, not until he was certain her soul was on the mend. But she'd taken the first step tonight, and Henry was filled with a new sort of hope. Eve's unwillingness to leave her child had been the gust of air that his candle needed, and it lit up the darkness around them.

The boat was pulling close to the other shore, and he could see Jonah waiting patiently for them.

"Jonah, I have some bad news, fella," Henry said with a laugh as the other man held out a hand and helped him maneuver the pirogue onto the shore. "All that stuff's going to need to go back in the truck, my friend. I hope you don't mind."

"Ah, course not, Henry, if that's what you want. You have a nice visit?" Jonah asked.

"Yeah. Yeah, you might say we did, Jonah." Henry looked back over his shoulder at Eve. He couldn't seem to wipe the grin off his face, and he knew he was acting like a fool.

Eve didn't notice, though. She was looking back over her shoulder, staring into the deadly beauty of the swamp in the darkness.

"You leaving Noah at our place for a sleepover, then? That'll be a treat. Me and Aunt Helen, we sure do love that little guy," Jonah said.

Henry turned back to Jonah and tilted his head a bit to the side. Ms. Watson must have said something to him after all. Henry hoped Jonah wouldn't be disappointed.

"Jonah, I'm sorry, man. There's been a change of plans. Noah's not staying. He's coming home with us. Isn't he, Eve?"

As Henry turned his head to smile at Eve again, he barely noticed the confusion on Jonah's face.

Eve was still looking away, back at the swamp in the direction they'd come.

It was then, only then, that Henry recognized that something was very, very wrong.

Eve didn't look like a woman who'd just discovered a connection to her young child, in spite of everything. She looked like a woman haunted.

The baby carrier was gone.

Henry stared at the place it had been, the place where he'd set it himself, safe and secure to make the trip back across the marsh. He'd put it right there. Right there between them.

It was gone.

His head whipped around, his eyes searching the ground on the shore next to Jonah. He must have handed it over without thinking about it.

But there was nothing. Only his friend. Jonah was speaking again, but Henry couldn't make out the words. A rushing sound was filling his ears. If he'd had time to examine it, he would have said it was the sound of the world catching fire. His world. Theirs.

"Where's Noah?" Henry asked frantically. He rushed at Eve and grabbed her by the shoulders. The movement pulled the little boat away from the tenuous hold it had on the shore, and they began floating through the water, drifting. He was yelling, screaming in her face. He didn't know what words he was saying, he'd never know. They were like blackbirds released from a cage, fluttering and pecking at both of their faces.

It didn't matter. Eve only stared off into the darkness, not even acknowledging Henry as he shook her by the shoulders.

"Where is he? Damn it, Eve! Where's Noah?!"

Henry turned to search the darkness, looking for any sign.

His eyes followed Eve's. And there it was, floating on top of the water yards behind them. He could barely make it out. Then, like an optical illusion that finally comes into focus, he realized what he was looking at.

There, with just enough moonlight to illuminate its whiteness, was the blanket that had been laid over the top of Noah's baby carrier. Just the blanket. The rest was gone.

The splash, Henry thought dazedly. The splash. That was no alligator. That was Noah's carrier going into the water. Eve had picked up the carrier that held her son, and without saying a word, she'd dropped it into the water behind the boat.

But that was so long ago, Henry thought. *So, so long ago.* Minutes, hours, a lifetime ago. And she'd stayed silent through the rest of the trip, letting him move the boat farther and farther away from where she'd dropped him into the water. She'd never made a sound.

"What have you done?!" Henry screamed into her face. "What have you done?!"

Slowly, she turned her face to his.

There were no tears now. She'd left those behind at the house on the swamp with Ms. Watson, the friend who'd tried to help them. Now, there was only Eve. Broken, broken Eve. The girl with no name.

She tilted her head and looked up at him.

"I left him behind," she said, in a maddeningly calm voice. "He couldn't come home, Henry. If he came home, he'd only grow up. Like a weed, he'd grow, and he'd breathe, and he'd take. Men only take."

"Why?! Why couldn't you just leave him there? She was willing to keep him, Eve! Why?!" he yelled.

She shook her head at him slowly, and her brows drew together at his confusion.

"It was too close," she said. "Too close. He would always be between us. You love him now, and your love would only grow. But he'd always be a monster, don't you see? He could never be anything else. He couldn't deserve your love."

And with those words, she broke him.

His hands came up of their own accord and wrapped themselves around her throat. He saw them, watched in fascination as they tightened. She didn't fight him, only squeezed her eyes shut. An act of love, he realized. So that he wouldn't have to look into her eyes.

His hands fell away, and he dropped to his knees in the boat, and he sobbed.

He felt the light touch of her hand upon the back of his head. And he sobbed harder.

He'd been wrong. He'd been wrong all along. He couldn't fix her. Who did he think he was? No amount of love would erase what had been done to make her this way, and he'd been a fool, an arrogant fool, to think it would.

And now he was paying for that arrogance.

It was the wrath of Livingston Doucet's vengeful god, visited upon his head in one swift blow.

"Shh," Eve whispered in a soothing tone. "It's okay. It's over now."

He couldn't bear to look at her. He couldn't face the truth he'd see in her face.

He felt her hand when it pulled away from him. He felt the rocking motion of the boat beneath them as she walked the few steps it took to reach the edge.

He looked up, forced himself to see.

He felt it in every fiber of his being when she stepped up onto the edge of the boat. He felt it as if he were standing there with her. Because he was.

"Forgive me," she said, her hair blowing in the breeze behind her just as it had done the night he'd realized his life would never be the same. And those words tore through what was left of him.

He knew what she was going to do. Knew, because she was him.

He didn't move to stop her.

This was the only ending their story was ever destined to have.

With one last glance in his direction, Eve stepped off the boat. The swamp took her greedily, and she didn't fight against it, giving herself over freely to the death that waited there.

And Henry let her go.

After a moment, he stood himself, listening to the sounds of life around him. Life that served no master but death. It lay in wait for all of them, knowing it held the winning hand. Always.

Henry stepped off the boat to meet it face-to-face.

CHAPTER
SIXTY-FOUR

The brackish water filled Henry's mouth and his nose, tasting of death and whatever comes beyond.

Henry let it fill him, pull him down, as he gave himself into its hands.

But his eyes opened, searching, even through the darkness of the murky water around him, for one last glimpse of Eve.

A calmness fell over him, and all thoughts drifted away. He thought of his parents, of Livingston and Del. He thought of Noah. And he drifted.

It was Jonah who had other plans.

With a jerk, Henry was pulled back from the destination he so desperately sought. He fought against the hands gripping him.

No! he opened his mouth to yell, but nothing emerged. He had no breath left to yell with.

And no more strength to fight. As the blackness finally took him, his lungs and his heart burning, he realized that it wasn't meant to be.

Death wouldn't be his escape. Jonah would pull him from the water, breathe life back into him.

Life would be his punishment. Life without Eve.

A coldness filled him as he lost consciousness. A coldness that he would carry with him for the rest of his days.

CHAPTER

SIXTY-FIVE

Jonah was sad for Henry.

He'd pushed on his chest the way Aunt Helen had shown him, when he'd dragged him from the marsh, and he'd breathed in his mouth, but Jonah wondered if he'd done something not quite right.

He didn't understand what had happened at the swamp, but he knew that the Henry who'd awoken, vomiting up water, wasn't the same Henry who'd gone in.

And that made him sad.

"Eve," Jonah had said, once he'd realized Henry wasn't dead, turning to head back into the water.

"No," Henry told him, coughing and grabbing him by the ankle. "No, Jonah. She's gone."

And that made him sad too.

He'd tried to walk Henry back to the boat. He'd take him to Aunt Helen, she'd know what to do, but Henry had other ideas.

"No, Jonah. Alice. Take me to Alice," he'd said, leaning his weight against Jonah.

"But, Henry, you don't look to be in a fit state to drive," Jonah had told him.

"Keys are in the truck," Henry said, shivering and coughing. "You can drive me."

"But . . . but, Henry, I don't know how to drive."

"It's easy. You just point and steer. Please, Jonah."

And he couldn't say no to that.

So with a lot of starts and stops, and a few close calls, Jonah had driven for the first time in his life, across town to Alice's house.

"You did good, Jonah," Henry murmured when Jonah stopped the truck in Alice's driveway.

Jonah grinned. He thought he kind of liked driving.

Henry lurched to the side, reaching to open the passenger door, but Jonah thought he might fall out on his face if he managed it, so he hopped out and ran around to help Henry out of the truck.

He carried his friend's weight as he helped him toward the house.

The front door opened, and Jonah could see Alice outlined by the light that shone from inside.

"Jonah? Is that you?" she called.

"Alice," Henry called.

"Henry?" The worry in her voice was clear, and she ran down the steps toward the two of them. "Oh God, Henry, are you all right? What happened to you?"

Henry released his hold on Jonah and fell into the woman's arms. He cried. Jonah had never seen a man cry before, and it made his heart hurt something terrible.

"How could she, Alice? He's just a baby," Henry cried into his sister-in-law's embrace.

"Noah? Henry, you're not making any sense," Alice said, pulling back to look at Henry's face. "Jesus, you're freezing. Let's get you inside. Jonah, can you help me with him?"

He nodded, happy to oblige.

With Alice on one side and Jonah on the other, they helped Henry stumble up the steps to the front door. Jonah could hear the sound of a child laughing from inside, and that made him a little happier, although he was still worried about his friend.

The lady named Camilla came to the door. Jonah had met her before. She was nice.

"Mary, honey, can you fetch me a blanket?" Alice called into the house as she settled Henry into one of the chairs that sat on the porch. "Now somebody better tell me what happened. Where's Eve?"

Henry dropped his head into his hands, so Alice looked up at Jonah. He could only shrug.

"Eve's gone, Alice," Henry said from the chair. "She's gone, and I just . . . I just let her go." A sob caught in his throat. "I couldn't help her, Alice. I couldn't fix her."

Alice lifted a hand to her mouth, and Henry looked up into her shocked face.

"Noah. She couldn't let him live. There was something broken inside of her, and the baby . . . She . . . she'd rather let him die . . ."

Alice looked over her shoulder at Camilla, the woman who'd become her friend in the last few months. With wide eyes, she gestured toward Henry with a nod.

Camilla walked forward and stood in front of him. When Henry looked up, she leaned down and gently placed a warm, sweet bundle into his arms.

Noah's dark eyes stared up at him in fascination, and his mouth opened and closed, like he was tasting what life had to offer.

Jonah smiled when a tiny, chubby hand reached up and grasped Henry's finger in his fist.

"Noah," Henry breathed, holding the baby tightly while silent tears ran down his cheeks.

"She didn't know. Thank God, she didn't know," Henry said, with a look at Alice. "She didn't know I left him here."

Alice shook her head, looking as sad as Jonah felt.

"I'm so sorry, Henry. I wanted it to work as badly as you," she said.

"I was a fool," he said quietly, holding the baby like he might never let him go. "I thought I could shock her into being whole. That the experience of leaving her child would bring her back to me. But I expected too much, Alice. She could never be that girl. Because that girl didn't exist. Not anymore. Only in some unremembered place, where unbroken souls hide."

Alice laid a hand on Henry's shoulder, and they watched in silence while Henry held the child and sobbed like his heart might never be whole again.

Jonah didn't understand. But that was okay. There were a lot of things he didn't understand, so he didn't worry much about it.

He knew that he was with friends. And that was enough.

CHAPTER

SIXTY-SIX

"What the hell are you saying, Henry?" Brady demanded as he paced across Alice's living room.

Alice was there too, looking pale and shocked.

"I'm saying it was me," Henry said, his voice a barren and parched wasteland. "I'm the one who took Livingston's body to the shack. I wanted to make it look like the traffickers had done it. But I knew, I knew the whole time, and it got Del killed."

He glanced over at Alice, who was staring at her hands, fiddling with her wedding ring.

"I know it doesn't fix anything, Alice, but I'm sorry. I'm so sorry."

Alice huffed out a breath and stood from the couch, straightening her blouse and walking over to stare out the window.

He didn't expect her to forgive him. But she deserved the truth. They all did.

"I couldn't let you think Jonah did it," Henry said to Brady. "I couldn't live with you thinking that."

Brady sat down in an armchair with a huff.

Henry waited. He'd said everything there was to say, and he knew once it sunk in there'd be questions they deserved answers to, recriminations and accusations that he deserved to answer for.

So he stayed silent, and he waited.

It got a lot harder when Alice started to cry. She was quiet about it, but Henry could hear the faint sniffling, and he could see her back shake with the sobs.

He wanted to go to her, to tell her again how sorry he was, but she wouldn't want to hear that now. And he didn't deserve to ask for her forgiveness.

The clock ticked, and Henry waited.

"I put in my resignation yesterday," Brady said in a dazed voice. "It was always Del and me, side by side. Without him . . . I just don't want to do it anymore. Tinker said he's looking to sell his place. Thought maybe I'd take out a loan, put it together with my savings."

Brady shook his head. "Alice," he said. "It's up to you. You want me to arrest him? I've still got a badge until the end of the month. You say the word, and I will."

Henry could only stare at him. He'd never considered that Brady might not arrest him. He was an accomplice to murder, or an accessory, or whatever the hell it was when you hid the truth from everyone you loved and made one bad decision after another and ended up getting your brother killed.

But Brady wasn't looking at him. He was looking at the wife of his best friend. His dead best friend.

Alice gave a bitter laugh.

"Isn't that just like a man?" she said, still staring out the window. "Just fine walking around like you're in charge, until things get sticky. Then you want to dump the whole thing in my lap, shift the responsibility off yourself."

Brady looked abashed. "I . . . well, I mean . . . ," he stammered.

Alice sighed, then turned back to the two men. "It's fine, Brady," she said. "It's fine. I'm used to it. You and Del really were two peas in a pod, weren't you?"

Brady shut his mouth. Henry supposed there wasn't much he could say to that.

Alice turned her attention to him. "Henry," she said. "Henry. Look at you."

She walked over and took his hand.

"I love you, Henry, but you are a stupid, stupid man. Henry, you can't fix everybody. You don't have to carry the weight of the world on your own shoulders. Did you kill Livingston?" she asked.

He shook his head.

"Did you kill Del or those men at the shack?"

"No," he whispered. "But—"

"Stop it. Stop it now. Whatever you've done, whatever punishment you deserve, I think you've got that and more. Right there inside that stupid head of yours. Now, if you'll excuse me, I think I'll go check on Noah."

And with that she walked out of the room.

Henry watched her go, marveling at the strength of her.

CHAPTER
SIXTY-SEVEN

The day that Henry walked away from his life was crisp and cool, the promise of winter around the corner.

He locked the doors at the empty house, the house that had been his father's and his grandfather's before that. He put a padlock on the shed that held the still and his mother's loom.

Before he did, though, he took the small strip of fabric from the loom, the one Eve had been working on at the last. He ran his thumb down the brightly colored threads, woven together to form something beautiful. Some physical thing that showed she'd existed.

Lifting it to his nose, he breathed in the smell of the fabrics, then held it tightly in his hand. He tucked it into his pocket. He knew there was no point trying to forget Eve. But he did try not to remember quite so often. It was difficult. Impossible, really. But he tried all the same.

He'd said good-bye to everyone already. Everyone who mattered. They'd made noises about his going, but he knew they could all see that he was only existing there, rattling around in the old house alone.

Noah was with Alice now. She was a good mother. He'd always known she would be.

Brady and Camilla were engaged. The wedding was going to be in the spring. Mary would be the flower girl.

When he'd told Ms. Watson that he'd been to see the army recruiter, she'd smiled and given him a hug.

"You're gonna be just fine, son," she said. "I know you don't believe it now, but time really does heal. You'll see."

He thought she was probably wrong, but he smiled back at her anyway, though it didn't reach his eyes.

He'd found a rare sense of joy, though, when he'd handed Jonah the keys to his truck. He'd spent some time teaching him to drive over the past few months, and he trusted him not to hurt anyone on the road.

"I can't take your truck, Henry," Jonah had said.

"I want you to have it," he told him. "But be careful, okay? Remember, this one's not a toy."

"No," Jonah said, shaking his head vigorously. "Not a toy. I'll remember, Henry, I will. You're a good friend, Henry. A real good friend."

The big man's words had brought a bittersweet smile to Henry's lips.

"No, Jonah. Not me. Everything I know about being a friend, I learned from you."

He was leaving now, and he didn't know when he'd be back, if ever.

But the army called to him, as it always had, though for different reasons now. He longed to be just a face in the crowd, a soldier whose only responsibility was to do what he was told. He thought maybe he could do that.

But one way or another, life wouldn't be denied. It was his punishment, and he would serve his time—life, without Eve.

Together they'd been one. Together they'd burned their world down around themselves, and there was no going back. The only way was forward.

So Henry walked forward, one step at a time, with the bitter taste of ash in his mouth.

EPILOGUE

Four years later

The bell rang above Henry's head as he entered the diner. Everything looked exactly the same, down to the waitress he'd gone to school with. Only Henry had changed.

His family didn't know he was back yet. He was looking forward to surprising them. Especially Noah. Alice had sent pictures, letters, and handmade drawings that had reached him in the far-off places he'd been. He'd kept each and every one, chronicling the journey of a happy dark-haired boy.

Eve had been wrong. About a great many things, but mostly about her son. He was no monster. He was whole, and he was beautiful.

Henry often thought of Eve, though the sharp edges of the memories had dulled with time. Ms. Watson had been right about that. Mostly, he was haunted by the girl she could have been. If she'd been given the chance.

Henry took a seat at a booth.

The waitress walked over. The tag on her blouse said "Becky," though he would have remembered anyway.

"Just coffee, please," he said.

Her eyes lit with recognition. "Henry Martell. Well, I'll be damned."

He smiled. "How are you, Becky?"

Her eyes twinkled. "I'm good, Henry. I'm real good."

She brought him his coffee, then glanced around the empty diner. She bit her lip, obviously debating something with herself. When she straightened her shoulders slightly, Henry could see she'd made up her mind.

Becky slid into the seat opposite him and smiled. And just like that, Henry's life changed course once again.

There was a sorrowful corner of Henry's heart, marred by shadows and scars, where Eve lived—and always would. But in the days and years to come, Henry would occasionally hear a faint echo. It was the voice of an old man named Apollo, who'd once given him a piece of advice at a truck stop in Louisiana.

You'll never appreciate the daylight till you've walked on the dark side of the night, without even the stars to show you the way.

Dawn, at long last, was breaking on the horizon.

ACKNOWLEDGMENTS

I've heard a rumor that it takes a village to raise a child. I can attest that it takes a village to raise a book too.

Many grateful thanks to Katie Shea Boutillier, Faith Black Ross, Danielle Marshall, Miriam Juskowicz, and the rest of the Lake Union village.

It could also be said that it takes a village to raise a writer. To my village, you know who you are, and I hope you know I love you all the best.

ABOUT THE AUTHOR

Eliza Maxwell is the author of *The Grave Tender* and *The Kinfolk*. She writes fiction from her home in Texas, which she shares with her ever-patient husband, two impatient kids, a ridiculous English setter, and a bird named Sarah. An artist and writer, a dedicated introvert, and a British cop-drama addict, she enjoys nothing more than sitting on the front porch with a good cup of coffee.